The Falconer's Knot

Also by Mary Hoffman
The *Stravaganza* Series

Stravaganza: City of Masks
Stravaganza: City of Stars
Stravaganza: City of Flowers

The Falconer's Knot

Mary Hoffman

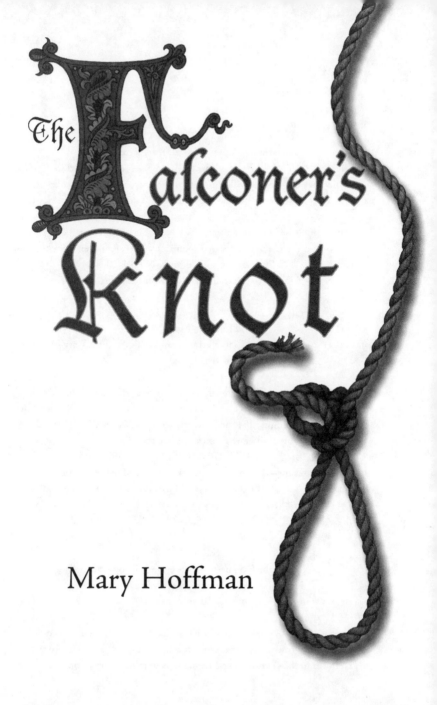

Text copyright © 2007 by Mary Hoffman
Map illustration copyright © 2007 by Peter Bailey

First published in Great Britain by Bloomsbury Publishing Plc
Published in the United States by Bloomsbury USA Children's Books
175 Fifth Avenue, New York, NY 10010
Distributed to the trade by Holtzbrinck Publishers

Library of Congress Cataloging-in-Publication Data
Hoffman, Mary.
The falconer's knot : a story of friars, flirtation and foul play / by Mary Hoffman.
— 1st U.S. ed.
p.   cm.
Summary: Silvano and Chiara, teens sent to live in a friary and a nunnery in
Renaissance Italy, are drawn to one another and dream of a future together, but
when murders are committed in the friary, they must discover who is behind the
crimes before they can realize their love.
ISBN-13: 978-1-59990-056-8 • ISBN-10: 1-59990-056-4
[1. Religious life—Fiction. 2. Love—Fiction. 3. Murder—Fiction.
4. Renaissance—Italy—Fiction. 5. Italy—History—1268–1492—Fiction.
6. Mystery and detective stories.] I. Title.
PZ7.H67562Fal 2007   [Fic]—dc22   2006016365

First US Edition 2007
Typeset by Dorchester Typesetting Group Ltd
Printed in the USA by Quebecor World Fairfield
2 4 6 8 10 9 7 5 3 1

Acknowledgements

I am grateful to Dr Cathleen Hoeniger of Queen's University, Kingston, Ontario, for generously sharing relevant parts of her PhD dissertation, 'The Painting Technique of Simone Martini', and to my invaluable Italian researcher, Dr Manuela Perteghella, for a wealth of useful facts and comments on my text. Jeryldene M. Wood, Associate Professor of Art History at the University of Illinois, Urbana-Champaign, kindly answered my questions on the Poor Clares.

The London Library sent a stream of books to this country member and the British Library and Bodleian provided relevant books not only in English but Italian. And the Sackler Library most of all.

I have taken Joel Brink's theory about the references to Siena in the fresco of *St Martin Reviving the Dead Child* from his paper in *Simone Martini: atti del convegno*, 1998, L. Bellosi ed.

Contents

For Stevie, my falconer

'He enters and exits the tale
astonished
at being a part of it'

From 'Simone' in *Viaggio terrestre e celeste di Simone Martini*
by Mario Luzi
(Dual language edition by Luigi Bonaffini, 2003)

UMBRIA, ITALY, THE YEAR OF OUR LORD 1316

CHAPTER ONE
Courtly Love

ilvano da Montacuto was not just young, handsome and rich. He was young, handsome, rich and in love. As he rode on a grey stallion along the main street of Perugia one evening in high summer, a hawk on his pommel and his hound pacing behind him, he could hardly have been happier.

Silvano was sixteen years old, slim and elegantly dressed, with a feather in his hat and a silver dagger in his belt – he was his mother's darling only son and his father's pride and joy. And he was on his way to the house of Angelica, his beloved.

But first he was to meet his best friend, Gervasio de' Oddini, to show him his new hawk, Celeste, and ask his advice about how to pursue his courtship of Angelica.

'Like a hunter,' Gervasio was sure to say. 'Study your prey, learn her habits, accustom her to your presence by seeming harmless and kind. And then, when she is tame and off-guard, you pounce!'

'But I *am* harmless – at least I mean her no harm,' Silvano would say.

Gervasio would just smile. He was a year older than his friend and liked to play the world-weary older man, experienced with women, accomplished in the arts of courtly love as well as proficient in the skills of hunting, fighting and running up debts at the local inns.

The Eagle was where they were to meet this evening, their favourite inn near the main square of the city, the Platea Magna. Silvano tied up his horse outside but took the hooded Celeste in on his wrist, Ettore the hound padding after them. The inn was an ideal place for a private conversation, full of loud-voiced drinkers and smoky with candles.

Silvano made out his friend through the gloom and threaded his way past wooden tables, stepping over outstretched legs. Gervasio was drinking with a man Silvano had never seen before, who slipped away silently as soon as he approached. Gervasio called for more wine and the two young men moved to a table in a quieter part of the room.

'Nice bird,' said Gervasio, admiring Celeste's barred breast feathers.

'From Bruges,' said Silvano casually, while bursting with pride. 'She was trained in Brabant, of course.'

'Of course,' said Gervasio ironically. His own hawk was a small hobby, a lesser bird, but all his father could afford as his family were minor nobility and Gervasio was the sixth and youngest son.

Silvano was the only son and heir of the wealthy Baron Montacuto, and his clothes, his horse and now his new peregrine all declared his status to the world. The friends spent a good ten minutes discussing the qualities of the falcon, who had been a birthday present, before getting on to the subject of the fair Angelica.

'If only a certain lady could be induced by soft words and compliments to bend to your will like Celeste,' said Gervasio, at last changing the subject to an area in which he did feel

14

superior to his friend.

Silvano fetched a deep sigh in agreement. He was quite happy to discuss Angelica all night long but did not feel any confidence that she really knew of his existence. She was married to a wealthy sheep farmer, much older than her, who bought her fine dresses and jewels and perfumes, but that was not the problem. In Silvano's eyes she was as much above him in beauty as he was above her in station and he could not believe she would ever look kindly on his devotion, even if she were free.

'Write her a poem,' suggested Gervasio, looking keenly at his friend. He was much more cynical than Silvano and couldn't see how a well-dressed and good-looking boy with money and a title to inherit could fail to impress a young woman married to a middle-aged farmer with a paunch and a wart at the side of his nose.

And there was no doubt that Silvano was good-looking. His light brown hair was cut so that it fell straight to just under his jaw and his eyes were a silvery-grey with long dark lashes, both features inherited from his Belgian mother. The Baronessa Montacuto was delicate in face and form and her fragility, which had caused her to lose three other sons and a brace of daughters before they drew breath, gave to her surviving boy a grace of movement and a fineness of feature that fitted his destiny perfectly.

He rode, fenced, hunted, sang like a dawn bird and could read Latin almost as well as a monk. But his future would not lie in the Church. No, Silvano would be Baron Montacuto, with a household of servants, the rents from substantial lands north of Perugia and a beautiful Baronessa to raise his brood of children. Only she would not be Angelica. The sheep

15

farmer's wife would be fat before she was twenty-five, but Silvano would have moved on by then.

Gervasio's mouth curved as he thought of her ample charms. 'Write her a poem,' he said again. 'She'll be impressed.'

A faint pink flush had tinged Silvano's prominent cheek-bones.

'You've done it already, haven't you?' laughed Gervasio. 'I knew it! Come on, let's hear it.'

Silvano dug into the purse at his belt and produced a piece of parchment, much scraped and criss-crossed with black ink. He pretended not to be able to read his verse properly but actually he knew the words without the parchment:

'Twice wounded lies my bleeding heart
And suffers still its secret pain.
Amor himself shot the first dart
My lady's eyes then aimed again.
The god has left for Heaven's gate
Who now his work on earth has done
For me to heal it is too late
Unless to mercy she should come.
One glance would mend the second scar
Or could if it were soft and kind.
One rose but thrown from out her bower.
The first I'll bear till end of time.

'That's all there is so far,' said Silvano, his cheeks now burning.

'That should do the trick,' said Gervasio, trying to keep a straight face.

'You really think she'll like it?'

'She will if you read it to her in your most pleading voice

and flutter your long eyelashes at her. In fact,' said Gervasio, getting to his feet, 'let's go and find her now and strike while the iron is hot.'

Angelica lived in the west of the city, near the Porta Trasimena, a short walk from the inn. The two young men walked past the vast bulk of the Church of San Francesco, with its friary alongside it. It held a special horror for Gervasio, who feared that he might one day be sent to live there as a friar, once his father had died and his brothers had shared out the patrimony. And he had no taste for poverty or obedience, let alone chastity.

Two young friars, in their dingy grey habits, walked barefoot out of the great church as they passed and Gervasio grimaced at the sight. He hurried Silvano along the road west.

Angelica sat at the window of her husband's town house feeling bored. Tommaso was off negotiating sheep prices in Tuscany, but she refused to set foot in the old-fashioned stone farmhouse outside Gubbio, even when he was not away. Buying the fashionable palazzo in the city had been part of their marriage contract. Old Tommaso brought the wealth and substance to the match; Angelica the beauty. Her family were well aware that she had nothing else to offer: no name or breeding, no particular skills or accomplishments, just her perfectly oval face with the springy blonde curls that framed it and her perfectly rounded limbs.

Tommaso wanted an heir; his first wife had been barren and he had waited patiently until she died. Angelica wanted a nice house, servants and pretty clothes to wear. In her

17

parents' home she had been little more than a servant herself and she had sworn not to have hands as coarse and red as her mother's. So the town house had been purchased and for the first year of her marriage Angelica had enjoyed buying furniture and hangings for it almost as much as she had revelled in the silks and lace and fur she could wrap around her pampered body, according to the season.

But now she was bored. The expected – the bargained for – baby had not arrived. There had been the beginnings of one but it ended in pain and blood a few months into its life and Angelica had used that as an excuse to keep Tommaso out of her bed for many months. And she was beginning to wonder if all the pretty clothes in the world could make up for having a short fat middle-aged man for a husband.

Angelica glanced out of the window and immediately turned pink with pleasure. There were two good-looking young men in the street below and she knew that one of them was in love with her.

Silvano looked up and saw her. She was dressed in a light blue gown with white muslin at the breast and she wore a double string of pearls round her throat. In his own throat his voice died and he knew that he could never recite his poem to her.

'You do it,' he hissed to Gervasio. 'You'll say it better than I will,' and he thrust the parchment into his friend's hand, turning away from the palazzo to hide his confusion.

'I won't, I won't, I won't!' said the girl, glaring at her brother. 'You can't make me!'

18

'I think you will find that I can,' said Bernardo. 'I am your brother and your guardian and, if I say you are to enter a convent, who will argue with me except yourself?'

Chiara was weeping with rage and fear. 'Then you will have to tie me up and take me there in a sack,' she spat. 'For no one will ever say I went there willingly!'

'If that is what I have to do, then I shall do it,' said Bernardo, quite unperturbed. 'There is no other choice. Father did not leave enough money for a decent dowry for you. The pittance that the Poor Clares are willing to accept as a donation would buy you no kind of husband. And you wouldn't want to be married off to a hideous old man, would you?'

Chiara stopped her raging for a moment. Could it really be that Bernardo was being kind and considerate in his way? But she knew his way of old and there had been little enough kindness in her life since their father had died six months ago. And not much before that.

'But why can't I stay here with you and Vanna?' she asked, subsiding into sobs. 'It is my home and I could help you with the children.'

'We've been through all this before,' said Bernardo wearily. 'I can pay a servant girl to do that for far less than it would cost to keep you in meat and wine and decent clothing.'

'Then let me eat bread and drink ale and wear homespun!' cried Chiara. 'Only don't send me away.'

'You are being ridiculous,' snapped Bernardo. 'I am not selling you into slavery. Many girls like you enter religious houses and live devout and useful lives. Why should not you?'

Because I am not without a family, thought Chiara. And I don't have a vocation. But she was too proud to beg for her

19

brother to show her some affection. She had been starved of that since the death of their mother when she had been a little girl just losing her milk teeth. Their father had been like his son, a man not given to tender caresses or shows of emotion. Chiara wondered fleetingly how her sister-in-law Vanna could bear being married to such a cold fish.

But she pushed the thought down along with her own feelings of rejection. She had been silent for some minutes and the tears were drying on her face. Her future as a nun stretched drearily out in front of her, empty of adventure or romance, and she felt deathly tired, as if she really had fought her brother physically and lost.

'I see you have no answer,' said Bernardo. 'That is settled then.'

He had won.

Silvano turned aside, biting his lip while Gervasio recited his verses to Angelica. They sounded banal now to his ears, and impossibly naïve, when said in Gervasio's light, slightly mocking voice, and yet he had filled them with all the passion in his heart while he was writing. Silvano couldn't wait to be properly grown up with a mistress of his own and a beard on his chin and some property to manage.

With his girlish features and slight body he was an easy target for his father's friends, who were all prosperous middle-aged men with chests like barrels and legs like tree trunks. Men of substance, who could drink all night and show no ill effects and get up at dawn to ride out hunting the next day. Yet Silvano was stronger than he looked and

20

fearless, and could wield the dagger he wore at his waist and a long sword when occasion arose. He just wished he could learn how to keep his feelings out of his face.

But what was this? Angelica was clapping her hands, her soft white hands, and laughing. She was saying that his poem was pretty. And now that he looked at her, he could see that she was picking a red flower from a pot on her balcony. True, it was a geranium and not a rose, which did not smell as sweet, but it sailed through the air gracefully enough, before being caught by Gervasio.

His friend handed it to Silvano straightaway, along with the parchment, indicating him as the poet. Did Angelica look a little disappointed? Silvano put the pungent flower in his hat and bowed to her with a flourish before putting the cap back on.

'Come away,' hissed Gervasio. 'We must leave now. That's the husband coming back.'

Tommaso was indeed toiling up the hill and Angelica's expression told the friends that she was surprised and displeased to see him in equal measure. She would have much preferred to spend the sunset hour flirting with two young men. Now she would have to organise dinner for her husband and listen to him grumbling about the price of sheep. And if she were unlucky, later than night he would come to her room and slobber over her, ruining her complexion with his stubbly face. She shuddered.

As the two friends strolled back down the hill, the farmer lifted his cap to them and they, in a gesture that he took quite rightly as irony lifted theirs to him with a flourish. Nobles didn't display much courtesy to farmers. Tommaso looked sharply at the flower in the younger man's hat and thought he

21

caught a glimpse of a blue dress vanishing from the balcony of his house.

Sister Eufemia was in charge of the novices at the little convent in Giardinetto. It was a small community; in spite of what Bernardo had said to his sister, not many women entered the Order of the Poor Clares unless they had a real calling. The community at Giardinetto had only twenty nuns and three novices. Chiara would be the fourth.

'This girl from Gubbio,' said the Abbess to Sister Eufemia. 'I doubt she has any real vocation.'

'Didn't the brother say she was a devout child, so racked with grief still for her dead father that she wanted to withdraw from the world?' asked Eufemia.

'I think the brother would have said anything to get her off his hands,' said the Abbess drily. 'But if we don't take her in, he'll find some other convent that will. And at least we can be kind to her. If she doesn't seem fitted to the religious life, she can be a lay sister. Perhaps she'll be useful in the pigment room?'

'Well, Sister Veronica could certainly do with the help,' said Eufemia. 'You'd think those painters in Assisi *eat* the colours we prepare for them – Sister Veronica simply can't keep up.'

'We must not complain about that, Sister Eufemia,' said the Abbess, in a tone of mild reproof. 'It is all to the glory of the Blessed Saint Francis himself. It will be a wonder that brings many more pilgrims to Assisi when all the frescoes are finished.'

22

'True, Mother,' said Eufemia. 'Nothing is too good for the Saint, God rest his noble soul.' She crossed herself matter-of-factly as all the sisters did so many times a day they hardly noticed they were doing it. 'But you know the brothers here have started their own pigment room? There will be work enough for both houses before the Basilica is complete.'

The Abbess looked out of her window: she was the only person in the house whose cell had one. The familiar outline of the friary just across the vegetable garden from the convent met her eye. Abbot Bonsignore had mentioned only recently that his house had agreed to take on production of pigments for the artists who swarmed over the Basilica being beautified in neighbouring Assisi. His new friar, Brother Anselmo, had the necessary skill and would be Colour Master. Abbess Elena had felt a momentary twinge of jealousy that her own convent would no longer be the only local religious house with a colour room; but, as she had just told Sister Eufemia, anything to the glory of Saint Francis could only be a blessing.

There was nowhere else in the whole of Italy where a Franciscan house and one of the Poor Clares sat so close together. Most Clares found it difficult to hear Mass the seven times a year they were bound to, but in Giardinetto, there was a friar free to come and celebrate whenever the sisters asked. And that friar was now Brother Anselmo.

The friary was the older foundation but the sister house had grown up next door when two women had decided together to renounce worldly life and came to the brothers for help. At first they lived in what was no more than an out-house of the friary and used the same chapel as the brothers, taking turns to say the Office, so that the sisters were always

23

half an hour later with their Hours.

But with time, more women wanted to join them and several had their own fortunes, which they used to build a proper convent and a small chapel of their own. In addition to their work on the land and with the poor people of the parish, they had specialised in the grinding of colours for the artists who were flooding into Umbria from Tuscany, to decorate the many new churches being consecrated.

The present Abbess was the great-niece of one of the convent's founders and she ran a peaceful house. But in the few weeks since she had received the visit of Bernardo from Gubbio, she had felt uneasy. This was the first time she had agreed to take a girl without having met her first. The three existing novices were quiet and obedient; someone less so could disrupt the serenity of the Poor Clares of Giardinetto.

Angelica lay wide awake and dry-eyed in the large bed, whose yellow silk hangings she had chosen so happily a few months earlier. Beside her, Tommaso snored with his mouth open.

'I cannot bear it,' she thought. 'Did God give me beauty just to waste it on a wild boar like that?'

She thought about the handsome young men and the poem, which she hadn't fully understood but which was full of the sort of pretty words she liked – flowers and wounds and love and sighs. Then she remembered what had just happened and a single fat tear trickled down her grazed cheek. It was like living in two different worlds and Angelica longed for a chance to escape from one to the other.

24

CHAPTER TWO

Red-handed

hiara rod beside her brother Bernardo, mute and miserable, on the way from Gubbio to Giardinetto. She had taken very few possessions – only the dress she was wearing, her undergarments and the prayer-book that had been her mother's. Bernardo didn't know that she also had with her, sewn into the hem of her petticoat, a few small pieces of jewellery. The pearl and ruby cross and the gold earrings might come in useful one day in getting her out of the convent.

I expect he thinks he can give them to Vanna once I'm locked up with the Poor Clares, thought Chiara. Or sell them. It gave her a quiet satisfaction to imagine Bernardo going into her old room and opening the wooden jewellery casket on her window sill and finding it empty.

A cluster of buildings came into view as they rode down into the valley. It was a pretty spot, with the river winding through it and the bell tower of the friary chapel rising up among the whitewashed houses where the friars and nuns lived, surrounded by their neat gardens. True there were more marrows than flowers to be seen but even they looked charming at a distance, a broad circle of greenery, neatly hoed and tended.

This will be my home, thought Chiara. It was somehow

not as hateful an idea as she had imagined.

Silvano was out hawking with Celeste. It was only a small hunt, a few local nobles gathered together by the Baron and no other young men. Gervasio hadn't been invited. There was a dawn mist rising from the marsh and Ettore the hound was splashing through the water flushing out the wildfowl for Celeste to bring down.

It was a few days since Gervasio had read the poem to Angelica and Silvano hadn't seen her since. He shivered pleasurably in the early morning chill, remembering her reception of his words. The geranium flower, squashed now, was tucked inside his shirt, where it was making a red stain and giving off a faintly unpleasant smell.

Standing by the tree where his horse was tethered, Silvano watched his breath forming little clouds in the cold early morning air. But the sky was blue and clear and it would be another hot day, like most of the days of his life. He had the feeling that nothing would ever change, that he would always be young, that his life would roll out in front of him without adventure or incident under the blue skies of his native Umbria.

A heavy hand clapped on his shoulder startled Silvano out of his reverie.

'Boo!' said his father. 'I would pay to know what you are thinking.'

Silvano jumped and coloured up as guiltily as if he had been planning a murder.

'I can save my scudi, I see,' said his father much more

26

loudly than Silvano would have liked. 'Clearly there's a woman in the case. But regain control of yourself now – there are birds to be taken home for the pot.'

In Assisi, the friars were also up early, saying Prime in the Lower Church of the magnificent Basilica. Around their observance, the building was already swarming with workmen, from stonemasons to the most skilled artists from the great cities of Tuscany.

In a side chapel, one of these artists stood before a wall, red-loaded paintbrush in hand. This was in some ways the hardest part of any commission, transferring his vision from brain to wall, by way of the sketches he had brought with him. He knew how far they fell short of what he had in his mind. And no matter how much that image could be clothed in beautiful colours and his trademark embossed gold, it was the sinopia that would lay down the outlines of all that was to come and he wanted to get it right.

'Ser Simone,' said the priest in charge of the Basilica, interrupting the artist's thoughts. 'You were inquiring about more pigments, I believe?'

The artist wrenched his attention away from the swirl of forms and colours in his mind.

'Indeed, Father,' he answered. He had brought a good supply of already ground pigments with him when he came from Siena, but he had long since used them up and was going to need vast quantities more to finish the walls of the Chapel of Saint Martin in the way he imagined them.

'There is a convent in Giardinetto,' said the priest. 'A

house of Poor Clares, where they are skilled at preparing colours. They have been supplying the painters from Messer Giotto's workshop here in the Lower Church. And by great good fortune, their brother house of friars next to them has also started to produce pigments. Between them they should be able to meet your needs.'

'Excellent!' said the artist. 'And how far is Giardinetto from here?'

'Only a few miles,' said the priest. 'It lies towards Gubbio.'

'Then I could travel there to speak to the Colour Master,' said the artist. 'I should like to do that as soon as I have completed this sinopia.'

Chiara was woken on her first morning at the convent by the harsh clanging of the rising bell. The sisters rose at three to say Lauds, the first Office of the day, and again at dawn to say Prime, but as a novice she was allowed to get up later. She turned over on her thin, straw mattress and went back to sleep. It seemed only five minutes later that a hand was on her shoulder shaking her awake, not roughly but insistently.

It was Elisabetta, one of the other novices.

'What's the time?' asked Chiara, but Elisabetta shook her head and put her finger to her lips.

She waited, face turned away, while Chiara put on the shapeless grey robe she had been given the night before. Then she beckoned her to follow.

Chiara was shown first to the garderobe and then into the refectory where the sisters were already sitting at a long wooden table. Breakfast was taken in strict silence and it was

28

not much of a meal but Chiara was young and hungry. Her bowl of coarse porage and cup of goat's milk vanished quickly.

Then Sister Eufemia beckoned her and took her to the Abbess's room. Chiara had not met the Abbess on her arrival and was careful not to say anything until she was spoken to; she wasn't sure of the times at which the sisters had to keep silent.

The Abbess was tall and what could be seen of her hair under her veil was grey like her robe. Her face was almost fleshless, the countenance of one used to a life of fasting and prayer. But her dark eyes were bright and intelligent and Chiara instinctively wanted the Abbess to approve of her.

What has that brute Bernardo done? Abbess Elena was thinking, looking at her new charge. Nothing less like a girl with a vocation could be imagined. She looked at you full in the face, forgetting to lower her eyes, which were full of spirit. Her pretty young face was framed by dark curls and something about her brought back to the Abbess a wilful young girl of some thirty years ago, who had not expected to be called by God.

'You may sit down Chiara,' she said not unkindly. 'How are you finding it here?'

'It is pretty in Giardinetto,' said Chiara, her voice already feeling rusty and unfamiliar, 'but I don't expect I shall see much of it.'

'Why not?' said the Abbess. 'Although we are a closed order, as a novice you may leave the confines of the convent if you need to. You will be expected to work and that work could take you outside the convent walls. As long as you behave decently and respectfully among the people you meet,

29

and remember your calling, you may still play a part in the outside world.'

This was better than Chiara had dared to hope. But it was still not enough to lift her spirits. What work could a Poor Clare do that would bring any kind of excitement to her life? Tending vegetables or sick children would be very worthy but hardly romantic. And once she was professed, even that escape would be denied her.

'When you take your vows in a year's time, you will have a new name,' the Abbess was saying. 'We have chosen the name Orsola for you; you might like to start using it now.'

A tear slipped down the side of Chiara's cheek in spite of her best efforts to stop it; she hated the name Orsola. Little bear, it meant. Why would any girl want to be called that? Her own name meant bright and that was how she had always seemed to herself, like a candle in darkness, like sunshine on a spring day. She had always managed to remain cheerful even in the unloving home she had grown up in and now she was afraid of the convent snuffing her spirit out.

Besides, Chiara was the name of the patron saint of the Poor Clares so why should she change it? But 'Sister Orsola' felt like her destiny – a dark, shapeless, unimaginable form.

She bent her head submissively.

'And now we must cut your hair,' said Sister Eufemia.

Chiara looked at her in open horror; she hadn't thought about that.

'It is the custom,' said the Abbess, gently. 'Not too short while you are a novice. But no sister may retain such flowing locks. It encourages vanity. There is no shame in it, child. It is what the blessed Saint Francis himself did for your namesake, the founder of our Order, when she chose to leave

30

her family and follow him.'

There was no escape. Chiara would suffer enough humiliation having her hair shorn off; she wouldn't add to it by struggling. She took off her simple white veil and stood quietly while Sister Eufemia, who was rather short, stretched up to cut her hair into a ragged halo. The curls, no longer held down by their own weight, sprang even more wildly about her face. She felt literally light-headed and a bit cold. She was glad of even the flimsy veil to protect her vulnerable neck.

Poor child, thought the Abbess, looking at the luxuriant hair on the floor while Sister Eufemia took her charge off to instruct her. She bent down impulsively and gathered up handfuls of the glossy dark curls, feeling their weight and texture before casting them out of the window. 'Let the birds build their nests with them,' she murmured.

Tommaso the sheep farmer was puffing up the hill from the market-place to his home. He was humming to himself; his fleeces had fetched a good price earlier in the summer and now his vegetables were doing well. And he had another little business that was thriving too. He would have significant wealth to leave to a son. Now that Angelica had let him back into her bed he was hopeful that he might have a son at last.

It was early afternoon and there were few people about; most were taking their midday meal or were already enjoying their rest. It was not the time of day to fear attack and, when he heard light footsteps behind him, Tommaso paid no attention. Even when he felt the blow at his side, he thought that some young bravo had just bumped into him by mistake.

31

He turned to curse the careless youth and saw someone running back down the hill. His legs felt weak and, looking down, he saw red flowering from his tunic. He put his hand to his side uncomprehendingly, and sank to his knees. It didn't hurt, but there was a silver dagger-hilt sticking out from between his ribs. He grasped it and then the pain began.

He was a few doors from his house. He roared like a bell-wether. He looked up and saw a face he thought he recognised, a good-looking face. Tommaso clutched at the young man's arm, not caring that he was splattering blood on the other's clothes.

'Murder!' he whispered, feeling his voice gurgling in his throat.

'Murder,' echoed Silvano, gazing stunned at his lady's husband dying in the street.

And then there was the sound of running feet all around him and a woman started screaming.

'This is where we grind the colours,' said Sister Veronica. She was tiny, several inches shorter than Chiara, with the bone structure of a twelve-year-old and hands and feet to match. She was neat and deft in all her movements and Chiara understood why she was valued by painters.

As she was shown round the pigment room, Chiara discovered that the preparation of colours was a serious business. Elisabetta the novice worked there already, as did two older fully professed sisters, Lucia and Felicita. But there was plenty of work and Chiara could see why Sister Veronica needed another pair of hands.

32

The sisters sat at a long wooden table, like the one in the refectory, but instead of a wooden platter, each had in front of her a square slab of a red veined stone.

'Porphyry,' said Sister Veronica, following Chiara's glance. 'It is harder than marble and ideal for grinding colours. You take another piece – like that one Sister Lucia is using, see? – and grind the natural minerals on the slab until they are a fine powder. Then you add fresh spring water and mix them together.'

Chiara looked round the room and saw shelves lined with little bottles, each stoppered with a cork and labelled in spidery writing. She went to take a closer look, fascinated.

'Vermilion,' she spelled out. 'Terra verde, azurite, dragonsblood. Dragon's blood?'

'Not much of that, you see,' said Sister Veronica. 'It is not used by the fresco painters in Assisi. The friars use it for illuminating manuscripts.'

'But is it really made from the blood of dragons?' asked Chiara, wide-eyed.

'According to some,' said Sister Veronica, 'it is the result of battles between dragons and elephants. But it seems more likely to be a resin that comes from a shrub.'

Chiara looked disappointed. She liked the explanation about dragons and elephants better.

'But it is a shrub that does not grow in these lands,' said Sister Veronica. 'It grows only on hot islands in the East.'

Well, that was something, Chiara thought. At least it came from somewhere exotic, even if not from real dragons.

33

Baron Montacuto was roused from his afternoon rest by his manservant tugging at his sleeve. The Baron had only just drifted into a refreshing dream about boar-hunting and was tetchy at being disturbed.

'A thousand apologies, my lord,' said the servant nervously. 'But it is the young master. They say he has killed a man.'

The Baron was instantly awake, shaking his head like a wild boar himself, one with something caught on his tusks. He motioned towards a pitcher of water and the servant fearfully obeyed his master's gestures to throw the contents over his head. The Baron ran downstairs, buckling on his sword and shaking the water drops out of his grizzled hair and beard.

'Where is Silvano?' he demanded of the servant.

'Disappeared, my lord. They say he ran away when people came to help the dying man.'

'And who was this man?'

'Tommaso the sheep farmer. They say – forgive me, my lord – that your son was enamoured of Tommaso's wife.'

The Baron stopped in the hall and wiped the remaining moisture from his face. The servant cringed.

'I have heard something of this. But my son is no killer. He is mild as milk. Why do they put the blame on Silvano?'

'It was his dagger, my lord, with the family crest.'

The Baron looked instinctively up at the coat of arms above his mantel: the jagged summit of a mountain between oak trees. He had given Silvano that dagger himself.

Just then Silvano himself appeared, white-faced and red-handed. Blood stained his elegant jerkin and his long fingers.

'What the devil does this mean?' demanded his father, relieved though he was to see the boy alive. He hustled him

34

into a side room where they couldn't be overheard.

'I . . . I came in through the stables,' stammered Silvano. There is a mob after me. They think I . . . they say I killed a man.'

'So I've heard,' said the Baron testily. 'Well? Did you?'

Silvano looked miserable. 'No. I found him dying. I tried to help him.'

'Dying from your own weapon, as I hear,' said the Baron. 'Do you swear it was not by your hand?'

'I swear it,' said Silvano passionately. 'You know I would not kill anyone – unless to save my mother or sisters. I don't know what happened to my dagger. I knew it was missing only when I saw it in the body.'

'I believe you,' said the Baron. 'But you are in severe danger. It looks bad against you. Weren't you fooling with the man's wife?'

Silvano looked anguished. 'Not exactly,' he mumbled. 'But why would I kill her husband in broad daylight, with my own dagger?'

'The Council will not concern themselves with such fine detail,' said the Baron. 'You will be arrested and, unless we can find the real assassin and force him to confess, you will be executed.'

There was a furious knocking at the great wooden door.

'Quick,' said the Baron. 'Go and wash all that blood off. Give your stained clothes to the servants to burn. Then take refuge in your mother's chamber.'

Cautiously he led Silvano back into the hall and summoned the servant who was waiting.

'I need you to take a message to the Franciscans in the city,' he ordered, thinking fast.

35

The Baron turned to Silvano. 'No one is going take my son from me without a fight,' he said grimly. 'Now, hurry, or it will be too late.'

The Abbot of Giardinetto was standing at his window when he saw a member of his Order riding at full tilt towards the friary. It was unusual enough to see a friar on horseback; they were encouraged to walk everywhere, unless they were sick. Such a messenger must bring urgent tidings.

The exhausted friar was shown into the Abbot's room and given a blessing before being poured a cup of wine. He waited until he was alone with the Abbot before spilling out his message.

'I come from the brothers in Perugia,' he said. 'My name in Christ is Ambrogio and I am sent by my Abbot. You know the Baron Montacuto, I think, Father?'

'I do indeed,' said the Abbot. 'We were at university together in Bologna, more years ago than I care to remember. Bartolomeo da Montacuto has been generous to the friary here too.'

'And now he begs a favour of you, Father,' said Brother Ambrogio. 'His only son is in mortal danger, accused of a murder he swears he did not commit. The Baron asks that you give the boy sanctuary here in Giardinetto until the real culprit can be found.'

'Bartolo's boy,' said the Abbot, half to himself. He had not had much contact with his old friend in recent years but he knew of the many children conceived and lost by the delicate Baronessa, knew how much this boy – Silvio, Silvano? –

36

meant to the friend of his youth. Titles, property, inheritance – these were all baubles the Abbot had renounced when he accepted God's calling but he understood what his only son and heir meant to Bartolomeo da Montacuto.

'We will take him,' he said decisively. 'If Montacuto says he is innocent, then he is and we shall shelter him until it can be proved.'

❧

Chiara was walking with Elisabetta back from the colour room to the living quarters, when she saw two horsemen riding into the yard of the neighbouring friary. She looked up with interest in spite of Elisabetta's shushings and frantic gestures to turn her eyes away from the visitors. Both were dressed in the grey habits of the friars of Saint Francis, but Chiara was not so long out of the world not to recognise that the younger one was a most unlikely religious.

His robe seemed to have been thrown on over some more fashionable clothes and he was wearing boots of fine suede. His horse was of a much better quality than his companion's and there was a hawk on his pommel. Chiara peered through the dusk unable to believe her eyes, but it was true. There really was a hunting bird, probably a peregrine, tethered to this 'friar's' saddle. It was the most interesting thing she had seen since entering the convent.

Silvano looked up, as if aware of a gaze fastened on him. He saw two sisters of the Poor Clares, one modest, with downcast eyes, agitatedly trying to pull her companion away. The other stood boldly looking out towards the friary, frankly assessing him and his horse.

37

In that moment he knew that there was one person in Giardinetto who would never believe he was a Franciscan novice. But it did not alarm him; he found it comforting, as if there would be someone in his new home who could be a friend.

CHAPTER THREE

Sanctuary

ommaso the sheep farmer was buried with great pomp and solemnity for someone of his station. His widow Angelica hid her relief and excitement by paying, out of what were now her own full coffers, for a Requiem Mass in the Cathedral and elaborate black mourning for herself, her mother and her two younger sisters. Even her father had a new black velvet hat.

After the service, the few mourners went back to the fashionable town house, where Angelica had ordered a feast. Truly, there was not much mourning being done, except by Tommaso's two nephews, who had hoped that Fate might have removed their uncle's second wife before him and given them the farm and the fat flocks of sheep.

But Fate had not leant kindly in their direction; she had instead decided to favour the unhappy bride, at least for the time being. In spite of the sudden and violent manner of Tommaso's death, Angelica had to concentrate hard on not skipping for joy. The thick black widow's veil was invaluable in disguising her smiles.

Her family were equally far from desolate. Angelica's parents were hoping to move into the palazzo soon; the bargain with poor, rich, dead Tommaso had been their idea and they looked forward to gaining handsome interest from their

39

small investment of a child.

Angelica had different ideas. She didn't mind helping her parents and sisters a little but she had become increasingly fond of her own way the less she had been allowed to exercise it, and was getting ready to be equally fond of having her own money. When the period of mourning was over, she would emerge as a woman of business, familiar with her late husband's account books. And that would be the time to welcome a second suitor.

Sanctuary was a blessed-sounding word, thought Silvano. He felt safe, protected from the summary justice that the Council would have meted out to a man caught red-handed beside the body of his enemy – especially one whose dagger was in that enemy's chest.

He had been a counterfeit novice for a week but his mind was far from thoughts of prayer and repentance. Over and again he relived the moment of finding Tommaso bleeding to death in the street; it troubled his dreams and even by day he found himself checking his hands to see if they were free from blood. As well as the ghastly image of a man's bloody death, he was haunted by what had followed – the screaming of a woman (had it been Angelica?), the running feet and his own decision to leave the scene as quickly as possible.

Should he have stayed and defended himself? With the blood dripping from his hands and his own dagger in Tommaso's chest, he just couldn't have risked it. Not that he knew it was his dagger straightaway. But it had looked familiar and as soon as he returned home he saw that his own was missing from its sheath.

When he wasn't thinking of Tommaso, his mind strayed to Angelica. Did she know he was supposed to have killed her husband? Did she hate him? Did she miss him? Did she even think of him at all? How he wished he could get a message to Gervasio in Perugia and ask him to plead his cause with the beautiful young widow!

These people, the characters in the most interesting story of his life so far, were more vivid to him than the grey-clad friars who lived at Giardinetto. He found it hard to take in the new names when everyone dressed the same. But gradually they became clearer to him. Father Bonsignore, the Abbot was easy to remember. He was kind with a round face and a steel grey tonsure fringing his head.

Brother Ranieri, a tall thin friar, was the Novice Master. He knew Silvano's true story but was as welcoming to him as if the young man had been a genuine novice, with a calling to follow Saint Francis. As far as Silvano was aware, no other friar knew of the fate he had come to Giardinetto to escape.

He was friendly with the real novices like Brother Matteo, and the younger professed friars like Brother Taddeo, who was Assistant Librarian, but most of the others were still just a grey blur of names and titles to him.

❧

Chiara had a week or so's advantage of Silvano and there were fewer Poor Clares to remember than there were friars next door. Gradually she had settled into the routine of the convent and was surprised to find how little she missed her previous life in Gubbio.

41

There were still things that irked her, of course. The poor food for one and the keeping of silence between Compline after supper and Terce after breakfast the next day. She was always forgetting that Poor Clares must also not speak in the dormitory or refectory or in chapel except to say the words of the Office.

But for one who liked to chatter and to hear gossip all around her, it was surprising how easily she had given it up. She missed her sister-in-law Vanna, of course, and her little niece and nephew. But the grey-robed sisters were not unfriendly or unkind and she positively liked the other novices, Elisabetta, Cecilia and Paola, even though she was constantly shocking them with her bold behaviour.

'She'll learn,' said Sister Eufemia, any time one of the other novices drew Chiara's failings to her attention. 'She'll have to.'

And it really seemed as if she might. Already the routine of trooping into the little chapel to say the Hours of the Office seemed normal and her life as a young girl in the outside world was slipping away.

The highlight of Silvano's days now was to go to the stables every morning and rub down his horse and take Celeste out in the yard to fly for her daily ounce of meat. Sometimes he met a kindly friar called Brother Anselmo there. He seemed to like horses and was interested in Silvano's falcon.

'Falcons need exercise,' Silvano told him, tying a piece of meat to a lure on a long length of cord. 'Celeste must fly every day or her feathers will go out of condition. It gives her just

42

enough exercise when I swing the lure for her to fly to. But she should really fly further.'

He might have said the same of himself. The life of a religious brother was very alien to him. This was the other side of the rich coin of sanctuary: even after a week, he was missing his hunting and riding, his regular visits with his father to inspect the work on their farms. Here he had no more exercise than the walk from dormitory to chapel, from chapel to refectory, and he missed the sun on his back and the breeze in his face.

He had to get up with the dawn to say prayers and his meals were scanty and without meat. At least his hair had not been tonsured; he thanked God for that. But his coarse grey robe and bare feet were a long way from the elegant clothes and soft leather boots he was used to. Truly he felt his own feathers drooping like a mewed hawk.

Once, on one of his limited journeys within the walls of the friary, he had seen the bold-eyed girl again. She was walking in the convent garden, with two other novices, gathering herbs. The others put what they culled swiftly and efficiently into their baskets but this girl stopped and sniffed every leaf and branch. He caught her eye, as she crushed a verbena leaf and held it to her face, inhaling in a kind of ecstasy.

When she saw his eyes upon her, she turned away in confusion, dropping the verbena and all the other herbs from her basket. The novices knelt to gather them up with little cries like those of the grey doves their robes made them resemble, while the bold girl remaining standing, turned away, her shoulders drooping. It pained Silvano to see her dejection, since it mirrored his own.

'I have a commission for you,' a voice broke in on the

young man's thoughts. Father Bonsignore, the Abbot, was making an unaccustomed visit to his stables. 'How would you like to hunt some fowl for the brothers' table?'

'I thought you didn't eat meat,' said Silvano, startled into abruptness, his mind still on the dove-grey girl with the drooping shoulders.

'We, Brother Silvano,' said Father Bonsignore, 'do occasionally treat ourselves to flesh, especially on Holy Days and High Festivals. And Brother Rufino likes to keep a few delicacies in the infirmary for the older or ailing brothers.'

'And could I really take Celeste out?' asked Silvano. It was a blessed vision of liberty under blue skies amidst the safe but grey life among the holy brothers.

Father Bonsignore sighed. 'You are here as our guest, Silvano, and we have no wish to confine you. You may take your horse and hawk once a week to bring back fowl for Brother Bertuccio's kitchen. But you must not stray far from the walls of our house. Remember that you are still suspected of a terrible crime. Our protection covers you only within these walls. Still, a few hours early in the morning once a week, while the brothers say Prime, should not be too risky.'

'Thank you, Father,' said Silvano fervently. 'I shall be careful. When may I go?'

'You may start tomorrow,' said the Abbot. 'But you must be back in time for breakfast. Now I think it's time I assigned you some work to do.'

❧

The huge silver epergne in the shape of two dragons fighting sat in the middle of one of the finest dining tables in Gubbio.

44

Monna Isabella gave silent thanks for it, as she did at every meal, while her husband said grace. 'Thank you, God, for putting it into Ubaldo's mind to buy that hideous great thing when we married. And for saving me the sight of him for twenty years.'

It was not a very pious prayer, but deeply heartfelt. Ser Ubaldo was an immensely rich merchant, who had been wealthy even when he first set eyes on the lovely Isabella. And then he had decided he must have her as an ornament for his home, just as he might have determined to buy a large silver decoration for his table. It hadn't mattered a jot to him that she had been promised to a young scholar. The promise had been made by the lady herself and not sanctioned by her family. The scholar was poor and Ubaldo was rich. That was the end of the matter.

Isabella had hated her husband for so long it was second nature to her. The image of her first love still burned brightly in her memory after all these years – his dark brown eyes and slender hands, his sensitive mouth that had spoken such tender words and given her such passionate kisses. Ubaldo was not hideous or coarse but he was cold as the marble floor of the dining hall.

He treated her as a possession, not cruelly, but indifferently, after the first six months of their marriage, during which his passion had never once been rewarded with a spontaneous caress. He accepted that she would never love him and had long since ceased to have any feelings for her other than those of ownership. She was treated with the minimal politeness that her position as his wife merited. But he had a young mistress, not the first, and it was to her that he went to find the warmth lacking in his marriage bed.

45

Isabella gave thanks for the young mistresses, who had saved her from Ubaldo's presence in her chamber for so many years. She was in her mid-thirties, still beautiful, her figure rounded only a little by the birth of her four children. They were at table with her now, two on each side, and she could at least look on them with pleasure. It had surprised her every time she gave birth to discover the force of the love she felt for children born out of such indifference. But the three sons and one daughter she had dutifully given her husband were the greatest source of pleasure in her life.

It was to the friary's colour room that the Abbot took Silvano.

'This is Brother Anselmo, our Colour Master,' he said, introducing him to the friar Silvano already knew from meeting him in the stables, a middle-aged brown-haired man with an intelligent, bony face. 'He too has only recently joined us at Giardinetto. But he ran a colour room in his previous house.'

Behind Brother Anselmo five other friars sat at a long table with slabs of stone in front of them. They were all grinding something, like cooks in a kitchen crushing spices.

But the colour room wasn't full of pungent cooking aromas, delicious enough to bring water into the mouth. The smells were acrid and fairly unpleasant.

'As we discussed, Brother,' said the Abbot, 'I am assigning young Silvano here to assist you with the pigments.'

'Welcome,' said Anselmo. 'I shall be glad of another pair of hands.' Silvano wondered if the Colour Master knew why

46

he was there in the friary. Was it still only the Abbot and Brother Ranieri who knew he wasn't a real novice but a suspected murderer?

'You have joined us on an auspicious day,' said Brother Anselmo. We are to receive an honoured visitor today. The famous painter Simone Martini is coming to the colour room to inspect our work. And if we satisfy his high standards, he will order many pigments for his work in the Basilica of the Blessed Francis, our founder.'

The brothers looked up from their work on the wooden bench. The three real novices and two lay brothers were more interested in the impending arrival than that of a new novice. But by the end of the morning Silvano felt very much at home in the colour room. His hands were fine and dextrous, and the work of chopping, grinding and mixing was something he picked up easily.

It was indoor work though, which was frustrating. Thank goodness he had tomorrow's hunt to look forward to.

'Tell me everything you know about my son and that man's wife,' said Baron Montacuto.

Gervasio de' Oddini stood before the Baron in the great hall his friend called home. Even as Gervasio cleared his throat and fiddled with the hat in his hand, he couldn't help letting his gaze stray to the vast mantelpiece with the Montacuto arms above it, the brightly coloured tapestries of boar hunts and the heavy carved wooden chair in which the Baron sat to quiz him.

'I know that Silvano was infatuated with her,' he said

hesitantly. 'He wrote her a love poem.'

The Baron sank his grizzled head in his hands. 'Poetry!' his muffled voice said. 'Where is that poem now?' he asked, his voice suddenly clear again and his eyes raised bright to Gervasio's face.

'I don't know, sir,' said the young man.

'It could mean his death warrant if it fell into the wrong hands,' said Montacuto. 'If he had any sense, he would have burned it. But if he had any sense, he wouldn't be in the mess he's in now. See if you can find it, will you? Go to the man's widow and see if she has it and get it off her. I don't care what it takes.'

Gervasio's mouth curled into a smile, quickly suppressed. Silvano's father was issuing orders to him as if he were a servant rather than another member of a noble family, but the Baron was actually sending him to the beautiful Angelica, with his blessing! And all the while the poem was inside his own jerkin.

'We all know my son didn't do it,' continued Montacuto. 'This is killing his mother and sisters. They spend all day weeping over him. But it is far too dangerous for him to return.'

'May I ask where he is, sir?' asked Gervasio politely.

'You may ask,' snorted the Baron. 'But you'll excuse my not answering. Safest if no one knows who doesn't have to.'

'Welcome, Maestro!' said Brother Anselmo. He had never seen any of Simone Martini's paintings himself but the artist's reputation was great all over Tuscany and Umbria.

48

Rumour had it that he had just completed in Siena a Mary in Majesty so beautiful as almost to rival that of his old master Duccio in the Cathedral there. And Anselmo had seen that one of Duccio's installed himself.

The painter walked among the friars and novices watching their hands deftly grinding minerals on their porphyry slabs. He was a slight figure, with a down-turned mouth that made him look as if he were sucking lemons, thought Silvano. But he was not a miserable man; far from it. His grey eyes held the spark of great intelligence and liveliness of imagination.

'I brought with me to Assisi a great supply of colours,' he said in a high, light voice. 'But that was over a year ago and I am running out, in spite of the deliveries I've had from Siena since then. It would be very convenient to have a source of supply so near at hand.'

'It would be an honour,' said Brother Anselmo. 'We can supply most pigments that you are likely to need, I think. May I ask exactly what you are working on?'

'A chapel,' said the painter, waving his arm in an arc from left to right. 'I am telling the story of the life of Saint Martin on its walls. Fresco – the most difficult of all techniques. I have a workshop outside the Basilica where my journeymen mix the gesso for the walls. But they are not skilled in grinding pigments and I need them for humbler tasks like preparing the lime-white. And my assistants I need working with me on the frescoes if we are to be finished in time. We have been here many months already.'

Silvano racked his brains to recall something about Saint Martin but could not. Was there something about a cloak? Or was that Saint Francis himself? He couldn't remember.

'Rose,' the painter was saying. 'Purples, blues, greens. I

shall need ochres, cinnabar, vermilion, green earth – but most importantly, I must have some ultramarine. Can you supply me?'

'If you can provide the necessary lapis lazuli,' said Brother Anselmo, and he and the painter might have been speaking a foreign language for all that Silvano understood. 'But I'm sure you know how expensive it is.'

'Money is not a problem,' said the artist. 'The late Cardinal Gentile has left me well supplied with soldi. I can get you the stone. But do your brothers have the skill to make the ultramarine – the true blue?'

His piercing eyes raked the group of lay brothers and novices and lingered for a moment on Silvano's unshorn head.

'I can teach them, Maestro,' said Brother Anselmo.

Chiara had seen the false novice only once since he arrived, that day she dropped the herbs. Her cheeks burned to think of it, as they had then. Her knowledge of young men was very limited – and unlikely to become any more extensive now – but she had never seen any more pleasing to look on than the unconvincing brother in the house next door.

She asked Sister Cecilia, another novice, about him. But Cecilia was scandalised.

'We do not look at the brothers,' she whispered. 'Only the new friar, Brother Anselmo, who comes here to hear confession and celebrate Mass. Before him it was Brother Filippo, but he's too old and infirm now. And we know Father Bonsignore, of course. But we must never look at any of the

50

younger brothers, particularly the novices like us who are not yet professed.'

'But I'm sure that one is not a real novice,' said Chiara. 'He has a proper nobleman's horse. And a hunting hawk! How can a friar, even a novice, have such worldly goods?'

Sister Cecilia shook her head. 'I can't imagine. But it is wrong for us to speculate. It is not our concern, Sister Orsola.'

So many things seemed no longer to be Chiara's concern. Her world had never had very large horizons but now, within a week or so, it had shrunk to the little chapel, the sisters' house and the garden of the convent in Giardinetto.

Still, there was also the colour room. She did like working with Sister Veronica. The work grinding the pigments was dull enough, but the bright colours that sprang out when the water was poured on to the powders in the jars made her catch her breath, and ever since her first day, she had loved the names of them.

'Green earth,' she would murmur, as they worked on the pigments. 'Blood stone, cinnabar, red lake, death's head purple.' It was like a litany to her.

'Sister Orsola,' reprimanded Sister Veronica that afternoon. 'Silence while you work. We have an important visitor coming to see us.'

❧

Brother Anselmo watched as the artist crossed the short distance separating the Friary of Saint Francis from the Convent of Saint Clare.

'Oh well,' he said, shrugging his shoulders as he turned to

51

Silvano. 'It was not to be expected that he would entrust all his orders to us. The sisters have had a colour room much longer than we have and he will need a lot of paints if he is to cover the chapel he described.'

'I wish I could see it,' said Silvano. Listening to Simone describing the stories he was painting on the walls in Assisi had taken his mind off the murder for the first time since he had arrived in Giardinetto.

'Oh, but you will,' said Brother Anselmo, smiling. 'We are to take the first consignment to him at the end of the week. I thought you might like to come with me.'

CHAPTER FOUR

Saint Martin's Cloak

he morning air felt fresher to Silvano than a draught of pure spring water. It was a clear sunny day with a sharp tang of cold because of the early hour and he laughed as he rode his grey stallion flat out. The horse shook his head and snorted as he galloped, as happy to be away from the friary as his master was.

'We are free, Moonbeam, free at last,' cried Silvano, his novice's tunic streaming out behind him and revealing some very unreligious brown knees. Even Celeste, gripping the pommel of the saddle with her yellow talons, seemed to enjoy the feeling of the wind ruffling her feathers.

After a while the road began to climb into the hills and Silvano slackened the horse's pace. He found an open spot near a small stream and took the hood off his falcon. 'Fly, Celeste,' he whispered, releasing her jesses and casting her off into the sky.

She soared heavenward on a current of warm air and was soon lost to sight. Silvano wished for the hundredth time that he had been allowed to bring Ettore with him. The hound would have flushed out a good eating bird for Celeste in no time. As it was he had to hope that the falcon would return to his sight before she found prey on her own.

He listened for the silvery sound of the two bells on her legs and was soon rewarded. Celeste had flown in a wide circle and Silvano could just see her hovering high above. And even as he searched in vain for another bird in flight, his falcon, with her keen eyesight, went into a stoop; she had spotted something below her.

Silvano ran in the direction of Celeste's rapid descent, crushing grasses and twigs beneath his clumsy friar's sandals. He found Celeste sitting on a plump partridge and let her take a bit of the warm flesh before skilfully making the substitution with a bit of chicken wing he had brought in his pouch.

He stuffed the still bleeding bird into his saddlebag and let Celeste take a break. The day was warming up and he raised a heartfelt prayer of thanks to God above for letting him be out here in the Umbrian sunshine instead of inside the dark chapel of the friary in the company of several dozen pious men all older than him.

❧

Monna Isabella ran her household as well as any woman in Gubbio. Once she had accepted that she could not escape her marriage, she had become like a trained hawk; she would obediently return to her master's fist with something good for him to eat. Which is to say, she kept a good table. Ubaldo's money meant that she could order the finest food and the richest clothes. She and her children went about in velvet, silk and lace, like nobles, and their dinners were as lavish as a bishop's.

And this was because Isabella supervised everything

herself. No selection of food from the market or cloth from the merchant was made without her eye upon it. Not a chicken could be plucked in her kitchen without her knowing where every feather ended up, according to her servants.

It was a way to fill her days but that didn't mean she was happy. Thousands of women before her, she supposed, had endured marriages to men they didn't love – or even disliked – but every now and again a rage would rise in her heart that took her by surprise. It made her rail against her fate so hard that she had to hide away in her private sitting room till the fit passed.

On these days she thought of the young scholar with the brown eyes more than usual. It was a private dream of hers to imagine what marriage to her Domenico might have been like. It was a dangerous fantasy, because of the descent into reality that had to follow. But for a few hours she could picture the two of them sitting side by side poring over an illuminated book, while Domenico talked to her of poetry.

She remembered the terrible day when they met for the last time and she told him that she must marry Ubaldo. Domenico had told her the story of the Umbrian poet Jacopone da Todi, to console them both.

'Imagine, my darling,' he said. 'Jacopone, a wealthy young man, had married the lady of his heart's desire, the woman he had loved for years. They pledged themselves to each other for all time. But not long afterwards, at a grand feast, the platform where his bride was standing collapsed and she was crushed to death.'

'How dreadful!' said Isabella.

Domenico took both her hands in his. 'When the body of his wife was unearthed from the rubble, Jacopone found that

55

she was wearing an instrument of penance under her beautiful dress. Even on that day of rejoicing she had clothed herself in such a way as to mortify her flesh, in memory of Our Lord's suffering and because she feared Jacopone was too attached to the pleasures of the world.'

Isabella had been confused. What woman could be so pious and yet love a mortal man carnally, enough to marry him? 'What did Jacopone do?' she asked.

'For ten years he wandered like a beggar, sleeping rough,' said Domenico. 'And then he decided to devote the rest of his life to God. He turned his back on this world of personal desires and possessions and dedicated himself to the service of Our Lord. He joined the Franciscans. If he wrote poetry before to his beloved's beauty, since her death he writes only in praise of God.'

'And this is a tale to cheer me?' asked Isabella, her throat aching from all the tears she had shed.

'It is to show you that life must continue – even after great grief,' said Domenico. 'Yours and mine. You shall be another's but I shall never marry. I shall carry your image in my heart for ever and it will comfort me whenever my life is hard.'

And that was how they had parted, with a kiss that had to last them for the rest of their lives; they had not seen each other since. Domenico's lips had remained unkissed ever after, if he had been true to his vow, and Isabella's had suffered the unloving touch of Ubaldo's.

When her first son had been born, she had wanted to call him Domenico but her husband wouldn't hear of it.

'He is my son, not the bastard of your miserable swain,' he had said. 'Let him be Federico, after my father.'

Federico was followed swiftly by Giovanni and then there was a lost child. Ubaldo had been almost tender towards her then in her new grief. Was it because of that or the indifference he later felt for her that she was allowed to call their third boy Domenico after all?

Isabella neither knew nor cared. It was enough that she could say the name caressingly to her little boy. In spite of all her care not to show it, he was her favourite child. Her little daughter, Francesca, was a great joy and she loved all her sons, but Domenico had a special place in her heart.

He looked least like Ubaldo of all their children, having her rosy complexion and chestnut hair, while the others were all dark. And he was his father's least favoured child, which endeared him all the more to his mother. It was almost as if this little Domenico had been the result of her unfaithfulness, though this was entirely imaginary; she was not a fond wife but she was an honourable one. Whenever she retired to her sitting room in one of her black moods, it was of little Domenico that she thought, pretending that he was the son of her dream husband with the same name.

It was on one of those days that she heard an imperious knock at the door and started to her feet in surprise. Ubaldo never visited her here and yet there was no mistaking the master's knock. He did not wait for Isabella to open the door but came in, a dark presence shadowing the pretty space she had created for herself. There was no painting or relic of her first love and yet she was conscious that the room was a kind of shrine.

Ubaldo seemed to sense it too, curling his lip with disdain. But he made no reference to her setting. 'I have to go on a journey,' he said. 'To the friars in Assisi. The Franciscans will place an order for even richer altar cloths now that the Basilica is nearing completion. They want the best silks and I must have them embroidered according to their designs. I shall be away three days.'

'Thank you for telling me,' said Isabella politely, but exulting that she would have three whole days without her husband. 'When do you leave?'

'Tonight,' said Ubaldo. 'I shall ride as far as the friary at Giardinetto and lodge there.'

Chiara was walking to the refectory when she sensed the aroma of roasting partridge on the air; it made her mouth water. But the smell of cooking was not coming from the little wood oven at the convent. Meat was even more of a rarity for the grey sisters than for their brothers next door. But that was where the partridges were being roasted, turned on a spit over an outdoor fire by the false novice.

Chiara felt her stomach growl. She cast down her eyes as she went on towards the refectory, but not before she had seen the boy smile at her. He seemed happy, she thought, and she was sure that he hadn't been when he came, that first night when she had seen him riding in on his grey horse. Perhaps she would have had cause to smile too if there was roast fowl to dine on in the convent; there was nothing to look forward to but a sort of savoury gruel, lumpy and rather gritty.

Chiara found herself sitting at the refectory table opposite Sister Veronica. The sisters ate in silence but the Colour Mistress cast a sympathetic glance at the young novice toying

58

with the gluey mess with her wooden spoon. As soon as they were both outside again and walking back to the dormitory for quiet contemplation, Sister Veronica spoke to Chiara.

'Would you like to come with me when I take Ser Simone's colours to Assisi?'

Chiara looked at her in surprise. 'You may leave the convent, Sister?' she asked. 'I thought all the professed sisters had to remain enclosed.'

'I have a special dispensation from the Abbess,' said Sister Veronica. 'I may go outside the convent in the service of the Lord. So, would you like to come with me?'

Chiara nodded gratefully. Just to have a change of scene from the convent would be a treat. 'Yes please, Sister,' she said. 'I should like that very much.'

❧

The wooden cart was laden with boxes and barrels filled with glass jars. It didn't really take two friars to transport them from Giardinetto to Assisi but the Abbot was quite content to let Silvano go with Brother Anselmo. And his strong young arms would be useful for the unloading.

It was not a long road but Silvano had not travelled it before; in fact he had never visited Assisi in all his sixteen years, although it was not far from Perugia. Brother Anselmo was telling him about the Basilica, as he occasionally flipped the reins on the back of the horses.

'The Lower Church, where Ser Simone is working, was built first. In fact they started building it within two years of Saint Francis's death. But the whole Basilica was only finished less than forty years ago.'

59

'Finished?' said Silvano, surprised. 'How can it be finished? The painters are still working there.'

'I suppose in one sense a great church is never completed,' said Anselmo. 'It is always being added to and beautified. But the Basilica was consecrated before I was born. And the frescoes of the Upper Church are already a sight that pilgrims come from miles around to see.'

'You have seen them yourself?'

'Oh yes, many times. They were painted by Giotto di Bondone. Ser Simone speaks of him with almost the same reverence we use towards Saint Francis.'

'Forgive me,' said Silvano. 'But I am rather ignorant about saints and their lives.'

'That's understandable,' said Anselmo. 'You didn't expect to be joining a religious house.'

Silvano looked at his bony profile. 'You know about me?' he asked quietly.

'Father Bonsignore told me a little when he asked me to take you on in the colour room. I know you are not really a novice.'

'And you know what I am supposed to have done?'

Anselmo nodded.

'Well, I didn't,' said Silvano.

Anselmo smiled. 'Of course not,' he said. 'You are no murderer.'

Silvano felt his heart lift. No one had said that to him since he found Tommaso dying in the street. Even his father had needed to ask him. He felt a warm rush of affection for Brother Anselmo, who accepted him so calmly and believed in him so completely.

'Who else knows why I am in Giardinetto?' he asked.

'Only Brother Ranieri,' said Anselmo.

'I know about him,' said Silvano. 'As Novice Master, he needed to know that I was seeking sanctuary and had no calling.'

'Then there is just him, myself and the Abbot,' said Anselmo.

'I wonder how long I'll have to stay here,' said Silvano.

'Do you hate it so much?' asked Anselmo.

'Oh, no,' said Silvano, flustered and wondering if he had seemed rude or ungrateful. 'Not at all. It's just that I can't bear not knowing what's going on in Perugia. Have they found the real murderer? Or is my name still slandered? It seems cowardly to hide away in the friary when I am not guilty. I would have stayed to plead my innocence but my father wouldn't let me take the risk. I am his only son.'

'You are precious to him,' said Anselmo simply. 'I can understand that. I wasn't born a friar, you know.'

Silvano wondered if the Colour Master was one of those religious who had been a married man and lost his wife. Perhaps he had even had children of his own. 'You would be a good father, Brother,' he said impulsively, making them both laugh.

The hill of Assisi was coming into view, with its fortification at the top. Silvano could see the Basilica even from this distance, looking as if it had grown out of the rocks at the side of the hill, rather than being built by the hands of men. As they got nearer, Silvano could see that large numbers of people were swarming round the great church.

There were pilgrims, barefoot and wide-hatted, leaning on staffs. And there were people selling food and wine, and others selling carved wooden crosses and likenesses of Saint

Francis and Saint Clare. Then there were artisans who Silvano guessed were working for the artists, stirring barrels of plaster. He felt very proud to be bringing the colours that would bring the plaster to life.

Brother Anselmo left Silvano in charge of the horses while he went to find Simone Martini. He soon returned with the artist, who was clearly delighted to see both of them.

'Welcome to Assisi, Brother Silvano,' he said. 'I hear you have not visited here before? You must let me show you my work. But let's get these pigments unloaded first.'

He beckoned to one of the young workmen making gesso. 'Marco, come here and give our young friend a hand. He brings colours from Giardinetto.'

The four men made short work of unpacking the cart and then Marco took the horses off to a nearby stable. Silvano stretched in a rather unfriarlike way. He had been carrying in barrels without taking much notice of his surroundings and his arms ached.

But now he turned and looked around him. Simone was ordering the new materials on a long bench. They were in a chapel off the nave of the Lower Church. The windows had no glass in them and the light streamed in. That and the wooden scaffolding obscuring part of the walls made it difficult to see the wall paintings at first.

Silvano looked closer and he could see that each one was a miracle of colour and story-telling. The ceiling and the higher parts were completed and the round wooden platform where Simone stood to work was only just above Silvano's head.

Simone saw him looking at the pictures and invited him up on to the platform to show him more closely.

'You see, Brother Silvano? There is Saint Martin cutting his cloak in half for the beggar.'

There on the left was the Saint, on horseback, taking his sword to his cloak. Saint Martin was turned round looking backwards over his right shoulder at a poor shivering man, just as his horse had his neck turned round too.

The Saint's horse reminded Silvano of Moonbeam. It too was a grey horse with a proud neck and flared nostrils. The cloak concealed its hindquarters but Silvano was sure it was a hunting stallion too. It made a contrast with the Saint, whose mild face was framed by curled golden hair and a decorated halo.

The whole picture was a mass of pinks and greens and golds, offset by the dark blue sky behind. Silvano's gaze travelled upwards and he gasped. Peeping out from behind the scaffolding was Ser Simone's own face, with what Silvano thought of as his 'sucking lemons' expression. He was wearing a fashionable green and blue berettone on his head, quite different from the working clothes the painter was in now.

Simone caught his eye and laughed. 'You must read the pictures in sequence,' he said. 'Not up from that one but along to your right. You are not to look at my ugly face yet.'

He indicated a picture of the Saint lying in a bed having a dream. It was startlingly realistic and Silvano, who knew nothing about painting, could not believe that he was seeing a flat wall. There was the Saint in a nightcap, lying in his bed, his body making the chequered bedspread rise and fall round its contours. He had elegant and expensive embroidered white pillows and sheets, and a gold halo surrounded his nightcap.

Saint Martin's eyes were closed but there in his room was

63

Christ the Lord, surrounded by angels and wearing the very half of the blue cloak that Martin had given to the beggar in the other picture. Silvano was entranced. 'So the beggar was really Jesus?' he said to the painter. 'And Saint Martin had a dream of him?'

Simone looked pleased. 'You didn't know the story before? That's good. It means I've told it properly.'

'I've heard it but I couldn't remember all of it,' admitted Silvano. 'But it's very clear. Martin was kind to a poor man and then it turned out to be the Lord.'

'It is as we read in the Evangelist,' said Brother Anselmo, smiling. 'Our Lord said, "Whenever you have done something for one of my least important brothers, you have done it for me." So Saint Matthew tells us.'

Silvano suddenly felt safe between these two men, as safe as he felt in the friary. They were wise and good and could tell him of wonders. It was a world far away from blood and murder.

A shrill voice interrupted his thoughts. 'Ser Simone, we are here with the colours.' He turned and saw a grey-clad nun. By her side was another and he suddenly found himself staring straight into the eyes of the pretty novice from the convent next door.

CHAPTER FIVE

A Stab in the Dark

hiara was as astonished to see the novice friar as he was to see her. She didn't take in a word of the rather awkward introductions, except to notice that the painter, Ser Simone, was embarrassed and amused that both his suppliers of pigments had turned up at the same time.

Sister Veronica obviously knew Brother Anselmo and they were stiffly polite to each other, each a little wary of treading on the other's area of expertise.

Then Sister Veronica had gone off to supervise the unloading of her cart, with the painter and the young novice, leaving Chiara with the older friar in the chapel. It felt as if she were standing inside a jewellery box. Colours cascaded from the walls, sparkling with stamped gold and rich with azurite, cinnabar, red lake and malachite.

Chiara was suddenly flooded with sadness for the absence of colour in her present life and the future that stretched before her. For weeks now, apart from when she was in the colour room, she had been living in a sea of grey, the only brighter hues the occasional blue-eyed sister or glimpse of an illumination in the convent's psalter. She felt the tears spring to her eyes.

Fortunately, Brother Anselmo was not surprised to see

someone moved to tears by fine fresco painting.

'It's magnificent, isn't it, Sister Orsola?' he said gently.

'What? Oh, yes, Brother, it is quite wonderful,' said Chiara, sincerely.

'Ser Simone was explaining to Brother Silvano the order in which the scenes are to be read,' said Anselmo. 'Shall I show you?'

So his name is Silvano, thought Chiara, but she had the presence of mind to say out loud, 'Thank you, Brother. Please do tell me. I have never seen wall paintings before.'

Over the next half hour, more supplies of pigments were carried in by Silvano, Simone and the convent's cart-driver, under the fussy supervision of Sister Veronica. There were so many that they had to be stacked along underneath the bench. And yet Simone assured them he would soon use the colours up. Every time Silvano came back into the chapel, he was intensely aware of the pretty novice and of her conversation with Brother Anselmo. Every so often, the painter lingered to explain a detail of one of his pictures. During one of those breaks, when Silvano stopped to stretch his muscles, he spotted a falcon in one of the paintings. It was on the right wall of the chapel, on the lowest level.

'The Saint is receiving his knighthood in this one,' the painter was saying. An important-looking man in a rich red and gold robe was girding a sword round the Saint's waist. 'The Emperor Julian,' said Simone.

Silvano was confused by the picture. How could a man be a saint and a knight at the same time? The short time he had spent in the friary had made him believe that the religious life and the life of action were as different as red and blue. But this clearly was the Saint again, with his hands raised in

66

prayer even at the moment of his investiture, and his gold halo surrounding his almost equally golden hair.

Another figure was putting a spur on the Saint's left foot and in the background were colourfully dressed musicians and singers. It was a figure on the left who was holding the bird of prey. It was beautifully painted, with every feather clear and separate, the jesses and the bells, the leash and a golden hood all shown.

'He isn't wearing a glove,' said Silvano, before he could stop himself. 'You need a glove or the bird's talons grip your hand.' Instinctively, he held up his left arm; he could almost feel the light weight of Celeste on his wrist.

'I'm sure you're right,' said Simone, smiling. 'I'm no falconer. You sound as if you keep a hawk yourself.'

Silvano realised he was on dangerous ground and cast a quick look at Brother Anselmo. He saw that the young novice nun was listening intently.

'Brother Silvano takes his falcon out once a week to bring back food for the ailing friars,' said Anselmo.

'I trust there are not many of those,' said Simone and the moment passed.

❧

While Silvano and Chiara were being amazed by the art in the Basilica, Ubaldo the merchant was concluding a very successful meeting with the head of the friary at Assisi. The order for the altar cloths was going to make him a lot of money. He left and ate an early dinner at a local inn, fearing that the fare offered to him in Giardinetto would be as scanty as the night before. After many goblets of wine, he heaved himself up on to his horse with some difficulty and ambled towards the Gubbio road. The horse, who knew his master's moods well, adjusted himself to Ubaldo's slumped posture and did not break into a trot until they were on the main road.

On the way back to Giardinetto, he overtook two horse-drawn carts, one with two grey friars and the other carrying two Poor Clares. For some reason, the sight made Ubaldo laugh and he began to wobble in his saddle.

'What a lout!' whispered Sister Veronica. 'You'd think a man who can afford clothes and a horse like that would have better manners.'

It was not the sort of thing that nuns were supposed to say and Chiara was delighted to discover that Sister Veronica had this human side. It had been a most interesting day, what with the trip to the Basilica and meeting the painter and seeing the handsome novice.

'Ser Simone was very agreeable, wasn't he?' said Chiara. 'I liked him.'

Nuns weren't supposed to have personal likes and dislikes either, but Sister Veronica let it pass. It seemed as if all the rules were relaxed a bit once they were outside the convent.

'And a great artist,' added Veronica. 'It will be wonderful to see the chapel when it is all finished.'

'So we can go again?'

'Oh yes. I think Ser Simone will need several more loads from us and the brothers. We are going to be kept busy in the colour room.'

68

Brother Landolfo was the Guest Master at Giardinetto. He was a small, plump friar with a silver tonsure, who did not often have to offer hospitality to outsiders. But two days ago Abbot Bonsignore had told him to make a room ready for a rich merchant, saying that the house's reputation was at stake.

The first night, their guest had been brought supper in his room and had seemed to look down his nose at it a bit. So Landolfo was determined that the stranger would eat in the refectory tonight with all the brothers and that their fare would be richer than usual. He had discussed the meal with Bertuccio and Brother Nardo, the Cellarer.

Franciscan friars were not supposed to own anything but they were often given gifts, particularly of food and wine, in return for prayers said or acts of healing performed, and there was nothing against using the items they received. Since Giardinetto had a skilled Herbalist and Infirmarian there were plenty of such gifts.

Brother Landolfo fussed around the kitchen, driving the cook, Bertuccio, mad. But a commotion brought him out into the yard. Their distinguished guest had returned – and fallen off his horse. As Ubaldo staggered to his feet, helped by the friary's stableman, it was clear that he was inebriated. He waved graciously to Brother Landolfo.

'Good evening, Brother,' he said, his voice slightly slurred. 'How are you faring this evening? It has been a lovely day, has it not?'

Landolfo was pleased to see that Ubaldo was the kind of man who became mellow with drink rather than mean-tempered.

'Good evening, Ser Ubaldo,' he said. 'We are glad to see

69

you safely back from Assisi. I trust your business went well?'

'Excellently well, thank you,' said Ubaldo, swaying slightly.

'I hope you have not already dined,' said Landolfo anxiously. 'The brothers hoped to have the pleasure of your company at table tonight.'

'I shall be happy to join you,' said Ubaldo, aware of the rules of hospitality. He was so pleased with his day's work that he wouldn't mind eating a second dinner. And he thrived on the deference and respect the friars showed him. He never experienced anything like that in his own home, with his wife's quiet hostility always there like a murmuring underground stream.

He weaved his unsteady way across the courtyard as the bell rang for Vespers and all the friars scurried to the chapel.

'I shall join you in the refectory,' he said, 'when you have finished saying your prayers.'

Brother Anselmo and Silvano were back only just in time for Vespers themselves and the younger man found it even harder than usual to concentrate on the Office. Why couldn't he get the novice Clare out of his mind? Try as he might, he was finding it difficult to visualise Angelica's face and an altogether darker and rosier one was superimposed on his pink and white image of beauty.

This was madness. He loved Angelica. And where was the future in being attracted to a nun? Admittedly she wasn't professed yet, but she would soon be 'a bride of Christ' and out of any man's reach. These were very unholy thoughts to be having in a chapel and Silvano struggled to discipline his mind.

The visit to Assisi had been a welcome change but it was unsettling to be back in touch with life outside his sanctuary.

70

Simone's paintings with their vivid colours and their narrative of knightly adventure had made Silvano wonder afresh when he would be able to resume what he thought of as his real life. And yet he knew that he would miss the friars once he was back in Perugia, especially Brother Anselmo.

It was a shock when he entered the refectory after Vespers to see, at the top of the long table, the richly dressed merchant who had ridden past them on the road. So this was the visitor some of the younger friars had talked about! In spite of his wealth, Silvano hadn't thought much of the merchant's manners. In fact even Brother Anselmo had commented on the man's obvious consumption of liquor.

But as Silvano took his place at the bottom of the table, with the other novices and heard the name 'Ubaldo' mentioned, he was surprised to see the Colour Master's reaction. Brother Anselmo, as a senior friar, was seated much higher at the table and he was clearly having to fight to restrain some very strong emotion. Perhaps no one else would have noticed but Silvano had spent a lot of time with Brother Anselmo and felt he knew his moods.

Abbot Bonsignore took the head of the table with Ubaldo the merchant, as guest, on his right. Close by were the Lector, the Librarian, the Illuminator, the Guest Master and the Colour Master. Down Silvano's end, as well as the novices, sat the Assistant Librarian, the Herbalist, the Novice Master, the Cellarer and the dozen or so professed friars who had no assigned title within the friary. The Infirmarian was tending a couple of elderly brothers and was not present. The lay brother, Bertuccio, was still toiling in the kitchen.

The introductions, which took place after Grace, seemed to go on an inordinately long time. Silvano felt his stomach

71

rumbling. Ubaldo was the only man who had come to table without being particularly hungry and he took his time understanding who each brother was and what was his name and function, while Bertuccio fumed in the background, worrying about the food spoiling or getting cold.

At last, he was allowed to bring in his game-bird stew. Silvano couldn't believe the delicious smells coming from the dishes. His partridges had been consumed days ago and he hadn't been hawking since but Bertuccio had somehow got hold of some more fowl and worked kitchen miracles with them.

Ubaldo seemed more interested in having his wine cup filled than in what was on his plate, but at least he no longer looked disdainful and ate a reasonable amount, to Brother Landolfo's relief. In spite of what Sister Veronica thought, Ubaldo was not a lout. He was a rich man with expensive tastes, used to getting his own way. But he respected learning and piety, which is why he preferred to lodge with the friars rather than stay in a more comfortable inn.

He took pleasure in describing the Assisi altar cloths to the Abbot, who listened intently, along with Brother Fazio, the Illuminator, who had an interest in all decorative schemes.

Silvano didn't take much notice of the guest at first; he was more interested in how much stew would be left by the time the dishes reached his end of the table. Once his appetite was satisfied and he was more aware of his companions, he saw that Brother Anselmo had scarcely touched his food but was consuming much more wine than usual. He did not seem to be joining in any conversation with the merchant Ubaldo but was listening with intense concentration.

At the end of the meal, the Abbot said to his guest, 'I gather you will be leaving us early tomorrow morning and I am likely to be at Prime, so I shall say my farewell now. Convey my best wishes to your wife, Monna Isabella. May God go with you on the road to Gubbio.'

Brother Anselmo jumped up hastily from his chair, knocking his wine cup over.

'Forgive me Father Abbot, honoured guest,' he muttered. 'I am not well.'

And he hurried out of the refectory, leaving Ubaldo staring after him.

The friars went to bed early because they had to get up in the middle of the night to say the Office. Silvano still wasn't used to such a strict routine and usually didn't get enough sleep, even though he was excused Matins and Lauds. But he was young and healthy and not ready to go to sleep while the sky was still light.

When it was time to retire, Silvano hesitated at the door of the dormitory then turned away in the direction of the senior friars' cells. He had never approached Brother Anselmo's cell before, but he was worried about him. He knocked lightly at the cell door, but there was no reply. He saw that a light was burning in a cell a few doors along, which he knew to be the guest room.

While he stood uncertain in the corridor debating whether he should lift the latch on Brother Anselmo's door, the Colour Master returned. He started when he saw Silvano, then relaxed.

'I came to see how you were, Brother,' said Silvano.

'You're a good boy,' said Anselmo, patting him on the shoulder. 'I am much better now, thank you. I think the rich

73

fare at supper disagreed with me. But you must get to your own bed, or you will be yawning in the chapel again.'

Silvano went on his way not quite satisfied; he knew that Brother Anselmo had eaten very little of the 'rich fare'.

'Father Abbot, Father Abbot!' The Infirmarian was knocking at Bonsignore's cell door long before Matins.

The Abbot came to the door in his undershirt, his grey tonsure a tousled halo. 'What on earth is it, Brother Rufino? Don't tell me one of the friars has gone to his Maker?'

'Not a friar, Father,' said Rufino. He looked ghastly in the light from his flickering candle. 'It is our guest, Ubaldo the merchant.'

'Ubaldo? By Our Lady, what ill luck! Under our roof! What was it – a seizure?'

'This is the dreadful thing, Father,' said Rufino. 'I was on my way back to my cell from the infirmary, when I noticed the door to the guest room was open. I glanced in to check whether he was unwell or just out at the garderobe and I saw him stretched out on the bed.' Rufino's hand holding the candle shook so hard he spattered hot wax on himself. 'The merchant was dead.'

'Come inside, Brother,' said the Abbot. 'We shall light a lantern and go and see him together. Perhaps he had just fallen back to sleep without shutting the door? He had consumed rather a deal of wine.'

'No, Father,' stammered Rufino. He allowed himself to be led into the Abbot's cell and accepted a chair. 'You don't understand. He has been stabbed. The dagger is still in his

74

chest. He is quite dead.'

By the light of the candle, Bonsignore saw that Rufino's hands and robes were stained red. The friar had obviously tried to revive their guest.

'We must not wake the other brothers yet,' he said quietly. 'I shall go and see for myself. You stay here.'

The Abbot was back within moments and poured two goblets of wine for Brother Rufino and himself. His own hand was shaking as he drank. He had never seen the result of a violent death at first hand.

'I shall give orders to toll the chapel bell,' he said, struggling into his grey robes. 'It shall suffice both as a passing bell for Ubaldo the merchant and to sound the alarm. The murderer may still be in the friary.'

Even as he said it, the Abbot remembered that he was giving sanctuary to a man accused of murder. And murder by stabbing in the ribs with a short dagger, just as the merchant had been killed. But he thrust the thought to the back of his mind.

❧

The bell of the friars' chapel next door woke the sisters from their deep sleep.

'Lord have mercy!' said Sister Cecilia, the novice who slept on a pallet beside Chiara. 'Old Brother Filippo must have died in the infirmary.'

'Who's Brother Filippo?' Chiara asked groggily, propping herself up on one elbow.

'I told you,' said Cecilia. 'He was our priest before Brother Anselmo came. He is an old man – at least fifty – and their

Infirmarian, Brother Rufino, has been treating him for the ague. We should pray for his soul.'

Chiara didn't quite see why she should get out from under her warm cloak and on to her knees on the cold floor for a friar she had never met.

'We don't even know it was him,' she objected. But Sister Felicita was awake now on her other side, and reaching for her rosary.

'Whoever it is, the Lord will know the right name,' she said, suppressing a yawn. 'We can just pray for a departed brother and say the Sorrowful Mysteries.'

But before the three young women had got far in their prayers, the Abbess herself entered the dormitory.

'Sisters in Christ,' she said, as calmly as she could manage. 'A messenger has come from the friary. Father Bonsignore sends to say that their guest, a merchant from Gubbio, has been stabbed in his sleep. The Abbot has sent two lay brothers to stand guard outside our door till daybreak. We shall not visit the chapel until at least Terce, but you may go to the refectory to break your fast as soon as it is light, unless I send to say it is not safe. The younger friars are searching the friary and grounds now for the murderer.'

Chiara had a vision of Silvano the novice out in the dark with a blade-wielding assassin at large. She shuddered and drew her coarse grey mantle over her shoulders.

'You may return to your prayers,' said the Abbess. 'And say the Mass for the Dead. A man has died unshriven and unprepared. Ubaldo of Gubbio will need all our help if he is to reach Heaven.'

CHAPTER SIX

Suspicion

aybreak found both the religious houses of Giardinetto in disarray. The normal disciplines of early rising and saying the Office had broken down and both the friary and the convent were no longer places of order, quiet and safety.

There had been deaths in the friary before, even deaths of visitors; in the early years of the fourteenth century, there were many reasons why a man's life might come to a sudden end. But murder was something else. And Ubaldo's blood left a stain on more than the flagstones.

Everyone was talking of an intruder, yet there had been no theft. The outer doors were never bolted at night, so any stranger could have entered without alerting the friars, but there was the unspoken fear that the killer might have come from within the friary. One by one, the Abbot called each friar to his cell and questioned them closely about whether they had seen or heard anything unusual. It was Brother Taddeo, the Assistant Librarian, who first mentioned that Silvano had not come straight to the dormitory after supper.

The Abbot immediately summoned the other novices, two of whom confirmed that Silvano had turned aside at the dormitory door and headed off towards the individual cells. Father Bonsignore sat in meditation for a while. He did not like to think that this personable young man, the son of his old friend, was a murderer. He had given him sanctuary at Giardinetto unhesitatingly and had not had any reason to regret it.

Silvano was an obedient and willing member of the house, doing anything that was asked of him with good grace. He had settled well to work in the colour room and had good relations with the other friars, particularly Brother Anselmo. Nothing that the Abbot knew of him sat well alongside the bloody corpse of Ubaldo the merchant. Why would this young man commit this crime? Even if by some unlikely turn of events Silvano had really been guilty of the murder he was accused of in Perugia, why in Heaven's name would he kill a visitor to the friary?

The only explanation was that Silvano might be the victim of insanity, but the Abbot felt sure there would have been some outward sign before now. He sighed deeply and prayed for guidance before sending for the young man.

❧

'What's going on?' asked Chiara, straining to see what was happening over the wall of the friary. The three other novices, unable for once to contain their curiosity, were all with her.

The two lay brothers who had stood guard over the convent through the dark hours were now breaking their fast in the sisters' refectory and the nuns had abandoned their daily duties. The friary seemed to be equally disordered. Once the chapel bell had stopped tolling for Ubaldo, it had not sounded again and the first three Hours of the Office had been unsaid, except by some of the brothers in private.

There had been many comings and goings of the friars across the yard between the refectory, where they had all been assembled, and the building where the Abbot and the other senior members had their individual cells.

'There goes that new novice of theirs,' said Sister Elisabetta.

Chiara was surprised. So Elisabetta had noticed Silvano, in spite of all her insistence on downcast eyes and lack of interest in men.

'He looks upset,' said Sister Cecilia.

'Of course he does,' said Elisabetta. 'It's a terrible thing to happen in a House of God.' She crossed herself piously.

'Or anywhere,' added Sister Paola.

'Perhaps he found the body?' suggested Cecilia.

'Why do you think that?' demanded Chiara.

'Only that he seems to grieve more than you'd expect for a passing visitor,' said Cecilia.

'Let me see,' said Chiara.

It was true that Silvano was pale; she could see that even from this distance. But that could have been from lack of sleep and he had a naturally fair complexion. Chiara knew that she was not supposed to think of the colour of a young man's face, but she couldn't help it. Her father, her brother, a few family acquaintances in Gubbio – these were the only men she had met and none was as fair as Silvano. He made the cluster of novices around her seem swarthy.

'Sister Orsola, what on earth do you think you are doing?' a sharp voice rang out.

Sister Eufemia, the Novice Mistress, was bustling across the courtyard to her charges. She looked scandalised.

'Come away from the wall!' ordered Eufemia. 'You are disgracing our sisterhood!'

Silvano was having a gruelling time with the Abbot. Since he had arrived at Giardinetto he had received nothing but kindness from the friars, especially Father Bonsignore, who often talked to Silvano about his university days with the Baron. Silvano had felt trusted and accepted and now all that was threatened by whoever had stuck a knife in Ubaldo the merchant. Silvano cursed his luck; if Ubaldo had to have an enemy and one who followed him to Giardinetto, why hadn't the villain used a club or some poison? Anything but a dagger in the ribs.

Immediately, Silvano felt ashamed of his thoughts.

'You admit that you did not go straight to bed after supper?' the Abbot was asking.

'I went to see Brother Anselmo,' said Silvano and instantly regretted it. He felt the colour rising in his face, even though what he was saying was true. 'I went to see if he was better as he said he was unwell at supper.'

'So Brother Anselmo will confirm that he saw you,' said the Abbot.

'Yes,' said Silvano faltering. 'He said he was feeling much better and that I should go to bed.'

He knew he was making a bad job of this and that Bonsignore was looking at him suspiciously but it was better this way than that the Abbot should know that Anselmo was not in his cell when Silvano arrived. He wondered what the Colour Master would say when questioned. And relieved as

80

he was to feel the burden of suspicion moving away from him, the last thing he wanted was to incriminate Brother Anselmo.

Silvano knew what it was like to be suspected of a crime you had not committed. It was a crushing feeling and one that made it difficult to appear innocent. But he knew Brother Anselmo, even after a few weeks, and he was sure that he couldn't have murdered anyone. Anselmo had said the same to him on the way to Assisi and Silvano remembered how much it had meant to him. He wanted to go and find Anselmo now and reassure him.

The Colour Master did not seem to have a reason to kill or even dislike the visiting merchant, other than remarking he had drunk too much wine. But that was no reason to stab a man! Still, Silvano remembered that Anselmo had looked startled when he heard the merchant's name. And he had behaved oddly at supper. Silvano hadn't seen him since their brief meeting outside his cell the night before and he couldn't help wondering where Anselmo had been.

'Is there anything else you want to tell me?' the Abbot was asking.

'No, Father,' said Silvano, feeling calmer now. Brother Anselmo would tell the Abbot everything, he was sure.

Isabella was out when the messenger arrived from Giardinetto. It was a fine, sunny morning and although it was early she wanted to be out of the house and down at the market with her cook. She always had a restless feeling when Ubaldo was away. The sense of freedom was wonderful but

81

always tinged by sadness, because it was an illusion. Her husband would be back.

So it was with dragging steps that she returned to the grand house. Its master would not actually be home yet but his return hung like a cloud over the fine morning. It was especially at times like these that Isabella wondered how she would endure the rest of her days. She needed to see her children; that would cheer her heart.

But there was a strange, still atmosphere in the house. It was unnaturally quiet. The children should have been up by now and making a noise. And the servants should have been bustling about their daily tasks. The man who opened the door cast his mistress a sympathetic look and her heart quickened. Something was wrong.

Isabella's maid hurried up to her. 'Madama,' she said.

'Are the children all right?' asked Isabella, her lips so stiff she could scarcely form the words.

'Perfectly well and safe,' said the maid. 'Have no fear on their account. But there is a messenger in the salon, from Giardinetto. He would speak with you.'

Isabella braced herself for whatever news she was about to receive. 'Has this messenger been brought refreshment?' she asked calmly.

'I will see to it immediately.'

Isabella moved slowly towards the salon, removing her cap and smoothing her hair. Although her mind was a whirl, she sensed that what awaited her in that room was about to change her life for ever.

'Come with me,' said Sister Eufemia, abruptly to Chiara and Paola. 'The Abbot has sent for some sisters to prepare the body for burial. You can come and help me.'

Paola looked as horrified as Chiara felt. A man who had been a warm, living, breathing person was now a corpse – and one who bore on him the marks of a violent death. Yet even as she recoiled at the idea, Chiara also felt a strange fascination. And, besides, this was a chance to see inside the friars' house.

The three sisters crossed the short distance to the friary and Sister Eufemia announced their arrival to the man at the gate. The Abbot himself came to meet them.

'Sisters in Christ,' he said, looking tired and grey. 'It is good of you to come. I trust the task will not be too much for you?' His eyes flickered towards Chiara.

'Not at all, Father,' said Sister Eufemia. 'I think you know Sister Paola and this is our new novice, Sister Orsola.'

Chiara bent her head dutifully but really to hide the flash of anger she always felt when that name was used. Would she ever get used to it? The Abbot led them to the upper floor of the friars' house, where the individual cells for the senior brothers were. There was a lay brother standing guard outside one of them.

The Abbot signalled for him to stand aside and, as he did, another friar came along the corridor.

'Welcome, Sisters,' he said. 'I shall accompany you.'

'Brother Rufino,' acknowledged Eufemia. 'These are my novices, Paola and Orsola. Brother Rufino is the Infirmarian.'

'And the person who found the body,' added Bonsignore, 'which has not been moved since. Though, of course, we have sent to his wife in Gubbio. We assume she will want the body

83

transported there for burial.'

His wife, thought Chiara. Of course. He was a rich man and even a poor one may have a family. It made the thought of what they were about to do much worse.

'And please come to my cell when your work is done,' said the Abbot. 'I shall be pleased to offer you a glass of wine.'

The door of the cell was pushed inward and Chiara strained her eyes in the gloom to see the figure on the bed. The cell had no window.

'Please leave the door open,' said Sister Eufemia, taking charge. 'So that we may have enough light.'

'I shall have water and cloths brought to you, Sisters,' said the Infirmarian. 'But first . . .'

Brother Rufino stepped in and moved towards the thing on the bed. He had a cloth in his hand. Chiara saw the flash of the dagger as he drew it from the body and it made a sound like her brother carving meat at table. Before she realised what was happening, the cold stone of the cell floor was rushing up to meet her.

When she opened her eyes, she was in the corridor again, with the not very reassuring sight of the Infirmarian standing over her with the dagger wrapped in a white cloth, which was slowly turning red.

Sister Eufemia fussed round her but Chiara struggled to her feet, mortified. Sister Paola hadn't fainted.

'I am perfectly all right,' she said. 'Do not let me hinder you.'

'If you are quite sure,' said Brother Rufino anxiously. Sister Eufemia nodded to him and he left, taking the dagger with him.

The corpse was much less frightening without it. The

84

merchant was just a man after all and a dead man can't do any harm. At least, that was what Chiara told herself. Then she saw with a shock that this corpse was the drunken man who had laughed at her and Sister Veronica on the road the day before. Chiara felt again how fragile life was, how a vigorous man could be snuffed out in an instant. The thought made her shudder.

Under Sister Eufemia's instruction, she helped wash the body, even round the wound, without feeling sick or faint again. They removed his clothes down to his undershirt and then Sister Eufemia pulled a long white shift, brought by a friar from the infirmary, over the dead man's head. Then they washed and combed his hair and beard, which was not too bad because Sister Eufemia had closed his eyes first. There were bad smells though: stale wine and sweat and something metallic that must have been the blood.

Sister Eufemia had saved one bowl of water to wash their hands in when the task was finished and she let the novices go first.

'Time to visit the Abbot, my dears,' she said, quite kindly.

Chiara was glad to get out of the cell into the comparatively fresh air of the corridor. The sisters walked to the far end, where Sister Eufemia knocked on a large wooden door. When they entered the room, she saw that the Abbot had another friar with him, the kind Brother Anselmo that she had met in Assisi. She felt very pleased to see him, though he was looking just as grave and strained as Father Bonsignore.

'It is done,' said Sister Eufemia simply. But Chiara saw that the hand with which she accepted her cup of wine was not altogether steady.

Brother Fazio, the Illuminator, was explaining to anyone who would listen to him, that the merchant Ubaldo had been perfectly well and in good humour when he had parted with him at the door of his cell.

'But that is irrelevant, surely?' said Brother Taddeo. 'A man may be as well or sick as he likes before he is stabbed to death. He will be just as unwell afterwards.'

Brother Fazio glared at him but conceded that he had a point. The friars were all gathered in the refectory, where the Abbot had asked them to wait. From time to time, Bertuccio brought them something to eat or drink. The daily timetable was ignored and they didn't know if they had eaten their midday meal or not. In spite of advice to pray and meditate, there was an air almost of holiday.

Not since he arrived in Giardinetto had Silvano seen all the brothers gathered together for so long with no task to do. There were several of them that he still didn't know by name and he wasn't at all sure what they all did. Since he spent all his waking hours when he was not praying or eating or sleeping, working in the colour room, he had made little contact with Fazio the Illuminator or Monaldo the Librarian or Valentino the Herbalist.

But they were all there now. And there was only one possible subject of conversation.

'Why is Brother Anselmo so long with the Abbot?' whispered Matteo, one of the other novices who worked with the Colour Master.

'Perhaps he is helping him to solve the mystery,' suggested Silvano, also in a whisper. And such was the veneration

86

Brother Anselmo was held in by all who worked alongside him, that it seemed only natural to them that he would be using his great intellect to discover the murderer of the merchant.

Silvano had not seen the body; no one in the friary had but Brother Rufino and the Abbot – and the killer, of course. But Silvano did not need to see it. He knew exactly what a man looked like when his life had bled out through his ribs. This new death, so far from Perugia, haunted and unsettled him. But whoever had killed Tommaso had surely not followed Ubaldo to Giardinetto from Assisi?

Yet perhaps the merchant had some business connection with the larger city? Try as he might, Silvano could see no link between the two killings except himself. He thanked the Lord that it wasn't he who had discovered this latest body, but he wondered how long it would be before others made the connection. He wasn't even sure that the Abbot believed in his innocence any more.

'Whose dagger was it?' Brother Valentino asked of no one in particular.

'His own, I think,' said Rufino, who had just entered the room, holding the weapon before him. It was cleaned of all bloodstains but still held a horrid fascination for every man in the refectory. 'See, there is the letter "U" engraved on the hilt and Father Bonsignore thinks he saw such a dagger at his belt when he arrived.'

'To kill a man with his own dagger!' said Brother Taddeo.

'The Abbot says you may disperse to your own occupations,' said Brother Rufino. 'We shall assemble in the chapel for Sext at noon and then come back here to eat. The bell will summon you in about an hour.'

Silvano was one of the first to leave and the first thing he saw was Father Bonsignore and Brother Anselmo escorting three grey sisters across the courtyard. He recognised pretty Sister Orsola straightaway. What on earth was she doing in the friary? The other two were unknown to him. She turned at the gate and looked at him, as if aware that he was there. And into that look she put such compassion and understanding that his heart began to race.

It was Brother Landolfo, the Guest Master himself, who had insisted on riding to Gubbio to break the news to the merchant's wife. Although he was no longer young and certainly no longer slim, he had been a great horseman before he felt called to the way of Saint Francis. And he felt such guilt that a guest had died under his protection that only a fast ride on one of the friary's surprised horses could relieve his feelings.

When Isabella had seen him in her home pacing the carpet, she knew that the news was bad but she prayed that it would be bad enough. A husband wounded, mutilated, incapacitated, she could have borne if she had loved him but not Ubaldo. He was hard enough to endure in his health; in sickness he would be insupportable.

But she need not have worried. Her husband was dead.

She drank deep of the wine she had ordered for the friar and he looked at her sympathetically. Shock. It did strange things to people. He might have expected this gracious and beautiful lady to weep and she did not do that. But turning pale and gulping wine and pressing her hand to her exquisite forehead were all good enough signs of grief.

'Stabbed, you say?' she said at last. 'Who did it?'

'Alas, Madama, we do not know. The Abbot has undertaken to investigate but I left before he reached any conclusion.'

'I must come to him,' said Isabella, more calmly than she felt. 'I must bring his body home. But I have things to arrange here first. I suppose I must see a priest, arrange the funeral. And I must tell the children.' Her voice cracked.

'There is no need for you to travel, Madama,' said Brother Landolfo. 'We can arrange to have him brought home if that would help. I believe the sisters from our neighbour convent have prepared the body.'

'Thank you; you are kind. But I must go and bring him myself in his own carriage.' Isabella looked down at her green dress with the yellow silk bodice. 'And I must change into more suitable clothes.' She rose. 'Please stay as long as you wish. Ring if there is anything you need. Let my servants bring you food. But you must excuse me. There is so much to do.'

And as she climbed the stairs to her children Monna Isabella felt bowed down by the weight of all her responsibilities. She did not wish Ubaldo back; she had often dreamed of this moment, not daring to hope it would come when she was still young enough to benefit from it. But now that it had, she felt no pleasure. Only apprehension and a terrible searing loneliness.

CHAPTER SEVEN

Illumination

ilvano sensed the change as soon as he joined the brothers in the chapel next morning. There was nothing specific: a few friars perhaps looked at him more closely than usual. But there was something in the air – a feeling that he was the subject of speculation. It wasn't until breaking their fast after Prime that anyone said anything direct.

His fellow-novice Brother Matteo whispered to him, 'Is it true? You are not really a novice?'

'Silence in the refectory!' called the Novice Master, saving Silvano from the need to answer.

But he caught up with Matteo on their way to the colour room.

'Who says that I am not a novice?' he demanded.

'Everyone,' said Matteo, not unkindly. 'We had all wondered, what with you being allowed to go hawking and keeping your horse. But now everyone is saying that you came here because of a murder.' He hesitated. 'A knifing in Perugia – like the one here.'

Silvano sighed. First his interrogation by the Abbot and now the common knowledge of his secret. It had been good not being under suspicion these last weeks, but it had obviously come to an end.

'I am guilty of neither crime,' he said and saw Matteo's worried expression clear. 'The man in Perugia I found dying and it looked bad against me because he was killed with my dagger. And,' he swallowed, 'I had been paying attention to his wife. But I did not kill him. And this man Ubaldo was completely unknown to me. I did not exchange a word with him. Why would I want to kill him?'

'Brothers,' said the Colour Master, appearing out of nowhere behind them, 'do not dawdle. We have much time to make up in the colour room if we are to keep Ser Simone supplied.'

It was a relief to return to work. Most of the friars had spent the day before in idleness and it did not suit them, as well as being against the rule of their founder. The lack of activity had bred speculation and gossip, which was no doubt how the word about Silvano had spread. He was aware of the glances of the other friars in the room and had to try hard to concentrate on the pigment he was making.

'We need large quantities of terra verde – green earth,' said Brother Anselmo, just as if no one had been horribly murdered in the friary the day before. 'Ser Simone uses it for under-painting the flesh tones of all the figures in his frescoes. It is the simplest colour to make. We have here a load of celadon rock from Verona,' indicating some sacks in the corner. 'Now, it is not exciting. It cannot be used for finished greens in wall paintings, like malachite or verdigris, because it won't last. But it is an essential part of the painter's art and we shall spend today grinding it for the glory of Saint Francis, in whose Basilica it will be used.'

It was a long speech for Brother Anselmo, and Silvano sensed that he was trying to bring the brothers back to earth

91

– literally – by giving them this dull clay-like stuff to work with. And there seemed to be a message about how much unexciting work was needed before a surface could be richly adorned. It was clear that he had no intention of discussing the murder and the friars worked diligently at their porphyry slabs till Sext at noon.

But there was no rule of silence in the colour room and, as long as the work was done, Brother Anselmo did not mind if there was a low level of conversation. The trouble was, from Silvano's point of view, that the main topic seemed to be him. Many of the brothers glanced towards him and held whispered conversations. He was gratified to see Brother Matteo talking animatedly under his breath to some of them and he hoped that his denial of the murders was being passed on. But no one spoke to him all morning and he felt very alone.

A visit from Brother Fazio was a welcome interruption. The Illuminator worked separately from Brother Anselmo and had his own novices to assist him. But he came into the colour room for supplies of dragonsblood, arzica, sandarach or saffron. Before Anselmo's arrival, he had got his colours from Sister Veronica at the convent. There was only one colour that he made himself and that was the lead-white used for the surfaces of his parchment.

When he had gathered up what he needed, Brother Anselmo said something quietly to Fazio and he beckoned Silvano to help carry his packages. Silvano was glad to leave the poisoned atmosphere of the colour room behind.

Brother Fazio led the way to his cell, the only double one in the friary. Silvano assumed that the inner room was where the Illuminator slept and prayed. The large outer room was a public one, full of activity. Two novices worked on scraping the animal skins that would become the parchment. In the middle of the room was a high wooden desk with a seat and on the surface was spread the page that Brother Fazio was working on.

'It is a New Testament,' Fazio explained, when Silvano had handed his parcels of pigments over to one of the novices. 'Here I am illuminating the words of Saint John the Evangelist.'

Silvano looked at the elaborate letter at the beginning of the chapter. Brother Fazio was an artist as skilled in his way as Simone Martini. There was a complete scene coiled within the shining golden letter: reds and greens and blues showed a grapevine laden with fruit; there was even a little man tending the vine and cutting off a dead branch with his billhook. It was so lifelike that Silvano could imagine the taste of the grapes in his mouth. Brother Fazio, holding a parcel of pigments in his right hand, picked up a pen in his left and added a tiny fleck of white to the wing of a miniature bird pecking at a grape. It seemed he was equally dextrous with either hand.

'It's beautiful,' said Silvano.

Fazio looked pleased. 'It is for the glory of God,' he said modestly. 'Would you like to see how we prepare the parchment and pigments?'

The novices were willing to show Silvano their work. He wondered if they had heard the rumours about him. Brother Fazio chattered on about the techniques of illumination. He was rather a fussy little man but friendly enough and clearly proud of his work. 'And we mix the colours with white of egg,' he finished. 'Yes, it is thanks to me that you have such bright yellow frittatas from Bertuccio's kitchen. All those leftover yolks.'

Silvano had been interested, in spite of his troubles. It was fascinating to see how a real artist like Brother Fazio could create beauty from such humble ingredients as part of an egg and the bits of rock that people like himself ground to powder in the colour room.

'Come and see where I make my white,' said Fazio suddenly. He took Silvano to an outbuilding at the far edge of the friary's grounds. The smell hit Silvano when they were still several yards away but it didn't seem to bother Brother Fazio. The Illuminator opened the door and the smell got much worse. Silvano held his sleeve over his nose.

'I am grateful to you, Brother Silvano,' said Fazio, 'for bringing another horse to the friary.

Silvano wondered if Brother Fazio was out of his wits.

'My horse?' he said.

'Yes, the white that I need is made from coils of lead in these special pots,' said Fazio. He pulled back some stinking straw and Silvano saw rows of clay pots stacked in tiers. 'Each one has a compartment in the base, which I fill with a solution of vinegar,' continued Fazio apparently unaware of the impression his handiwork was making on the novice's nose. 'I then pack the pots in straw and horse manure,' he finished triumphantly, 'and that is where your handsome steed comes in handy.'

'But how does that produce the white pigment you need, Brother?' asked Silvano, desperate to get out of the shed. Much to his relief, Fazio packed the straw back round the pots, like a mother swaddling a child, and led the way back into the fresh air.

94

'After a few months,' he said, 'white flakes appear on the lead spirals. I scrape it off then it is washed and dried. Then my novices grind it with linseed oil, under my supervision. It is not so different from what you do in the colour room. But lead-white – bianco di piombo – is not suitable for fresco painting. Your Simone won't use it.'

'Why not?' asked Silvano.

'Because on a wall, it will turn black over time,' said Fazio. 'It is already happening in the Upper Church in Assisi. You have to use lime-white – we call it bianco di Sangiovanni, Saint John's white, but I don't use it for his Gospel, oh no.' The Illuminator laughed at his own joke. 'Saint John's white is for walls only.'

'And do you need horse manure to make that too?' asked Silvano, glad that Brother Anselmo had not asked the workers in the colour room to produce any white.

'Oh no, the technique is quite different,' said Brother Fazio. But he seemed suddenly to have lost interest.

'I must say farewell, Brother,' he said absently.

'Goodbye,' said Silvano. 'Thank you for showing me your work.'

And he lost no time getting back to the colour room, out of the range of Brother Fazio's smelly shed.

❧

Isabella covered her bright hair in a black veil and peered through it at her looking-glass. She looked exactly as a widow should. She took a deep breath and smoothed the fabric of her taffeta dress. It was one made when she was in mourning for her father three years earlier but it would have to do. She

95

had already ordered more from the dressmaker. And now she must descend to the front door, which was already festooned with black silk ribbons, and take her place in the carriage.

A footman sat up in front with the driver but Isabella had the inside of the carriage to herself. She did not see the road to Giardinetto; her mind was still entirely turned in on itself, the way it had been ever since she heard the news from Brother Landolfo.

A part of her was quite frozen, unable to take in the fact that this man, to whom she had been shackled for so long, was never going to speak to her or look at her again. And the unexpected manner of his death was something else she could not comprehend. She had wondered from time to time, throughout their marriage, whether Ubaldo would die before her; he was older by some years. But if she had imagined how it might happen, it was always because of a seizure or a fever. At most, an accident on his horse. But never a murder. The fact that it happened under the roof of a religious house somehow made it worse, as if the world's order had been turned upside down.

The children had taken their father's death in different ways. Little Federico did not cry; he seemed to grow taller as he said, 'Don't worry, Madre. I am the head of the house now and I shall look after you.'

The younger ones had been frightened and disturbed but she had never known how they felt about Ubaldo. All the caressing and kissing and love had come from their mother. Some fathers, it is true, spent more time with their little ones and Isabella had often speculated about the very different bond they might have felt with Domenico.

Domenico. Her exhausted brain kept coming back to one

96

constant thought: Domenico, her first love. Where was he now? Had he kept his word and remained unmarried? Did he know what had happened to her? Below all her fears and worries about what the future might hold, there ran, like a powerful underground stream, the steady current that had never lessened: her feelings for Domenico. The vision that they might one day be reunited was more and more like a misty dream after all these years, but the fact remained that Ubaldo's death had left her a free woman.

She shook her head; these were impious thoughts in a woman going to bring her husband home for burial. She must do everything correctly, as she always had throughout the marriage. Nothing would be lacking in the outward forms of respect for Ubaldo. And curiously Isabella had never felt so warmly towards him as she did today; the fact that she had to endure his presence no longer made her determined to do everything fitting for his funeral and obsequies.

Chiara was in the sisters' garden when the carriage came down the Gubbio road. She was carrying out one of her favourite tasks, because it brought her out into the fresh air. Sister Veronica needed fuller's herb for a special yellow she was working on and Chiara was deft and neat at picking the plants. But she dawdled, always hoping to catch a glimpse of the handsome Silvano or at least see something to vary the monotony of life in the convent.

She had thought that, after the murder next door, everything would be different but, after the washing of Ubaldo's body, the sisters had gone back to their old routine. Chiara

97

shuddered as she thought of the task she had helped to perform the day before. And then she was rewarded by the sight of a carriage heading towards the friary.

It was drawn by two bay horses with rosettes of black ribbon on their harness and she knew immediately that this meant the arrival of Ubaldo's widow. Rumour had already circulated that Monna Isabella would be coming herself to fetch him home. I wonder if her heart is broken? thought Chiara. She tried to think of the thing she had seen the day before as a living, breathing man, loved by his wife.

Someone else had seen the carriage from her window. Mother Elena, the Abbess, realised as quickly as her youngest novice, that it signalled the arrival of the merchant's widow. Poor woman, she thought. What a dreadful journey for her to make! She made up her mind instantly to offer her condolences in person. Father Bonsignore is a good soul, she thought, but he will not know how to conduct himself with a woman of the laity, particularly one of her station.

As she swept through the courtyard, the Abbess found Sister Orsola standing open-mouthed in the garden, with a forgotten basket of plants at her feet. She had seen little of the girl since her admission into the convent and on impulse she decided to take her to the friary with her.

'Come, Sister Orsola,' she commanded. 'Let us go and offer our sympathy to the widow of Ubaldo. She will appreciate the presence of other women in that house of bachelors.'

Chiara couldn't believe her luck: two days running a visit to the friary! All the grisly business was over now and she was burning with curiosity to see the merchant's widow.

They walked the short distance to the brothers' house and were in time to see the footman help a very elegantly dressed woman out of the carriage and hand her ceremoniously to the Abbot, who had come out to greet her.

Monna Isabella would take no refreshment nor wash the traces of her journey from her before seeing the body of her husband. It had been moved to the chapel and was already in a plain coffin. The small procession of Abbot and Abbess, widow and novice, walked slowly towards the trestles on which the coffin lay.

The elegant woman gave an involuntary gasp when she saw the body and she pressed a lace handkerchief to her mouth.

What on earth would she have done if she had seen him the way he was yesterday? thought Chiara but, remembering the blood and the staring eyes, she wouldn't have wished that on Ubaldo's widow. How she must have loved him!

'I will take that wine now, Father,' said Isabella. She was struggling to compose herself. She glanced at the women, glad to have them near. 'Perhaps your novice might attend me, Mother,' she said to the Abbess.

Chiara took Isabella to the guest room, where Brother Landolfo had set a pitcher and bowl of water and a rare looking-glass ready for their lady visitor. Isabella looked round the room and shuddered while Chiara poured out some water.

'It was in here, wasn't it?' she asked, putting back her black veil. 'This is where he died.'

'Yes, Madama,' said Chiara, struck by the woman's composed beauty. 'I attended to him myself.'

'Really? And . . . and were his wounds very terrible?'

'Not too terrible, Madama,' lied Chiara.

Isabella gave a short laugh. 'You are a kind girl but there is no need to spare me. I have no idea who hated my husband enough to kill him but whoever it was has released me from a man I did not love.'

Chiara was astounded. She said nothing but encouraged the widow to splash water on her pale cheeks and white hands. Then she proffered the towel and saw that Monna Isabella expected Chiara to dry her hands and face for her. She submitted to the novice's care like a small child or helpless imbecile.

'It shocks you, I am sure,' continued Isabella. 'To hear the sacrament of marriage spoken of so slightingly. I should have felt the same at your age, before I had experienced love and had it snatched away from me.'

She paused and took a brush from her small carrying-case, then unpinned her veil. Chiara saw with admiration the glossy hair underneath.

'But I am forgetting, child,' said Isabella. 'You are married to the Church and must have no thoughts of earthly love.'

'Only against my will,' said Chiara, unable to help herself. She couldn't bear to have this elegant woman thinking of her as a nun with a vocation. Seeing Isabella's surprise, she plunged on with her explanation. 'My brother brought me here without my consent,' she said. 'And the sisters are very kind to me but I have no calling. I am here because there was no money for a dowry. Otherwise I should have been allowed to think of love as much as I might wish.'

It was the woman's turn to be astounded. 'But do not imagine you would have been able to choose your own husband, even if there had been dowry enough,' she said bitterly. 'It was my father who decided on Ubaldo for me, even though my heart was already given to someone else. We women have

100

no choice but to do as our fathers or brothers – or husbands,' she spat out the word, 'decide for us.'

Chiara was brushing the widow's hair by now with soothing strokes. How she had missed having her own long curls to tend!

'And what happened to him?' she felt bold enough to ask the back of Isabella's head. 'The man you really loved?'

'Domenico?' said the widow. 'I don't know,' and, putting her face in her hands, she wept for the first time since the news of her husband's death.

CHAPTER EIGHT

Widows

sabella and Chiara talked for a long time before Chiara led the widow to Father Bonsignore's cell. She felt very different now that she knew Isabella's secret. But, although the merchant's death had not grieved his widow, Chiara could not doubt that it had shocked and surprised her.

Now for the second time in two days, the novice found herself taking wine with the Abbot. The widow seemed reluctant to let her go and leant heavily on the young girl's arm. Father Bonsignore poured liberal measures of the best red wine his Cellarer could provide and looked relieved that Isabella had someone to look after her.

Isabella was having a whispered conversation with the Abbess about the funeral arrangements for her husband. Chiara heard the words 'Requiem Mass' and 'Cathedral'. But the Abbot had another pressing practical matter to discuss.

'Forgive me, Monna Isabella,' he said, 'for bothering you with such a matter at this time but what are we to do with your husband's belongings? His baggage and clothes can, of course, travel with you in the carriage but I was wondering about his horse . . .'

Isabella looked like someone who had just swum up to the

102

surface of a deep lake. 'His horse? Yes, to be sure. We must make some arrangement,' she said distractedly.

Then as if she had realised this for the first time, she suddenly said with anguish, 'Am I to travel in the carriage with his body?'

Bonsignore was nonplussed. There would be plenty of space for widow and coffin alike and he had assumed it would be the arrangement but now he saw that the idea filled Isabella with horror. He looked to the Abbess for advice.

'Can you ride a horse, Madama?' Mother Elena asked.

'I can,' said Isabella doubtfully. The journey home had become something enormous to accomplish.

'Forgive me, Mother,' said Chiara. 'But I don't think that Monna Isabella is well enough to ride alongside the carriage unaccompanied.'

'You are right, child,' said the Abbess. 'But Father, is there not a young novice here who can ride? Could he not accompany the lady and see that she travels safely on Ser Ubaldo's horse?'

'Excellent idea,' said the Abbot. 'I shall send for Brother Silvano at once.'

Silvano was back in the colour room, diligently grinding celadon rock into a dull green powder. He looked up from his porphyry slab when Brother Ranieri came into the room and whispered to Brother Anselmo. He saw the Colour Master turn pale and they both looked at him.

'Brother Silvano, come here a moment, will you?' said Brother Anselmo. 'Leave the green earth.'

103

He took the young man outside and said, 'Father Bonsignore has something to ask of you. Monna Isabella, the widow of Ubaldo, is here to reclaim his body. The Abbot wishes you to accompany her back to Gubbio on your horse. She will ride on her late husband's beast.'

Silvano was more than willing to go. It would be good to see Gubbio again and a ride in the fresh air, even with a grieving widow, would be more exciting than spending the rest of the afternoon grinding colours and praying.

And surely this meant the Abbot did not still think him involved in Ubaldo the merchant's death? He would hardly send a suspected murderer to accompany the victim's widow home.

He was surprised to see the pretty novice from the convent when he entered the Abbot's cell. It was as well that Brother Anselmo had already told him of his commission, because Silvano found it hard to concentrate on what Bonsignore was saying, under the young girl's scrutiny. She seemed always to be crossing his path nowadays and he more often found her features floating into his mind when he tried to remember Angelica's face.

He tried not to look at her, or at Ubaldo's widow, after the introductions. He was willing enough to ride with her to Gubbio but he didn't want to think about what she must be feeling.

The Abbot sent him to saddle up both horses. They were to borrow an ancient ladies' saddle from the convent, left over from Abbess Elena's secular life, so Silvano accompanied the sisters back to the convent to collect it. He walked silently and as respectfully as he could but it was hard to keep his eyes from sliding sideways for a glimpse of the novice.

'Sister Orsola' the Abbess had called her, and the widow of Ubaldo seemed attached to her. She had said, 'Please come back and say goodbye to me.' And the Abbess had nodded slightly, to give permission.

So it was that the two young novices found themselves walking back across to the friary unaccompanied. Silvano was perplexed. Since he wasn't a real postulant, he had no idea if he was allowed to address the sister but he didn't want to appear impolite.

'The lady seems grateful for your company, Sister Orsola,' he said and was rewarded by a deep sigh.

'I am not Orsola yet,' she said, glancing up at him. 'My name is Chiara and I like it a lot better.'

'So do I,' said Silvano impulsively. 'It is a beautiful name.'

She gave him a radiant smile.

'And it suits you,' he added rashly.

'Is Silvano your real name?' she asked.

'Yes, I have no other.'

'But you are not really a novice, are you?'

He stopped and looked at her.

'Does everyone know, in both our houses?' he asked, uneasy about his safety from prosecution if his disguise became the subject of universal gossip.

'No, I don't think so. But I saw you arrive, with your horse and your hawk, and I knew then that you were no friar.'

Silvano smiled. 'I remember,' he said. 'I saw you too and – forgive me, Sister Chiara – I thought that you too did not seem a very convincing novice.'

A shadow fell over her face. 'I don't know why you are here,' she said. 'But it is some kind of game to you and all in earnest for me. I cannot leave the grey sisters and one day I must be Orsola in reality for ever – a gruff and grim little bear.'

Silvano was moved by her sadness.

'It is not a game for me either,' he said seriously. 'The reason I am here is that I am accused of stabbing a man in Perugia.'

Chiara started.

'Don't be scared,' he reassured her. 'I am innocent and seeking sanctuary here with the brothers. And I had nothing to do with the merchant's death here.'

'But why did anyone think it was you?' she asked. 'That had murdered the other man, I mean.'

'Because my dagger was used,' he said. And then resolved to tell her the whole truth. 'And I had been paying attention to the man's wife, Angelica.'

Chiara felt a stab of pure jealousy. She would have liked to ask him more – what Angelica looked like and whether he still had feelings for her. But as they reached the stables, they met several people at once.

The elderly lay brother, Gianni, who worked in the stables, was leading out the bay horses to harness them into the carriage. He nodded to Silvano to go in to his own grey stallion and the merchant's brown mare.

The Abbot was leading the widow out to the stables and six brothers were carrying the merchant's coffin, now nailed up, behind them. Unaware of this procession, Brother Anselmo came round the corner from the colour room and called out.

'A moment, Brother Silvano,' he said. 'I would have another word with you before you leave.'

Chiara saw Isabella come to a sudden stop at the sound of

106

his voice. The coffin party nearly ran into her where she stood, a hand on her heart. 'Domenico!' She barely mouthed the name, but Chiara understood. In an instant she looked with new interest at Brother Anselmo, who stood fixed to the spot. So this was Monna Isabella's first love!

It was a strange tableau, whose meaning few members understood. Chiara hurried to Isabella's side, worried that this new shock would rob her of her senses. How was she to ride safely to Gubbio in this state? She persuaded the widow to sit down on a mounting-block.

'Father Abbot,' said Chiara, looking at Isabella's white face. 'I think that the lady needs a moment longer. The sight of the coffin might have been too much for her.' She flashed Silvano a look into which she put as much meaning as she could, indicating that he should go to Brother Anselmo.

Silvano took the older man's arm and led him aside, while the coffin was loaded into the carriage and the Abbot fussed around Isabella.

'What is it, Brother?' Silvano asked.

Anselmo answered through frozen lips. 'I, I came to warn you to be careful in Gubbio,' he said. 'There might be someone there from Perugia, who could recognise you and realise you are in disguise. It is dangerous for you to go and you must come back as soon as possible.'

'I shall take care, I promise,' said Silvano. 'But we must leave soon or I shall not be back before dark. Will you be all right? You seem upset.'

He looked towards the widow, who had recovered her composure. Brother Anselmo was looking at her too but she was turned away from them.

'I shall look after the widow Isabella,' Silvano said and was surprised by the pressure Anselmo put on his arm.

'You are a good boy,' said Anselmo. 'Treat her as if she were your own precious mother. She is all that their children have now.'

And Silvano wondered at how familiar he seemed to be with the circumstances of the merchant's life. He sensed that he was not the only one with a secret.

But now he must saddle the horses, help the widow to mount and escort her back to Gubbio. As the small cortège left the friary, Silvano realised with sinking heart that it was going to take hours to make the journey. A carriage carrying a man's body must go at a respectful pace and he wondered how he would fill the time ambling along behind it, beside a woman in deep mourning.

Being a widow was not as easy as Angelica had hoped. For a start, she didn't have full control of Tommaso's money and property, even though she was his only heir. His nephews were very keen that she should appoint one of them as her 'mundualdus', the man who would act for her in all financial matters. She was fiercely against having such a procurator, but the law insisted that a widow without children should have a man to undertake all transactions on her behalf.

However, she could have a say as to who that man would be.

When Baron Montacuto sent the young Gervasio de' Oddini to her, it seemed like manna from Heaven. He was too young to be her mundualdus himself but it took very little to persuade him to ask his father to act for her. So now she

108

had an ally, who was himself rather pressed for money and would do as she asked if suitably rewarded. He also had no connection with her nephews-in-law and as intermediary, Vincenzo de' Oddini could send his delightful youngest son.

This suited Gervasio as well as it did Angelica, of course. He had not asked her for Silvano's poem, for the simple reason that he still had it inside his own jerkin. He reported his failure to retrieve it to the Baron, who said only, 'I hope she has destroyed it.' But it had given him the perfect excuse to visit Angelica for the first time and now, as his father's representative, he no longer needed one.

And she did look handsome in her widow's weeds. The black veil was often pushed back so that her blonde curls escaped from it and she was delightfully dimpled and plump.

Today he was to escort her to Gubbio where on the following morning his father would sign on her behalf a deed selling one of the smaller sheep farms. It was Angelica's wish to move out of the smelly, animal husbandry side of wool production and to operate as a merchant. She had the makings of a shrewd businesswoman and had decided to use the money from the farm to establish a small trading post in Gubbio.

If it went well, she would gradually sell all the farms and become exclusively a merchant. Of course she would employ men to run the day-to-day business but she would be the first female wool merchant in Umbria – and a wealthy widow as well. Gervasio had no doubt that she would be much courted as soon as her period of enforced mourning was over.

He was to go with her and his father to an inn near the main wool market in the walled city so that they could visit the notary early in the morning and rent suitable premises for

109

trading. They were driven in the handsome carriage which Angelica had insisted that her late husband should buy. Two dappled grey horses pulled them smartly along the road.

They overtook a solemn funeral procession and the men doffed their caps. Angelica started. The young friar escorting the widow had for a moment reminded her of the good-looking young scoundrel who had murdered her husband. But it couldn't possibly be him. Silvano had disappeared on the night of Tommaso's death – a sure sign of his guilt.

Angelica remembered him fondly and had wondered if he really had killed Tommaso out of jealousy and love for her. She couldn't feel too harshly towards him since he had released her from such an irksome marriage.

'Whose body is it, I wonder?' asked Vincenzo. 'A wealthy man, by his carriage and his widow's clothes.'

'We shall find out in Gubbio perhaps? They are going the same way,' said Gervasio, who was still wondering where he had seen that grey horse before. It looked strangely familiar.

'Then he died away from home,' said Vincenzo. 'How sad for him!'

'Indeed,' said Angelica, with a great sigh.

'I'm sorry, Madama,' said Vincenzo, who was always scrupulously polite to this woman who was so much his inferior socially and yet so far above him in terms of worldly wealth. 'I have no desire to bring back your own sorrow.'

'Tell me about that friar you spoke to before we left,' the widow said to Silvano as soon as they were out of sight of Giardinetto.

110

'Brother Anselmo?' asked Silvano. 'He is the Colour Master of our house. I work with him, grinding pigments for the artists who work in Assisi.'

'Has he been in the friary long?'

'I have not been there long myself, Madama, but I believe it has been only a matter of months.'

'But he is a fully professed friar?' she persisted. 'He has taken the vows?'

'Oh yes,' said Silvano. 'He came from a house in the southern provinces, I believe, where he had been for many years.'

Isabella sighed.

'May I ask why you are interested?'

'I thought he resembled someone I used to know in Gubbio,' she said. 'But I must be mistaken.'

'He has never mentioned that he came from near here,' said Silvano, though he remembered that Brother Anselmo knew a great deal about the Basilica at Assisi. He wondered whether to say that he had thought Anselmo had recognised the widow too.

But then he remembered how Anselmo had seemed upset when the Abbot mentioned Monna Isabella's name to the merchant, the night that he was stabbed. And how Anselmo had not been in his cell at the time when Ubaldo had been killed.

He put the thought out of his mind. Brother Anselmo was no more a killer than Silvano was himself. But there was a history of some sort between him and Monna Isabella, he was sure.

'I'm sorry to take you away from your work,' she said and he was relieved that she had changed the subject. 'And to make you ride at such a slow pace. That is a fine horse you have and capable of great speed, I think.'

'It is no trouble, Madama,' he said. 'It is my pleasure to accompany you and do anything I can to ease your sorrow.'

He thought he saw the curve of her mouth behind the black veil.

'Thank you. But I hope you don't mind my saying you sound more like a courtier than a friar.'

'I am a very recent novice, with a lot to learn,' said Silvano humbly.

'And so not yet tonsured,' Isabella remarked.

He wished she would not be quite so personal with him but she was almost old enough to be his mother and he couldn't really avoid her questions except by saying nothing.

'And you keep your own horse?' she continued.

Silvano didn't know what to say. Chiara knew he wasn't a real novice and so did most of the brothers at Giardinetto now. He didn't want his secret to spread to Gubbio too.

'Don't worry,' said Isabella. 'We all have things we would rather that others didn't know. Let us talk of pleasanter matters. Tell me about the painters at Assisi. Have you been there?'

'Only once, Madama, but it is wonderful to behold. We are supplying colours for Simone Martini, who is decorating a chapel in the Lower Church. He is going to show me the frescoes by Maestro Giotto in the Upper Church when Brother Anselmo and I take him his next order.'

'He needs many pigments then?'

'Yes, so much that the sisters at Giardinetto are also supplying him. Sister Veronica has been running a colour room there for much longer than Brother Anselmo.'

'I didn't meet Sister Veronica, did I? Just the Abbess –

112

Mother Elena I think – and that sweet girl, Sister Orsola.'

'She works with Sister Veronica in their colour room,' said Silvano. 'We met them in Assisi.'

'I don't think she is at all suited to life in the convent,' said Isabella.

'Really?' said Silvano. 'Might I ask why?'

'She is very unhappy,' said Isabella. 'I should like to do something for her. She was so kind to me.'

Silvano was silent. He realised how sorry he would be to see Chiara go. But that was selfish of him since he didn't expect to be at Giardinetto for ever himself.

The sky was a dark royal blue by the time that they reached the merchant's house in Gubbio. The whole household came out to pay their respects and Isabella arranged for several menservants to transport the body into the parlour, where Ubaldo would be transferred to the much grander coffin she had ordered. Then, in the morning, the children could be taken to see him.

The journey had passed surprisingly quickly for Silvano after all. Monna Isabella could be a pleasant companion and he had enjoyed explaining Ser Simone's frescoes to her. She had even said she would like to go to Assisi herself when her period of mourning was over. And she seemed to be a woman of taste, quite knowledgeable about painting. She said she had seen Simone's Mary in Majesty in Siena the year before.

Silvano declined more than a hasty drink of ale and some bread and cheese because he wanted to get back on the road. The Abbess had said she didn't want the old saddle back so he was unencumbered on the homeward road and relished the thought of a proper ride.

Silvano walked out into the balmy night waiting for his

113

horse to be fed and watered. He strolled out into the main square and then ducked back quickly behind a building on the corner. He had seen Angelica! He was sure it was her. He had to fight a strong impulse to run over and throw himself at her feet.

It would have been madness. He had to maintain his disguise in order to save his own life. But it was hard. And then he saw that Angelica was accompanied by an older man, whom he recognised. As incredible as it might seem, it was Gervasio's father! And as he watched Vincenzo de' Oddini going into a tavern he saw that Gervasio himself was also one of the party. What could that mean?

And as he watched, he saw Gervasio bend down and whisper something in Angelica's ear and be rewarded with a smile.

His heart like a stone, Silvano turned back to the merchant's house. He would get Moonbeam out of that stable and ride him back to Giardinetto as hard as he could.

CHAPTER NINE

As Beautiful as Possible

ilvano spent a restless night at the friary. His limbs ached from the unaccustomed fast ride home and his mind could find no peaceful place to rest. He was no nearer to knowing who had killed Tommaso and the glimpse of Angelica had rekindled some of his old feelings for her. He could not understand why she was with Gervasio and his father. Silvano felt so cut off from his family and what was happening in Perugia. He knew that his father would have contacted him if the real killer had been found and that he wouldn't risk giving away Silvano's place of safety for anything less than that news. But it was so hard to wait, without any information.

And when he tried to think about things inside the friary, nothing was any better. There was another murdered man and he had a growing suspicion that Brother Anselmo knew more than he was telling. The only thoughts that did not distress him were of Chiara the reluctant novice.

Eventually he fell into a troubled sleep and immediately had a nightmare in which two women in black veils came towards him with blood dripping from their hands, pointing accusing fingers. He woke with a shout. The bell, which he

115

could usually ignore, told him it was midnight, time for Matins.

Although novices were excused from getting up for prayers in the middle of the night, Silvano was afraid of going back to sleep and went to the chapel to say the Office with the older friars. It did soothe him a bit, though he thought that Brother Anselmo still looked troubled.

They didn't speak then and Silvano went back to bed for another hour of tossing and turning. When the bell rang three hours later for Lauds, he gave up and rose with the other friars. Then he went to the stable and took Moonbeam and Celeste out on a morning hunt. He couldn't remember if it was the right day for it but he had to get away.

Angelica was feeling well satisfied with her morning's work in Gubbio. She had found suitable premises and appointed a manager. They had heard that the richest merchant in the city had recently died, leaving an excellent opportunity for a new trader to step in. As she walked back to the inn with Gervasio and his father, they passed a door with its lion head knocker tied up with black ribbons. It was just closing on a man leaving the house.

'That must be where he lived,' she said to Gervasio. 'The merchant who died.'

'That's right,' said the man, who had called to pay his respects. 'Ubaldo. Stabbed in his bed – at the friary in Giardinetto.'

'Giardinetto,' said Angelica, remembering the slow carriage they had passed the day before. 'Where is that?'

116

'A village on the way to Assisi,' said the man. 'Nothing there but some Franciscans and Poor Clares.'

'How sad. Had he a wife and family?'

'Oh yes. Monna Isabella went to bring him back yesterday and there are four young ones.'

'She must be broken-hearted.'

The man nodded and raised his cap to them before walking away.

'And yet wives are not always broken-hearted when their husbands die suddenly,' whispered Gervasio, so that his father should not hear.

If they could have seen Isabella inside her house, they might have been surprised nevertheless by how calmly she went about her domestic duties. There had been a constant stream of friends and neighbours coming to view the body and pray for the soul of her late husband.

But the worst had been taking the children down early in the morning, to see their dead father. He was now dressed in his finest lace-trimmed nightshirt and there had been sweet herbs burning all night but nothing could disguise the scent of blood and the incipient decay of his flesh.

The viewing was hurried through as soon as possible and then Isabella took the children to the kitchen for cakes and a mouthful of sweet wine. She had to supervise the provision of food and drink for all the expected visitors and think ahead to the funeral feast. The sooner Ubaldo was in the ground the better.

She saw in her mind's eye the long dining table spread with delicacies, the huge epergne in the middle. She would see Ubaldo on his way in grand style. And then she would give that thing away. She would not need it any more. Never again would there be anyone at her table she couldn't bear the sight of. As a rich widow, she might in time be courted. But if Isabella ever married again it would be for love.

The Abbot of Giardinetto had come to visit the Abbess. It was a rare enough event but these were extraordinary times.

They talked for a while about the upheaval affecting both their houses.

'Are you any closer to knowing who killed the merchant?' asked the Abbess.

The Abbot shook his head. 'It must have been an intruder – someone with a grudge against him. A successful businessman like him must have made enemies. Someone must have followed him from Assisi and waited till we were all abed.'

'And then fled from the friary,' said the Abbess. 'It would have been easy enough to escape without notice.'

'I have been thinking we should have a service of purification,' said the Abbot. 'Perhaps the sisters should come too? I feel that both our houses have been defiled.'

'It's a good idea,' the Abbess agreed. 'They are all very disturbed and frightened. I shall tell them that it is all over and the service will help to restore them to the proper frame of mind.'

'I hope it does the same for the brothers,' sighed the Abbot. 'I have never known them so disrupted. Rumours are flying through the friary.'

'Rumours?'

'Well, you know our young novice?'

'Brother Silvano?'

118

The Abbot shifted uncomfortably. 'Actually he isn't really a brother. We are giving him sanctuary at the request of an old friend of mine. Until it is safe for him to go back to Perugia, he passes for a novice here.'

'And why did he need sanctuary?'

'He was suspected of a murder,' admitted the Abbot. 'A man was stabbed in the street in Perugia and it was Silvano who found the body.'

'Stabbed!' exclaimed the Abbess. 'And you still say that Ubaldo's murderer came from outside the friary.'

'Silvano is no murderer,' said the Abbot. 'He's an obedient and good-hearted fellow. And what possible reason could he have had for killing Ubaldo?'

'For what reason did people think he had killed the other man?'

'There were rumours that he was, um, enamoured of the man's wife.'

'Well,' said the Abbess. 'At least that could not be the case with the merchant.'

'I am sure that he had nothing to do with it,' said the Abbot.

'But until they find out who killed the man in Perugia, there will still be a shadow over him, won't there?' said the Abbess. 'And however innocent he may be he can't stay in Giardinetto for ever. People will wonder why he remains a novice.'

The Abbot decided not to tell her that there was a second friar who did have a motive for murdering Ubaldo. He wanted to believe as she did that the killing was over.

119

The nuns and friars filed into the chapel of the friary the next day, filling it to overflowing. The Abbot led the service, solemnly intoning words of comfort. There was so little room that the novices had to stand at the back and Chiara managed to catch Silvano's eye. She wanted to talk to him about Isabella and Brother Anselmo but also hoped that he might tell her more about his life in Perugia. Chiara had already guessed from his superior horse and his hawk that Silvano was an aristocrat. And she wanted to hear him say that he no longer cared for the woman whose husband had been murdered. But it was virtually impossible for two young people of opposite sex in religious houses to speak alone, even though they lived so nearby.

An unexpected opportunity came later in the day, when both novices found themselves back in the Basilica with Simone Martini. The artist seemed much more pleased than either of them would have been about the quantities of dull green paint that Brother Anselmo and Sister Veronica had brought him.

'Do you make your own white?' Silvano asked the painter, remembering his conversation with Brother Fazio.

'My journeymen do,' said Simone. 'They mix the gesso for the walls in a workshop here at the Cathedral and make large quantities of lime-white.'

'Saint John's white,' said Silvano.

Simone raised his eyebrows, impressed. 'Indeed, though here it will be used for Saint Martin. It's not skilled work. They mix slaked lime and water in buckets and stir it for eight days. Then they make it into little cakes and put them to dry in the sun. We call it biacca.'

'Couldn't they make the colours for you too, Ser Simone?'

Chiara dared to ask.

'I would not entrust such a task to journeymen, Sister,' he replied. 'Of course my assistants have the skills but you see how I need them here.'

He gestured to the scaffolding where several men were working on the hands of figures in frescoes that were nearly finished.

'My brother, Donato,' said Simone, 'and my friends Lippo and Tederigo. They are part of my bottega in Siena. I could not finish this commission without them.' The artists looked down and smiled to acknowledge the visitors, then turned back to their delicate task.

When the day's load of colours had been brought into the chapel, Simone offered to take the visitors into the Upper Church and show them the life of Saint Francis. Sister Veronica was fascinated, dedicated follower of the Saint that she was, and even Silvano and Chiara were interested because the painter had made the scenes so real. Only Brother Anselmo seemed to have to force himself to be interested in the paintings.

'As beautiful as possible,' said Simone. 'That is the responsibility of all us mural painters – to beautify the House of God to the best of our ability. I am trying hard in the church below us but Maestro Giotto has given me a lot to measure up to.'

The nave was completely decorated – walls, ceilings, chapels, even the thin columns and arches that sprang up into the vaulted roof. Everywhere was a mass of bright colours and it took a while for eyes accustomed to the dimness of the Lower Church to make sense of it all. But the painter took them to the beginning of the sequence of the Saint's life on the north side of the nave.

It was a picture of the centre of Assisi, with a Greek temple in the middle, squeezed up between two modern buildings. The Saint walked from the left in a dark cloak, his head already haloed. On the right a man spread his cloak for Francis to walk on.

'He is a simpleton,' said Simone. 'Not a grand person like the other men in their red and gold and white robes. But he alone recognises the holiness of Francis and pays him homage.'

In the next picture the Saint, who had his own horse, gave a much grander, golden cloak to a poor knight.

'Just like Saint Martin!' Silvano exclaimed. 'Will he now dream that the poor man was Our Lord?'

'No,' said Simone. 'Francis does have a dream but it is of a palace filled with arms bearing the sign of the cross. It means that he has done a deed worthy of a knight and the arms are for him and his followers.'

He went on explaining the frescoes and gradually, as the Colour Master and Mistress became more involved in the story, the novices were able to linger behind.

'They are wonderful, aren't they?' said Silvano.

'Truly,' said Chiara. 'I have never imagined anything like it. But I don't understand why the church dedicated to the Saint is so full of light and colour while we, who are also supposed to dedicate ourselves to the Order he inspired, must live without either.'

'Do you hate it so much?' asked Silvano.

'It is different for you,' said Chiara. 'One day you will leave but I must stay for ever.'

'I don't know when that day will be,' said Silvano. 'And

maybe something will happen so that you can leave too. I know that Monna Isabella would like to do something for you. Perhaps you could write to her?'

Chiara looked up at him gratefully. 'Thank you. Perhaps I will. How was she when you left her in Gubbio?'

'Quite calm and composed,' said Silvano. 'She is a fine lady. I think she will recover from her husband's death.'

He heard what he thought was a very unreligious snort of suppressed laughter from the novice nun.

'Of course she will! She hated him.'

Silvano was amazed. 'Hated him? But she seemed so upset at the friary. I'm sure she nearly fainted when they put his body into the carriage.'

'Only because she had seen your Brother Anselmo,' said Chiara.

'But why?'

'His secular name was Domenico and they were in love when they were young,' said Chiara. 'It is a terribly sad story. Ubaldo took her from him. There was no way in which her family would let her marry a poor scholar when a rich merchant came courting.'

'And so Domenico became a friar,' said Silvano. 'That makes sense.'

'Yes but Isabella didn't know that, not till yesterday. And now she would be free to marry him, but of course he has taken a vow of celibacy.'

'Come, Sister Orsola,' called Veronica. 'You can see our blessed Saint Clare here.'

They hurried after the others so that Simone could show them the painting of Saint Clare and her fellow nuns encountering the funeral procession of Saint Francis. The Saint lay

123

on a bier covered in a gold-patterned cloth while Clare leant over, sorrowing and almost taking him in her arms. The other sisters whispered sadly to each other in the background. One of the ones on the right looked a bit like Chiara.

But Silvano could not keep his mind on the story. Monna Isabella and Brother Anselmo had once been in love! And Ubaldo had separated them. Anselmo must have hated him. Yet Silvano could not reconcile the kindly and devout man he knew with one who would kill out of jealousy. He tried to think how he would feel if another man took Angelica from him then chided himself. It was not the same. He had hardly ever exchanged a word with her; she was not his. She had been another man's before he knew her. And he had not killed that man.

They had reached the last pictures on the south side and were almost back at the stairs to the Lower Church. Simone was explaining that they showed miracles that happened after Francis's death. Sister Veronica was making sure that Chiara looked at every detail and did not dawdle behind again with the handsome novice.

As they descended back into the Lower Church and the painter showed the sisters where other new paintings were going to be, Silvano decided to speak to the Colour Master about what he had heard. He simply couldn't keep his curiosity to himself.

'Brother Anselmo, is it true that you ... that you knew Monna Isabella when you were young?'

It was perhaps the only thing that could have shaken Anselmo out of his reverie. He started and began to say, 'But how ...?' Then he changed his mind and sighed.

'It is true,' he said simply. 'I had not seen her for nearly twenty years, until she came to the friary yesterday. I have prayed and struggled with my feelings but the sight of her has undone many years of devotion to the service of Our Lord. I am deep in sin.'

'But not the sin of murder?' whispered Silvano.

Brother Anselmo looked at him reproachfully.

'I mean, I'm sure you didn't kill Ubaldo,' said Silvano hastily. 'But do any of the other brothers know your history with Monna Isabella?'

'Abbot Bonsignore does,' said Anselmo. 'I told him the reason I had first become a friar when I joined the house at Giardinetto. But he didn't know the name of the woman I loved or the man who married her. I told him only when he questioned me yesterday. He asked me about meeting you on the night of the murder and I told him I had been out for some fresh air. He asked me straight out if I had been to Ubaldo's cell.'

Silvano held his breath.

'I told him I had thought of it,' said Anselmo. 'The temptation was strong to find out how he had treated her over the years – just to hear him say her name would have been a sweet torment. But I struggled with it and took myself for a walk around the grounds instead.'

'She hated him,' said Silvano. 'She has never stopped loving you. She told Chiara, I mean Sister Orsola.'

Anselmo sat down suddenly on a step and put his head in his hands.

'It is like a nightmare,' he said. 'I told the Abbot about my past connection with Ubaldo and he believed in my innocence. But if this story gets out in the friary, I cannot trust that the other brothers will have such confidence in me, I am so recently come among them.'

'I shall tell no one,' promised Silvano. 'But wouldn't the best thing be if we could find out who the real murderer was?'

Anselmo smiled for the first time for days. Silvano's trust in him was balm to his bruised feelings.

'Yes, indeed. But how shall we do that? You are in the same situation yourself, are you not, with the man in Perugia?'

'Yes but I am not there and can do nothing about my case,' said Silvano. 'At least we are both here. We cannot let suspicion fall on you or any of the other brothers for that matter.'

'Unless one of them is guilty,' said Anselmo.

Simone had stopped to talk to a tall, red-haired man working on a wall in the south transept. He had introduced the sisters and now beckoned to the Franciscan brothers to join them. Silvano thought the man's long face looked vaguely familiar but he couldn't imagine where he might have seen him before.

'This is my old friend and rival Pietro Lorenzetti,' said Simone. 'I have known him and his little brother Ambrogio ever since we were all boys growing up together in Siena. For years now we have competed for commissions and I'm delighted to find him here in Assisi too.'

Pietro bowed courteously to both of them.

'Simone tells me that you and the holy sisters are supplying him with colours,' he said. 'Could you do the same for me? Now that I see the scale of the area I've been commissioned to decorate, I doubt that what I have brought with me will last for long.'

'I should be honoured to serve you,' said Brother

Anselmo, his composure recovered.

'I suppose we can manage to supply both of you,' said Sister Veronica. 'We must work even harder in the colour room, Sister Orsola. Mother Elena will be happy since it is all to the glory of Saint Francis.'

'How did you like the paintings of Maestro Giotto?' asked Pietro. 'Simone tells me you have just seen them for the first time.'

'They are beyond words,' said Anselmo. 'He is a genius of your art.'

'Did you ever meet him?' asked Silvano but the two Sienese shook their heads.

'Our master was Duccio di Buoninsegna,' explained Simone. 'We admire the work of the great Giotto but we were taught by Duccio.'

'It was he who painted the Mary in Majesty for the Cathedral in Siena,' Anselmo told Silvano.

'You have seen it?' said Pietro eagerly.

Anselmo nodded. 'I was there when they carried it into the Cathedral.'

'Ah,' said Simone. 'That was a great day! Five years ago and I remember it perfectly. There was a great procession from the Maestro's workshop through the streets of Siena up to our Cathedral of the Virgin on the hill. All the rulers of the city were there and all the other nobles and important people.'

'And all the common people came out to see it too,' added Pietro. 'Everyone carried a candle. It was like the greatest religious festival and we had a tremendous party afterwards in the workshop. Do you remember that, Simone?'

'Of course,' laughed the painter. 'And I remember the

127

headache I had the next day as well, saving your presence, Sisters!'

'We were no longer Duccio's apprentices by then, of course, though Ambrogio still worked with him occasionally,' said Pietro. 'Simone and I had our own bottegas. But we remain friends with him.'

'Is he still alive?' asked Chiara.

'Yes, but very old now,' said Simone, gravely. 'He paints little these days. But he and Giotto di Bondone are still the greatest artists in Italy. We just aspire to do anything as well.'

'And yet you have painted your own Mary in Majesty in Siena, I believe,' said Sister Veronica.

Simone inclined his head gracefully. 'I am honoured that you have heard of it,' he said. 'But I must get back to my Saint Martin or I shall not complete the chapel in time.'

And the visitors from Giardinetto took their leave.

'We should travel together next time, Sister Veronica,' said Brother Anselmo. 'It would save using two carts and taking up your man's time unnecessarily.'

Silvano and Chiara exchanged looks. That would give them more time together and surely they would snatch a few words. It was beginning to be important to them both.

CHAPTER TEN

Mundualdus

o, Brother Fazio told you something of the art of illumination?' Anselmo asked Silvano on their way back to the friary.

'He's very clever,' said Silvano. 'I saw the Gospel he is working on.'

'His Saint John?' said Anselmo. 'It is a masterpiece, isn't it?'

'Wonderful,' said Silvano. 'I liked it a lot better than when he showed me where he makes the white.'

'Ah,' smiled Anselmo. 'The malodorous shed. The brothers believe that Fazio has no sense of smell. It must help with that aspect of his work.'

'He's quite a character,' said Silvano.

'He was a bit suspicious of me when I came, I think,' said Anselmo. 'After all, he is an expert when it comes to colours. But the sort we supply to artists like Simone Martini aren't all suitable for illumination, and vice versa. So Fazio and I have settled down, each to his own speciality and I don't think he sees me as a threat any longer.'

'You don't have much ill-feeling in the friary, do you?' said Silvano. 'I've noticed the brothers seem to get along pretty well.'

'In the main, yes,' said Anselmo. 'Each has his own task to

129

get on with and that helps. But sometimes a brother might feel that another is treading on his toes. I believe that Brother Valentino and Brother Rufino don't always see eye to eye for instance.'

'Brother Rufino is the Infirmarian, I know,' said Silvano. 'But Valentino?'

'He is the Herbalist. You see that his role overlaps a bit with Brother Rufino's.'

'You said in Assisi that one of the brothers could be the murderer . . .'

'I should not like to believe such a thing,' said Anselmo quickly.

'Can't we try to find out?' asked Silvano. 'I hate the thought that anyone might suspect you.'

'They won't,' said Anselmo. 'As you know, I have told only you and Abbot Bonsignore about Monna Isabella.'

'But all the same,' insisted Silvano, 'wouldn't it be good to think we have found the real culprit?'

'You are a good boy,' said Anselmo. 'And I think it would ease your troubled heart to clear an innocent man. But how would we set about it? The Abbot has questioned all the brothers and apparently found nothing to suggest that the murderer came from within the friary.'

'Then there is nothing we can do?'

'Not now, I fear. The murderer has long fled.'

'We could ask Monna Isabella,' Silvano suggested hesitantly. 'At least Sister Orsola could. I'm sure she will see her again. She could ask about Ubaldo's enemies.'

Anselmo's brow creased with an old sadness.

'I should not wish to distress her,' he said softly.

Silvano was silent for a while, wondering when he would

see the pretty Chiara again.

'When shall we next go to Ser Simone?' he asked. 'Ser Pietro too now I suppose.'

'That has not been decided,' said Anselmo. 'We expect them to visit us next at the friary. Simone wishes to discuss the ultramarine with us. They will be with us the day after tomorrow.'

It was the day of Ubaldo's funeral. The principal mourners were Isabella and her four children and the merchant's younger brother, Umberto. He was a tall and grim-faced man with a forbidding air and Isabella had always sensed that he disapproved of her. She felt grateful for the first time that her husband had died away from home. She would not have put it past her brother-in-law to suspect her of a hand in Ubaldo's death otherwise.

It was very unfair, because she had spent so many years as a devoted wife, smothering her own feelings in order to serve Ubaldo and make his domestic life as comfortable as possible. The only thing she hadn't done was love him; he couldn't make her do that. But how could Umberto know that? She had always behaved impeccably in front of him.

And did so now, swathed in black, at the Requiem Mass. The children were so upset that she even managed to shed some genuine tears, out of sympathy for them. But Umberto, looking at her with his hooded eyes, seemed to see straight into her soul and she felt a fraud.

After the feast, when many toasts had been drunk in the merchant's memory and his passing suitably marked, only

Umberto remained of all the mourners. At his request, Isabella poured them both a goblet of wine and retired with him to Ubaldo's office. She went with a heavy heart, consigning the children to a servant. She doubted that she would want to hear what he had to say.

'Now, sister,' he began. 'We need to talk about my brother's business affairs. Firstly, you will need to appoint a mundualdus. I should be happy to offer my services.'

This was what Isabella had been dreading.

'Thank you, brother,' she forced herself to say as lightly as she could. 'You are most considerate. But I feel I need a little time to make up my mind. I have been so busy preparing for the funeral.'

'Yes, well, you did give my brother a good send off,' said Umberto grudgingly. 'But do not take too long to decide. I shall expect your answer within a week.'

And then he was gone, a dark presence removed from the house. Isabella took herself to bed and slept for ten hours.

She was woken by her maid who told her that there was a young woman to see her. 'A widow, Madama, like yourself and that only recently, I'd say by her mourning dress. The young gentleman accompanying her gave her name only as Angelica of Perugia.'

Isabella was puzzled but made haste to meet her unexpected guests. As she moved swiftly to the parlour, she couldn't help feeling her spirits lift. She could entertain guests in that pretty room now without any fear that Ubaldo would disapprove. The sun shone through the window and outside birds sang as if they had just been released from a locked cage.

Isabella had not recognised the name given by her maid and she did not recognise the plump and pretty blonde who

132

rose when she entered the room. Her widow's weeds were indeed as black as Isabella's own and the older woman recognised both the costliness of the materials and the style with which they were fashioned and worn.

'Madama,' she said to her guest, inclining her head.

'Forgive me for intruding on your grief, Madama,' responded the young woman.

'It seems that you have recently suffered the same loss,' said Isabella drily. She knew instinctively that this Angelica was no more grieving than she was herself. The young man bowing to her from the window was exceptionally good-looking, if a little foppish and there was an unmistakeable air of complicity between them.

'Indeed,' said Angelica. 'My husband died only a month ago – in similar circumstances to your own.'

Isabella's hand flew involuntarily to her mouth.

'He was murdered?' she asked.

'Yes, stabbed to death in the street,' said Angelica calmly. 'But I have recovered from the shock. It is not about his death that I wished to talk to you. I am going to trade as a wool merchant in Gubbio.'

Whatever Isabella had been expecting, it was not that. She could not reply.

'I wanted to tell you this because we are going to be in competition,' said Angelica. 'I thought it would be fairer.'

'And who is this?' asked Isabella, indicating the young man by the window. 'Will he run the business for you?'

'Gervasio de' Oddini at your service,' said the young man, with a flourish. 'And no. I am merely Monna Angelica's escort today.'

'His father is my mundualdus,' explained Angelica. 'We

133

have appointed someone to run the business in Gubbio. I wondered what your plans are? Will you continue with your late husband's wool business?'

Isabella had to admire this young woman, who had the confidence to confront her in this way. It was obvious too that she had her mundualdus in the palm of her hand if he let her be squired around by his handsome son. She could not imagine Umberto being so indulgent with her.

'How old are you?' she suddenly asked.

'I am not yet twenty, Madama,' Angelica replied, casting down her eyes in a practised pretence of modesty.

'Would you excuse us for a little, Messer Gervasio?' said Isabella, getting up to ring the bell. 'There are matters I should like to discuss with Monna Angelica in private. My servant will take you to my late husband's office and bring you refreshment there.'

When the two widows were left alone, the atmosphere immediately became more friendly.

'I know we would be rivals if we were both selling wool in Gubbio,' said Angelica. 'But we are both women trying to make a living among men. Perhaps we should think of going into business together?'

'Let us not be hasty,' said Isabella. 'You asked about my plans, but I find it difficult to plan anything until I know who will look after my legal affairs. My brother-in-law wants me to appoint him, but I know that he does not care about me.'

'Would he have your children's interests at heart?'

'Yes, I think so. After all they are his brother's children too. I don't think he would cheat us. But he would think nothing of what I wanted to do.'

'And what is that?' asked Angelica.

'It is not impossible,' said Isabella. 'I mean . . . in time . . . there is a remote possibility that I might wish to remarry.'

Angelica laughed, a high tinkling and most unbereaved laugh. Isabella envied her light heart and her youth.

'So I should think,' said Angelica. 'You are a beautiful woman, Monna Isabella, and a rich one too. I am contemplating the same thing myself.' Her eyes slid towards the door where Gervasio had made his exit. 'But what would your brother-in-law think of that? Especially if he were also your legal representative.'

Isabella was silent. Ever since her glimpse of Domenico at the friary her heart had been in turmoil. She had tried not to think of him as she prepared for her husband's funeral. It would have been disrespectful to Ubaldo and a departure from her sense of what was right. But whenever she had fallen short of her own high standards, she had come up against the immovable fact that Domenico was now a professed friar.

This meant two conflicting things at the same time: that Domenico had kept his promise never to marry anyone else and that he was as out of her reach now as when Ubaldo was alive. And yet she could not believe that Fate had brought them together at the time of her husband's death if they were not meant to find a way of being together.

'Monna Isabella,' said Angelica, startling her from her reverie. 'Would you forgive my impertinence if I were to offer you some advice?'

'Of course,' said Isabella. 'I am much in need of the counsel of another woman. And you seem very sure of your own course.'

'It might have been different for you,' said Angelica, giving

135

the other widow a shrewd look. 'But I did not love my husband. It was a marriage arranged by my family and he was much older than me. It was a relief when he died. My advice to you is this: choose as your procurator the father of the man you really love, if he still be living. In that way you have the protection of the older man and the company of the younger. And with the wealth you inherit from your husband, you can expect little resistance to your plans.'

Isabella smiled sadly. This rather brash young woman, brimming with crude vitality, saw everything through the eyes of someone who had not yet completed two decades on earth. It was doubtful that Domenico's father was still alive.

She was about to say something of the kind when an idea suddenly occurred to her.

'You might well be right,' she said. 'Thank you for that advice. I shall find a way to take it.'

Baron Montacuto was not happy. He had had several very uncomfortable interviews with representatives of the Council in Perugia and they were still seeking out his son for the murder of Tommaso the sheep farmer.

'I have absolutely no idea,' he said unashamedly, when they asked where Silvano was.

'But isn't that a clear admission of his guilt?' asked the Capitano. 'If he has run away from the city without telling even his own family where he was going? That is the action of a guilty man.'

'And what would the actions of an innocent man be?' asked Montacuto, enraged. 'To stay and answer questions

136

when his own dagger had been stolen from him to commit the crime?'

'You know that his dagger had been stolen?' asked the Capitano.

'It must have been,' said the Baron firmly. 'My son is not a murderer.'

But for all his bluster, he wished that he had some sort of evidence to offer that would clear Silvano of the crime he was accused of. He missed his son terribly every day and wanted him back from Giardinetto. But it clearly wasn't safe yet.

His own investigations had yielded one important piece of information. Tommaso, as well as being a successful sheep farmer, had started a second business as a secret money-lender. No records had been found of who owed him money; it was possible that he carried them with him and that they had been taken by his murderer.

But the Baron had found two people who had borrowed money from Tommaso at a high rate of interest and now there was no trace of the loans. Both had witnesses to testify that they had been elsewhere at the time of the stabbing, so they were not suspected of the murder. Needless to say they were very relieved that Tommaso was no more.

Montacuto was convinced there were many more debtors and, if only he could find them all, the murderer would be among them. But for the time being, Silvano remained the only person suspected of the deed and there were notices all over Perugia proclaiming him a wanted man. Baron Montacuto ground his teeth as he walked past one of them nailed to a tree in the square outside the Council. That debtor with the dagger had robbed not only Tommaso of his life and the Baron of his son, but also the House of

Montacuto of its honour.

If he ever found out who it was, that man would be made to pay for all three.

❧

Silvano still felt uncomfortable in the friary. Wherever he went, he found that brothers were looking at him or they broke off conversations when he drew near. Whatever Brother Matteo had said about him, it hadn't stopped the rumours. If he could have heard what they were actually saying, he might not have felt so disturbed. The friars of Giardinetto were so unused to anything interrupting their routine of prayer, preaching and attending to the needs of others that the arrival of both a suspected murderer and an actual murder had been like a fox invading a chicken coop.

Their feathers were ruffled and a certain amount of clucking was to be expected. But they had taken to this modest and willing boy from the city and it didn't seem as if any brother really believed him capable of one, let alone two murders.

The Novice Master, Brother Ranieri, let the gossip run for a while then decided to have a word with each of the postulants in his charge. But since he did not include Silvano, the young noble had no idea that anyone was trying to quash the rumours.

Late in the day, he decided to see the Abbot.

'Come in, come in,' Father Bonsignore welcomed him. 'How is everything?'

'I am not very happy, Father,' said Silvano.

'I am sorry to hear it,' said the Abbot. 'Can you tell me why?'

138

'Word seems to have got about among the friars as to why I am here. And I think they might believe I had something to do with Ubaldo's death.'

'Surely not?' said the Abbot, genuinely shocked. 'I must have a word with them. I don't know how they found out – certainly Brother Ranieri was under strict instructions not to tell anyone.'

'I don't think I can stay here if I'm under suspicion,' said Silvano. 'It was bad enough having to leave Perugia. I can't go through that again.'

'There is no question of it,' said the Abbot firmly. 'This is your home until it is safe for you to go back to your family.'

'I suppose there is no news from Perugia?' asked Silvano, without much hope.

'Nothing yet,' admitted the Abbot. 'But I shall go myself next week to see the Bishop, and it would be most natural for me to call on my old friend Montacuto. I can take him a message if you would like.'

'And to my mother?' said Silvano eagerly. 'And he can tell you about what is going on in the city.'

There was a knock on the door. Brother Gregorio, the Lector, came in with a roll of parchment in his hand.

'I shall leave you, Father,' said Silvano. 'Thank you for your kindness.'

As he passed Gregorio in the doorway, the Lector patted him awkwardly on the shoulder. 'Be of good courage,' he said quietly and Silvano left the Abbot's cell feeling better than when he came in.

'That is a troubled soul,' said Bonsignore, shaking his head.

'Indeed,' said Brother Gregorio. 'If only we could find out

who killed the merchant Ubaldo. Until we do, there is a cloud over Silvano.'

'And I see you know he came here under such a cloud already.'

'There has been some talk,' said Gregorio. 'But I have paid it no heed. I like the lad.'

'We all do,' said the Abbot. 'Now, what can I do for you?'

'This letter has come for you from Gubbio,' said Gregorio.

Bonsignore looked at the wax seal. 'That is Ubaldo's signet,' he said. 'It must be from his widow.'

'To thank you, perhaps?'

'Perhaps.'

The Abbot pulled the seal from the string and unrolled the parchment.

'By Our Lady and Saint Francis!' he said. 'Monna Isabella asks that I be her legal representative. She wants me to be her mundualdus.'

CHAPTER ELEVEN

From Beyond the Sea

rother Landolfo, the Guest Master, had been agitated when Brother Anselmo told him about the two distinguished painters coming to the friary.

'They will not stay overnight,' explained Anselmo. 'They are coming to see the colour room and discuss our production of the first batch of ultramarine. And they will want to see Sister Veronica's workshop too.'

'But they will join us in the midday meal, surely?' said Landolfo. 'I must speak to Bertuccio. And perhaps your young apprentice could get his hawk to catch a hare or two?'

'My novice,' corrected Anselmo. 'I'll see what he can do.'

It was astonishing how often Bertuccio or Brother Rufino came to Silvano to ask for a game bird or rabbit for the pot. He was indeed hawking more than once a week and the Abbot turned a blind eye to the pursuit. Celeste needed to be flown every day anyway and it was better exercise for her and Moonbeam if they went outside the friary walls.

Before the two painters arrived, the colour room was in good order. The friars who worked there had stopped gossiping about Silvano and spent the first hours of the day making giallorino.

'It is from a mineral found close to great volcanoes,'

Brother Anselmo explained to Silvano. 'This batch came from near Mount Vesuvius. It's much too hard to break up on a slab so you must pound it in a mortar.'

The friars took the large bronze mortars and worked hard to break up the yellowish rock. Brother Fazio's bird-like head poked round the door of the colour room.

'Sorry to disturb you,' he said. 'I have run out of verdigris.'

Brother Anselmo went to one of the long shelves and took down a jar of bluish green particles.

'What are you making today?' Fazio asked the room in general.

'A kind of yellow, Brother,' volunteered Silvano. 'From volcanoes.'

'Ah, giallorino,' said Fazio. 'All very well for walls, I suppose but I prefer king's yellow. Nothing less than the royal hue for the Word of God.'

He left with his jar of verdigris.

'What did he mean?' asked Silvano. 'What is king's yellow?'

'It is orpiment,' said Anselmo. 'We call it and its red brother, realgar, "the two kings". But they aren't suitable for walls.'

'Why not?'

'They turn black. I make small quantities for Brother Fazio and his helpers to use on parchment. But it is to be avoided as much as possible. The old Greeks called orpiment "arsenikon" and it is a strong poison.'

At that moment there was a tap on the door and the Sienese painters entered. The brothers had met Simone Martini before but they all had to be introduced to Pietro Lorenzetti. As when they first met, Silvano again had the strongest feeling that he had seen the tall red-haired painter before. He noticed that Simone was smiling at him.

'You have recognised our Pietro?' he said. And then Silvano remembered where he had seen that long handsome face before. 'Our Lord!' he exclaimed.

Pietro laughed. 'Yes, I'm afraid my Sienese friends took that liberty.'

'It was my assistants – the ones you met last time in Assisi,' said Simone. 'They painted Our Lord among the angels in that picture I showed you of Saint Martin's dream. And they decided to give him Pietro's features.'

'Isn't that blasphemy?' asked Silvano before he could stop himself.

'Not really,' said Simone. 'We are all made in God's image but I think He would have chosen to come to earth in a form more like Pietro's here than with a face like mine.' And he smiled his down-turned smile. 'But enough of paintings already done. I have a second commission in the Basilica. As soon as I have finished the chapel I must paint five saints and Our Lady in the north transept.'

'He can't keep out of my way,' said Pietro. 'It's always been the same. Wherever I go, I find Simone underfoot.' But he clapped the shorter man on the shoulder and Silvano could see that they were great friends.

'I shall not be under your feet,' retorted Simone. 'I shall be working across the aisle from you. But I shall be able to keep an eye on you and give you the odd word of advice if I see you going wrong.'

'And likewise,' said Pietro. 'I shall curb your excesses of gold.'

'Gold?' said Silvano. 'Are we to provide that too?'

'No,' said Simone. 'No one comes to a house of Franciscan

brothers for gold. But we are here to talk of something almost equally precious.'

'Ultramarine,' said Anselmo.

'Blue from beyond the sea,' said Simone. He took a small rock from his satchel that at first looked no more remarkable to Silvano then any other mineral the brothers had worked on in the colour room. 'This is the true blue, the only colour for Our Lady's mantle. Ordinary passers-by or bystanders might wear a cloak of azurite but for Our Lady it must be created from lapis lazuli and I ordered this consignment from Venice.'

'But there is no sea between here and that city, is there?' asked Silvano.

'No,' said Pietro. 'Only the sea that surrounds it. But the lapis comes from far away across the sea before it reaches Venice. It is hewn from rocks in the valleys of Khoresan, the Land of the Rising Sun.'

Silvano was silent. He had hardly ever been out of Perugia and he suddenly felt small and ignorant, his problems insignificant in a world that had such wonders in it. The strange names of places far beyond his imagining came easily to the lips of these great artists but even the great trading city of Venice, famed for its beauty and wealth, had sounded exotic to him.

'Look at your novice, Brother Anselmo,' said Pietro. 'We have bedazzled him with our talk of distant lands. Come closer, Silvano, and look at the stone. Some people believe that it is a fragment of the starry heavens themselves fallen on to the land from above. But those who work it say that it has to be hewn out of the rock like any other precious mineral.'

144

Silvano could see the dark, brilliant blue crystals shining in the dull rock. He yearned to turn it into a glowing colour that Simone and Pietro could use in their paintings. He could just imagine what an opulent robe Simone would give to the Blessed Virgin.

'May I grind some?' he asked.

'That will be only the beginning,' said Anselmo. 'When we have pounded it in mortars and ground it finely on the slabs, all we will have is a grey powder. You will think that we have spoiled it. But wait till we have mixed it with rosin and mastic and wax, and sieved it and kneaded it with lye. Then shall you see the true blue appear.'

Silvano looked appalled at the amount of work needed to turn the already beautiful blue stone into the equally beautiful pigment. But the two artists were nodding approvingly.

'We had no doubt about your expertise, Brother Anselmo,' said Simone. 'And I'm sure that you will use it to produce the finest ultramarine.'

The sisters were also expecting a visit from the Sienese painters. Chiara surprised herself by realising that she had something interesting to look forward to almost every day. And in between times the routine of the convent had become quite soothing to her. Even the regular visits to the chapel every few hours to say the Office, which she had thought she would never get used to, now felt like a natural punctuation of the day. She had stopped thinking of her brother and her first family and, although she was still in awe of Mother Elena, she was genuinely fond of Sister Veronica. And she enjoyed working the colours.

But her mind still went frequently to the friary next door and not just because of Silvano. A man had died horribly and so close to where she was living that it haunted her dreams. And all the more since she had seen the corpse and helped to clean it up.

'What are you daydreaming about, child?' asked Sister Veronica. 'We must keep up with our work or we shall not have enough to offer the painters.'

'I'm sorry, Sister,' said Chiara. 'I can't help thinking about the murder next door.'

'Natural enough,' said Sister Veronica. 'But there is no need to be afraid. Father Bonsignore is sure that the murderer has put a great distance between himself and Giardinetto.'

Chiara wasn't afraid but it was a good excuse for inattention. She bent over her slab determined to keep concentrated on the azurite she was grinding. It must not be too fine, Sister Veronica had said; the coarser the grains, the more intense would the blue pigment be. But not as intense as the costly ultramarine which the Sienese artists wanted for their most important figures.

Sister Lucia entered the room and whispered to the Colour Mistress. The two grey sisters turned towards Chiara, who had not yet trained herself not to be curious and was already looking at them. Sister Veronica beckoned her over.

'Sister Lucia comes with a message from the Abbess. She wants to speak to you in her room.'

Chiara wiped the blue-grey dust from her fingers on to her robe, where it became invisible, adjusted her veil, and prepared to face the Abbess. She hoped very much that she had done nothing wrong.

❦

Simone and Pietro sat down to a good meal with the friars; Bertuccio bustled about, shiny-faced, bringing more and more dishes from the kitchen. Brother Landolfo hovered in the background, smiling nervously. The painters were not richly dressed but they still looked like peacocks in a dovecote among the grey friars at table.

Usually the friars ate in silence while Brother Gregorio, the Lector, read from the Scriptures, but the rule was relaxed when they had visitors. Talk flowed around the table and the main topic was still that of the death of Ubaldo.

'So, your last visitor was murdered?' said Pietro. 'Should we be worried?'

'No, no,' said Landolfo hastily. 'That was a most unlikely occurrence. We have never had an intruder in the friary before and I'm sure it will never happen again.'

'Do not disturb yourself, Brother,' said Simone, frowning at Pietro. 'My friend is not serious. We are very comfortable here in your friary and grateful for your hospitality.'

'You go to visit the sisters next?' asked Landolfo. 'You must eat up here – they will have nothing to give you.'

'We shall have no need of anything from them after such a spread,' said Pietro, and Landolfo looked gratified. He eventually sat down at the long table himself in his usual place next to Brother Fazio and had a little to eat.

'Brother Anselmo tells me that your paintings in Assisi are of the utmost magnificence,' said Father Bonsignore.

147

'He is too kind,' said Simone and the conversation at that end of the table turned to art and great masterpieces seen by the brothers before they entered their calling. Brother Fazio was eloquent on the subject of Cimabue, who had also painted some walls in the Basilica.

Down at the lower end, Silvano strained to hear them but then caught another thread of talk that distracted him. Brother Taddeo, the Assistant Librarian, was whispering something to Matteo about Brother Anselmo. He heard 'Isabella' and 'Domenico' and his heart sank. Anselmo's secret was out.

When the novice came into her room, Mother Elena tried to assess how much Chiara had changed since the day she had thrown her curls to the birds. She still looked too boldly into other people's faces but now she remembered, after the first glance, to cast her gaze down. And she moved more slowly and was less impetuous. The Abbess thought that, with time, Chiara could make a good sister in the Order of the Poor Clares. She was willing and obedient but Mother Elena knew that she had still not felt the voice of God calling her to such a life. And she doubted that she ever would.

'Sister Orsola,' she said. 'I have had an interesting letter about you. From Gubbio.'

'From my brother?' asked Chiara, surprised.

'No, from a rich lady,' said the Abbess.

'Monna Isabella?'

'She writes to ask if you could be released from your novitiate,' said the Abbess gravely. 'What do you think of that idea?'

148

Chiara did not know how to respond. A few weeks ago and she would have been thrilled at the prospect of escape, as she would have seen it. Now she did not know if she wanted to leave. There was Silvano close at hand and the chance of seeing him both here and in Assisi. And there was the work itself, which had opened her eyes to the marvels of art. And her curiosity made her want to stay to hear the end of the story of Ubaldo's murder.

And yet . . . Isabella was offering her a way out of a life she dreaded. One day Silvano would leave and one day the paintings in the Basilica would be finished. In a year or two Chiara would be in the grey world of the sisters, growing older with no prospect of love or adventure. Wouldn't it be better to be a companion to a wealthy widow in Gubbio, if that was what was being offered?

'You are silent, Sister,' said the Abbess.

'It is a surprise to be asked, Mother,' said Chiara. 'What else does Monna Isabella say?'

'That if you wish to be released, she will make a donation equivalent to the one that your brother gave on your entry into the convent. And that she is willing to keep you at her expense in her house in Gubbio. Your duties would be light, I think, more those of a companion than a servant.'

'And would you agree to that, Mother?' asked Chiara.

'If that was what you wanted, yes,' said the Abbess. 'If you were sure that you have felt no vocation.'

Such kindness brought tears to Chiara's eyes. A part of her wanted to please the Abbess, to tell her that she would be happy to devote her life to God and end her days in the little convent at Giardinetto. But the other part beat wildly at the bars of its cage and yearned to fly away, even to so near a place

149

as Gubbio, and live the life of an almost free woman. Surely Isabella would be an undemanding mistress? And one day Chiara might find someone else to share her life with?

Here her imagination gave out. If she tried to visualise a man who might become her husband, only Silvano's fine features appeared in her mind, and even though he was not a real friar he remained an aristocrat – each equally out of the reach of a Poor Clare and perhaps even of Monna Isabella's dependent in Gubbio. She could not base a decision about the rest of her life on a good-looking youth who happened to live next door.

'May I have some time to think about it, Mother?' she asked.

The Abbess was surprised. She had thought that the novice would jump at the chance of her release. 'Of course,' she said. 'I shall send to Gubbio to let Monna Isabella know of our conversation. She expects to be here quite frequently, as she has business with Father Bonsignore. You can talk to her the next time she visits.'

'Well,' said Simone. 'We should leave your delightful table and visit Sister Veronica. We have brought the same amount of lapis lazuli for the grey sisters,' he told Anselmo. 'Perhaps it will inspire the spirit of competition?'

'Thank you again for the repast,' Pietro said to the Abbot.

The two painters went to say goodbye to the cook and Guest Master but Landolfo was unable to get to his feet. His face had gone a terrible colour and he was clutching his head. Brother Rufino was at his side in an instant.

150

'What is it man?' he snapped, pushing the other friars out of the way. He was a great friend of Landolfo's and the Guest Master was alarming him.

Landolfo looked at the Infirmarian as if he didn't know who he was. 'Silvano,' he said. 'Where is the young falconer?'

'I am here, Brother,' said Silvano, coming forward quickly. 'What can I do?'

'Take your hawk,' babbled Landolfo wildly. 'We need a couple of hares. Artists are coming from Siena.'

Silvano looked helplessly towards the Abbot.

Simone leant over the Guest Master. 'We are here, Brother,' he said. 'And have dined well.'

'Here already?' said Landolfo frantically. 'But we must cook the hares. Bertuccio, quick.' Then he slouched over the table and started to snore.

Silvano and the other brothers were amazed. It seemed as if Landolfo might be drunk but he was such an abstemious man and had hardly taken any wine at the meal. Certainly he was confused. Only Anselmo seemed to have an idea what was wrong. He went to Rufino and spoke to him and the Abbot urgently in a low voice.

'We shall take Brother Landolfo to the infirmary,' announced Father Bonsignore. 'My apologies to our distinguished guests but, as you can see, our brother has been taken ill.'

He summoned Taddeo, Matteo and Silvano, the three youngest members of the house to carry Landolfo out of the refectory.

Brother Anselmo followed, aware that he was receiving some strange looks from the other brothers. At a loss whether to stay or go, the two Sienese painters also followed

151

what was beginning to look like a cortège.

The young friars laid their brother on a cot in the infirmary and suddenly the room filled up with other people. The body on the bed, which no longer looked like Landolfo, began to convulse and a yellow liquid trickled from his mouth. Rufino and Anselmo exchanged desperate looks.

'Hold him down,' ordered Rufino, sending his assistants for cloths and water.

Landolfo was thrashing around, his eyes rolling up into his head.

'Is it a fit?' Simone asked Silvano.

'I don't know,' said Silvano, helplessly. 'I have never seen anyone like this.'

'Was it something he ate?' asked Pietro, surreptitiously passing a hand over his own full stomach.

'Perhaps,' said Rufino grimly.

Brother Anselmo took hold of one of Landolfo's wildly flailing hands and silently invited the Infirmarian to look at the nails. They were turning a purplish-blue colour.

Landolfo's back arched with another spasm and then he fell into a sonorous slumber.

'If it is as we think,' said Rufino, 'there is one thing we might try. Anselmo, do you have any sulphur in the colour room?'

Anselmo was beginning to shake his head when Brother Fazio broke in, 'I do, Brother. I use it in the manufacture of oro musivo – the gold employed on parchment. It is not the only component of course . . .'

'For Heaven's sake, man, we don't need a disquisition on how to make illuminator's gold!' said Rufino. 'Just fetch it will you?'

152

'Very well,' said Fazio, offended, but he trotted off at a great pace.

'Is he asleep?' Silvano asked Anselmo, looking down at Landolfo.

The Colour Master shook his head. 'No,' he said quietly. 'I think he is dying. Brother Landolfo has been poisoned.'

CHAPTER TWELVE

Poison in the Air

When Chiara left the Abbess and crossed the convent yard, she saw two brothers hastily carrying a plain coffin into the main house. She stopped for a moment and crossed herself, a cold premonition touching her spine.

But she shook off her fears. There surely couldn't be another death so soon. While she was still watching, the painter Simone and his friend Pietro hurriedly crossed the small distance between the two houses, looking desperately worried.

'Ah, Sister Orsola,' said Simone. 'Well met. Can you take us to Abbess Elena?'

'Of course. You want to see her before you go to the colour room?' asked Chiara, setting off to retrace her steps.

'I think our commission of ultramarine will have to wait,' said Pietro. 'We bring bad news from the friary.'

Chiara halted. 'Someone else has died, haven't they?'

The two painters looked at each other. 'Such news should be told first to the Abbess,' said Simone gently.

'Please!' insisted Chiara. 'If it is one of the brothers, tell me who. I have friends there.'

Pietro shrugged. 'It is Brother Landolfo.'

Relief flooded through Chiara's body. Then she felt

154

ashamed. She did not know Brother Landolfo but she was sorry that any of the friars had died and so suddenly that he must have gone unshriven. How awful to die unconfessed and unabsolved, she thought, especially for a friar. But perhaps, being a friar, he had very few sins to confess or forgive?

'How did it happen?' she managed to ask.

'It appears that he might have been poisoned,' said Simone, as the friary chapel bell started to toll.

'Another murder?' asked Chiara.

'We really should go to the Abbess,' said Simone.

'Yes,' said Chiara. 'I'll take you straight to her.' But her thoughts were in chaos.

Another murder meant another murderer – or the same one who had stabbed Ubaldo the merchant. But that meant it was one of the brothers – it was unthinkable! She wished she could talk to Silvano and Anselmo about it.

Once she had left the painters at the Abbess's door, she had to run to Sister Veronica and tell her what had happened. The sisters in the colour room had already heard the passing bell and were sitting white-faced, waiting to find out what had happened.

'Poison?' said Sister Veronica, as if she hadn't understood the word. 'He must have eaten something bad.'

Chiara lowered her eyes and whispered, 'I think it was another murder.'

The friars of Giardinetto were stunned. Brother Fazio had brought the sulphur but it had been too late. Brother Landolfo had never recovered consciousness and soon ceased

155

to breathe. For Silvano, it was the second time he had seen a man die and the third violent death to have occurred near him in a matter of weeks. His mind struggled to make sense of it. A small voice at the back of it said that at least it hadn't been another stabbing; he was sure suspicion would have fallen on him again if it had been.

But something worse was happening. All the brothers were looking at one another with doubt and distrust. And the rumours about Brother Anselmo grew. His early romantic entanglement with Monna Isabella now seemed to have become common gossip, making him the chief suspect for her husband's death.

No one had come up with a reason why he might have wanted to kill the Guest Master but Silvano heard more than one friar talking about how Anselmo had been the only one who knew what was wrong with Landolfo.

'That makes no sense,' he objected whenever he heard such gossip. 'Brother Anselmo was helping Rufino look after Landolfo. Why would he have done that if he had poisoned him?'

Silvano went to seek Anselmo out and eventually found him praying in the chapel where Landolfo's body lay. Silvano slipped on to a bench beside him and waited. He was appalled when he saw the face that Anselmo at last lifted from his hands; his mentor seemed to have aged years in the last half hour.

They left the chapel together in silence until Silvano dared to ask, 'How is it with you, Brother?'

'I am close to the sin of despair,' said Anselmo. 'There is a spirit of evil at work in this house that threatens to engulf us all.'

156

'You think it is the same person who killed Ubaldo?'

'How can it be otherwise?' said Anselmo wearily. 'It is bad enough to think that Satan has entered the heart of one of our brothers – I can't believe there are two.'

As they crossed the yard, Brother Anselmo noticed for the first time that other friars, who were loitering in groups of two and three, were looking at him and turning away as he passed.

'What does this mean?' he asked Silvano.

'I think that your history with Monna Isabella has become known,' said Silvano, embarrassed.

Anselmo stopped and looked at him.

'And how would that have happened?' he asked. 'I have told no one but Father Bonsignore and yourself.'

Silvano felt terrible. 'I didn't tell them, I swear to you, Brother.'

'I don't doubt you, Silvano,' said Anselmo. 'And I would swear it was not the Abbot. But that means that there was someone else who knew.'

'I have told them that you had no reason to kill Brother Landolfo,' said Silvano hopelessly.

'No reason in the world,' said Anselmo passing his hand over his forehead. 'He was my brother in Christ and I loved him. But perhaps they will say that it was Landolfo who knew my past and I wanted to silence him.'

Suddenly he turned on his heel and took Silvano by the sleeve.

'Let us visit the sisters,' he said. 'I know that the Abbot will not doubt me but I should speak to the Abbess before any rumours reach her.'

The painters were still with the Abbess in her cell, along with Sister Veronica and Chiara, when the friars arrived. In spite of the seriousness of the situation, Silvano could not help noticing that Chiara looked very pretty. Her hair, which had started to grow again, was escaping from under her veil and framing her face like one of Simone's burnished haloes. He saw that Simone was also casting covert glances at the young novice and he wondered for the first time if the painter were a married man.

'So it is true,' said Mother Elena. 'The Guest Master was deliberately poisoned.'

'I think so, Mother,' said Brother Anselmo. 'I was explaining – was it only this morning, Silvano? – why I don't make certain pigments in the colour room because they contain arsenikon. I have seen its effects in other places where I have worked on the colours and I recognised them in Landolfo.'

'Was that why Brother Rufino called for sulphur?' asked Pietro.

'Yes, but I could see it was too late. Landolfo must have taken a huge dose for it to kill him so quickly.'

'So it was in his food?' asked the Abbess.

'Either that or his drink,' said Anselmo. 'But he drank very little – every brother knew that.'

'Every brother?' said the Abbess. 'So you think it was one of your house that killed him?'

Anselmo did not answer.

'Forgive me but wouldn't Brother Landolfo have tasted the poison in his food?' asked Chiara.

'The dishes were rich and highly spiced today,' said Anselmo.

'So it was Landolfo's dish alone that carried the poison?' said the Abbess. 'The arsenikon was not in the serving dishes that came from the kitchen?'

The men all tried to remember the details of the midday meal.

'None of us has suffered any ill effects,' said Simone. 'Even those who ate without restraint,' he added, looking at Pietro.

'I must tell you that I am under suspicion,' said Brother Anselmo quietly, looking round the little group. 'And I must ask that you don't disclose that to anyone outside this room.'

'But why you, Brother?' asked Sister Veronica, appalled.

'Why any of us?' asked Anselmo. He spread his palms, resigned. 'No one wants to think that any follower of Our Lord and Saint Francis would plan to take another man's life. But some of the brothers believe they have found a reason that I might have wanted to kill the merchant.'

Silvano and Chiara exchanged glances. Brother Anselmo didn't say what the reason was but continued, 'And now that there has been another death my name is being linked to both.'

'That is ridiculous,' said Mother Elena immediately. 'You are our priest and our spiritual adviser and I would stake my life you are no killer.'

'Thank you,' said Anselmo. 'In days to come I may be glad to number those who think so against my accusers.'

'Are we in any danger here, Brother?' asked the Abbess.

'I fear we are all in danger,' said Anselmo. 'Since Landolfo was a man of God with a sweet nature, he had no enemies. We can only assume that his attacker was insane. And if there is a lunatic at large in the friary, he could strike at any one of us.'

'This is appalling,' said Simone. 'How are we to continue painting pictures to the Glory of God in Assisi while the Devil works in secret so nearby?'

'It is in all our interests to find the wrongdoer as soon as possible,' said Anselmo. 'In the meantime I shall suggest to Father Bonsignore that we keep a guard here on the convent gate.'

Isabella was enduring a most unpleasant interview with her brother-in-law Umberto. He was furious that she had appointed the Abbot of the place where Ubaldo died to be her legal representative.

'It is an insult to my brother's memory,' he fumed. 'That man might have been involved in his death for all we know.'

'Hardly,' said Isabella. 'He is a man of God.'

'So are they all in that place,' said Umberto. 'And yet one of them minced my brother's organs with his own dagger.'

Isabella winced. 'It was an intruder,' she said.

'So they say. But nothing was taken – no money or jewels. That does not sound like the work of a casual intruder to me.'

'I have no father or brother to act for me,' she said, as calmly as she could.

'But you have a brother under the law,' said Umberto. 'And I had already offered my services.'

'I did not think that you would place my concerns first,' said Isabella.

'Quite right,' snapped Umberto. 'My brother's children come first.'

'That is something that we can agree on, at least,' said

160

Isabella. 'But after them, I have decisions to make about my own life. And Father Bonsignore was kind to me.'

'So you prefer a doddering old friar who gave you a few sad smiles to a member of your own family?'

'If he did smile at me, that is more than you have ever done,' said Isabella.

'And what is there to smile at? A vain, arrogant, stubborn woman, who thinks that because she ensnared a man once with her looks she can play on them for the rest of her life? Believe me, the days of your beauty are fast approaching their end.'

'Are you accusing me of seducing the Abbot of Giardinetto?' said Isabella coldly, though a hot rage flowed in her veins.

'Anything is possible,' said Umberto sourly. 'I shall certainly investigate the Abbot and friars of that house now that you have put your business in their hands.'

Isabella could not help herself; she felt the colour leave her face. And Umberto noticed.

'It seems you do have something to hide at Giardinetto,' he said with bitter satisfaction. 'Trust me, I shall get to the bottom of it.'

And with that he stormed out of the room.

Father Bonsignore agreed with Anselmo's idea of mounting a guard on the convent and asked him and Silvano to take the first watch.

The artists rode back to Assisi, deep in conversation.

'We cannot expect much ultramarine from Giardinetto in

161

the near future,' said Pietro.

'No, nor much of any colour,' said Simone. 'At least not until they have found their murderer.'

'Well, it's not the Colour Master, I'll wager,' said Pietro. 'I'm with Mother Elena on that.'

'And I,' said Simone.

They travelled in silence for a while.

'I saw you looking at the little novice,' said Pietro.

'Isn't she perfect?' asked Simone.

Pietro had been his friend for a long time and he knew that Simone was a confirmed bachelor, who took little interest in women unless he had an ulterior motive.

'And what character does she suggest in your cycle?' he asked.

Simone laughed. 'You know me too well. I have to fill the entrance wall, in the archway to the chapel, and I want to put some saints there. I think she would make a perfect model for Saint Clare.'

'Too pretty for a saint,' said Pietro. 'Especially one who lived such an ascetic life as the friend of Saint Francis.'

'I disagree,' said Simone. 'Clare was a rich lady from a distinguished family. And she chose to renounce the world. Why should she not have been pretty? Surely there would have been less merit in closing herself away if she had been ill-favoured?'

'But a saint might have a beautiful soul without having a beautiful face,' suggested Pietro.

'As might someone less holy than a saint,' agreed Simone.

'And perhaps a pleasing countenance might conceal a wicked heart?'

'You are thinking of the friary, Pietro,' said Simone. 'We

162

seem to come back to that, whatever we do to escape it. It is a festering sore and we must help them to heal it.'

Anselmo and Silvano kept guard on the convent gate but each knew that if the murderer of Brother Landolfo came from inside the friary they would not know how to recognise a danger to the sisters if one of their brothers asked for admission.

They used the time alone to go through all the members of their house and pool any information they had that might throw light on the murders.

'We can leave out the Abbot, I suppose,' said Silvano.

'No. We cannot leave out anyone, not even ourselves,' insisted Anselmo. 'We must look dispassionately at what we know about each brother. Separate facts from feelings.'

'Well, I know that Father Bonsignore is an old friend of my father's,' said Silvano. 'And he has been kind to me. He never doubted that I was innocent of the murder in Perugia.'

'That is something else we should consider,' said Anselmo. 'Whether that murder can be in any way linked to the ones here. But to return to the Abbot, he knew about your situation and also about my history, though not all the details until after the merchant Ubaldo was dead. These are facts. But like you, I have never had anything but kindness from him.'

'So perhaps he told someone? Or maybe someone overheard him talking to you or me?'

'It is possible. But let us move on to ourselves. I had a motive to kill the merchant and I know how to get hold of

163

arsenikon. I do use a little in the colour room to make colours for Brother Fazio. These are bad marks against my name.'

'And I came here fleeing from the charge of stabbing so that makes me a good suspect for Ubaldo. But not for Brother Landolfo. Why would I want to kill the Guest Master?'

'Why would anyone? I have no motive either, even though I could have found the means.'

'What about Brother Fazio? He uses the orpiment and realgar,' said Silvano.

'Indeed, he has as much access to arsenikon as I do,' said Anselmo. 'More perhaps. But no reason to carry out either of the killings here.'

'As far as we know,' said Silvano.

'That is the point,' said Anselmo. 'The killer's reasons might be hidden in his past. Or as I said before, he might be lacking in reason altogether, completely insane.'

'Well, let's carry on,' said Silvano. 'What about Brother Rufino? He found the merchant and treated Brother Landolfo. Could he be the one?'

'If we continue to look at the facts, yes. But you saw how he tried to save Landolfo. I can't believe it's the Infirmarian.'

'The Herbalist then,' suggested Silvano. 'Valentino. He would have access to poisonous plants, wouldn't he?'

'Probably, though not arsenikon. He'd be more likely to poison with belladonna.'

'Do you know anything else about him?'

'No, not really. He's a quiet, pleasant companion and I believe him to be a devout friar.'

'This is hopeless,' said Silvano. 'They – we – are all devout friars and friendly people. Perhaps we should start with the least pleasant?'

'Well, Brother Nardo can be a bit surly,' said Anselmo dubiously.

'The Cellarer? Yes, I've noticed that. And Brother Gregorio, the Lector, is very strict. Though he has been good to me.'

'And I think Monaldo, the Librarian, resented me when I arrived,' said Anselmo. 'He is a scholar, like Gregorio, and I think they both feared I might intrude on their territory. But there has been no difficulty with them since.'

'We've left out Brother Ranieri,' said Silvano. 'Though I can't think that the Novice Master would be a killer.'

'We are treading in circles,' said Anselmo. 'The killer must be one of us yet none of us seems like a killer.'

'Then we must start at a different end,' said Silvano. 'We've agreed that we know of no one with a reason to kill either Ubaldo or Landolfo . . .'

'Except possibly me in the first case,' objected Anselmo.

'All right, but leaving you aside . . . I think we should look at opportunity. Ubaldo first.'

'Well that's me again,' said Anselmo. 'I was out walking in the garden. But I could be lying.'

'I was out of bed myself, coming to see you. Then there's Rufino.'

'Almost any brother could have been out of his cell.'

'But no one was missing from the dormitory except me,' said Silvano, excitedly. 'So that rules out all the younger brothers and the novices.'

'We hadn't begun to consider them anyway,' said Anselmo. 'That still leaves about a dozen, including you, me and the Abbot.'

'Well, let's for the time being rule out those three and we are down to eight or nine. We could try to investigate them.'

'What about Brother Landolfo's murder? Who had that opportunity?'

'You, Brother Fazio and perhaps Brother Valentino, if it was a plant poison instead of arsenikon,' said Silvano. 'But that's only the people who we know could get hold of poison. What about putting it in Landolfo's dish?'

'Then Bertuccio is the obvious person,' said Anselmo. 'As cook, he had the best opportunity.'

'Brother Nardo could have put it in the wine,' said Silvano. 'And Brother Fazio sits next to Landolfo so he could have put poison in his dish.'

They had been discussing the crimes so intently that they had not noticed Chiara coming up to them with a basket of food.

'Mother Elena sent me with some refreshment for you,' she said, unpacking bread, cheese and a flask of wine.

'Thank you, Sister Orsola,' said Anselmo. 'You must think us very inadequate guards since we didn't hear you approach.'

'You were talking about the murders, weren't you?' said Chiara. 'There is no other topic of conversation in either house tonight, I should think. Do you really think we are in danger here?'

'We have been going through all the brothers and have come to no conclusion,' said Silvano, smiling at her in spite of the question. 'Except that Nardo can be grumpy and Gregorio and Monaldo are fond of their books.'

He was not going to tell her that Anselmo had the most marks against him as a suspect.

166

'I am sorry to say,' said Anselmo, 'that however vigilant we may be, it might take another murder before we can find the killer.'

CHAPTER THIRTEEN

The Onlooker

fter two murders, the Abbot of Giardinetto had no choice but to send for the head of the Franciscan Order. He felt deeply worried about what was going on and ashamed that these things were happening in a house under his charge. Pray as he might, he could see no clear way out of the morass of sin that threatened to engulf the friary.

Several brothers had come to him to ask that Silvano or Anselmo or both should be expelled. One was known to be a murder suspect, the other had a past as the lover of the second victim's wife. Even though the two men were liked and had been welcomed into the brotherhood, it was believed they were more likely to be responsible for the two murders than any of the other friars.

Father Bonsignore sighed heavily. And now he must take on the additional burden of guiding the merchant's widow in her business affairs. Strictly speaking, he could refuse but the guilt he felt that the merchant had died while under his protection made that an impossible choice.

It seemed as if his thoughts had taken human shape when Ubaldo's brother arrived at the friary. Umberto resembled his older brother but had an even grimmer countenance. He pointedly refused all refreshment and said he would ride on to an inn in Assisi. 'Excuse me, Father Abbot,' he said, 'but I do not feel secure in the hospitality of the friars of Giardinetto. I hear there has been another death since my brother's. A poisoning?'

Bonsignore could not deny it.

'I am sure the deaths are not connected,' he said with as much composure as he could manage.

'Not connected?' said Umberto, his black eyebrows disappearing into his hairline. 'You have so many murders here that you can afford to say that? Giardinetto must be a charnel-house indeed!'

'It is just that the means were so different,' said the Abbot. 'I still believe that your brother was attacked by an intruder. The poisoning of a brother does look bad for all the rest, but this is a matter to be dealt with internally. The head of our Order, the Minister General, is on his way to investigate the case. Until then I can say nothing to you, except to repeat that I am sure your brother was not killed by a friar.'

'But how much do you know about your friars?' asked Umberto. 'I mean before they joined the Order?'

Bonsignore was very conscious of what he had recently found out about Brother Anselmo but he answered as confidently as he could. 'It is not I who admitted them to the Order,' he said. 'They would have applied to the Minister General of the time and each man's life and vocation would have been examined.'

'Then it looks as if your Minister General has overlooked at least one murderer,' sneered Umberto.

The Abbot made no reply.

'I am not satisfied that you are taking this seriously enough,' said Umberto. 'But, leaving aside the subject of my

169

brother's murder for a moment – and I don't care whether the rest of you kill each other off till there is only one man standing – what is this nonsense about your acting legally for my sister-in-law?'

'Monna Isabella has done me the honour of asking me to represent her in legal matters, yes,' said the Abbot. 'I took it as an act of trust, to let me know that she did not hold this house responsible for her husband's death.'

'The woman is a fool,' said Umberto.

'She struck me as very intelligent,' said Father Bonsignore. Umberto glared at him.

'And you will accede to her request?'

'I can see no reason not to.'

'Then there is nothing to detain me here. I see I can make no headway with you, Abbot. Perhaps your Minister General will be more interested in listening to me.'

He left abruptly. The Abbot drew a deep breath and walked over to the window. He watched his unwelcome visitor walk towards the stable. But Umberto stopped to talk to a couple of friars he encountered on the way. The Abbot frowned. His eyesight was not good and he could not make out which of the friars were talking to Ubaldo's angry brother. But since most knew of the rumours about the Colour Master, Bonsignore now had a new complication to worry about.

Monna Isabella was surprised when she read the Abbess's message about Chiara – Sister Orsola, as she insisted on calling her. Isabella had thought that Chiara would accept her

170

offer in an instant. She had made inquiries in the town and found that the girl's brother, Bernardo, was making a poor fist of handling the little of his patrimony that remained. Rumours were abroad that his debts were mounting.

On the other hand, the townspeople could not praise enough the wealthy widow from Perugia who was setting up as a trader in Gubbio. It was regarded as a daring venture, even though Angelica had appointed a man to manage the business. People treated Isabella with respect and deference and even some warmth; she was more popular than her husband had ever been. But they were wary of talking to her directly about Angelica, fearing that she might be anxious about the competition.

Isabella had not thought much about what would happen after her husband's death apart from certain hazy dreams about finding Domenico again. Now that she had found him she dare not dream any more. She must have a plan for the future that didn't involve him. And why not do the same as the little widow from Perugia? If a slip of a girl, not yet twenty, could run a business, and from another city, why should Isabella herself not continue with Ubaldo's successful trade here in Gubbio? She already had a procurator in Abbot Bonsignore, who had accepted her request. All she needed to do now was appoint a manager.

It would certainly take her mind off a middle-aged friar living in Giardinetto. But she would go there again soon to see the Abbot and try to have a private audience with the man they now called Brother Anselmo. She needed to resolve that question once and for all. She wished that she had a woman friend to confide in; it was a pity that Chiara was not coming to her, at least not yet.

171

While the friars waited for the visit of their new Minister General, Michele da Cesena, they went about their business as usual. They said the Office, tended the garden, visited the sick, preached in the local parishes and heard confessions. Brother Anselmo ran the colour room as he always had and had soon produced their first batch of ultramarine. In spite of the cares and worries oppressing him, Silvano was enchanted by the heavenly colour. It seemed to promise a better time.

Sister Veronica and the grey nuns next door had also made a batch and Anselmo proposed a joint trip to Assisi in the friary's cart. It was what Silvano and Chiara had both longed for but they felt self-conscious when they were at last seated in the back of the cart. Anselmo was driving, with Sister Veronica beside him. She was a little deaf, so that it was safe for them to talk. Silvano doubted that Anselmo would mind but he spoke in a low voice anyway.

'How are you, Chiara?' he asked. 'Are the sisters still afraid?'

'I am not afraid for myself, Brother,' said Chiara, uncertain how to address him but thrilled that he had used her real name. 'And if I were to become so, I have a way of escape. But some of the younger women are nervous living next to a house which now seems so ill-augured.'

'A way of escape?' asked Silvano. 'Are you leaving?'

'I might,' said Chiara. 'Monna Isabella has offered that I should live with her in Gubbio, as her companion. Mother Elena has said I may go.'

'But you are uncertain?'

'I am still considering it,' said Chiara in a way that closed the subject.

172

'Have you heard we are going to have a visitation from the Minister General?' asked Silvano.

Chiara nodded. 'The Abbess expects he will come to see us too. Normally it would be a cause for excitement, I believe. But everyone is jittery now. Suppose he disbands the brothers' house at Giardinetto? What would happen to the Poor Clares?'

'Disband the house!' exclaimed Silvano. 'Surely it won't come to that?'

Brother Anselmo turned slightly and put his finger to his lips.

'We are all in fear,' said Silvano quietly. 'And some of the brothers fear myself and Anselmo most of all. You can see it in their eyes.'

They travelled the rest of the way to Assisi in silence but they became more and more aware of each other's presence on the journey. They were sitting on opposite sides of the cart – anything else would have been indecorous – but that gave them ample opportunity to look at each other.

They kept catching each other's eye and then one would turn away, embarrassed and develop an interest in the Umbrian scenery. But that gave the other a chance to study unobserved a curve of cheek or sweep of lashes. It only confirmed what they had both thought: that the object of their scrutiny was very pleasing to look at indeed.

And Silvano now had to think that Chiara might not continue to be as out of reach as he had always thought her. She was not wealthy, certainly, but she came from a good family and she would have a respectable home if she chose to live with Isabella in Gubbio. He couldn't imagine that his father would put any obstacle in his way if he said he was going to

173

pay court to a merchant's ward. He checked himself from letting his thoughts run away with him. It was only a matter of weeks since he had thought himself hopelessly in love with another woman.

He looked into his heart to see how he felt about Angelica but had to admit that what he found there now was mostly hurt pride. If he was honest with himself, he found Chiara more attractive. And he was beginning to know her; they had exchanged far more words than he ever had with the widow of Perugia.

For Chiara, it was less complicated. She had never seen a man to her liking before Silvano and his face now seemed familiar and the very type she imagined when she thought of love and romance. She shouldn't have been thinking about either but she had never really believed that she could be a nun and now that she didn't have to accept that destiny, she let herself indulge those imaginings.

But something else was happening to her. Since living in the convent, contrary to what she had expected, her world had expanded. The riot of colour and form in the Basilica at Assisi had amazed her and meeting the painters opened her eyes still further. She had seen no art in her native city, except what was in the main church and had certainly never thought about how it got there.

And there were the murders. It was horrific, of course, but the notion that danger lurked so near was stimulating. It had broken up the routine of both houses and nobody knew what each new day would bring. She was not really afraid for herself and she didn't want to leave the convent with the mystery unsolved.

Simone was surprised to see them and delighted with the

ultramarine. As they visited him in the chapel devoted to Saint Martin, Chiara gasped. Her own face looked down at her from inside the entrance arch! The hair had been changed from brown to gold but it was certainly her face. It was a saint, with its halo already sketched in and waiting for Simone's famous gold stamping. She stood holding a lily and separated from another female saint by a slender spiralled column painted so convincingly on the blue background that it was hard to believe it had no volume or substance.

'I hope you will forgive me, Sister Orsola,' said Simone, 'for taking your likeness as my model for your patron, Saint Clare.'

'She is not just the founder of our Order,' said Chiara. 'I was named for her. I was called Chiara.' And shall be again, she thought.

'Then you were well named,' said Simone simply.

Silvano smiled at the painter; so that was why he had studied the beautiful novice so carefully! He wished he could have a copy of Simone's portrait of Chiara. If it were a miniature, he could carry it around with him.

While he was daydreaming, Simone was explaining to Brother Anselmo and Sister Veronica that the other saint, dressed more luxuriously than the woman who looked like Chiara, in green and white, red and gold, was Elizabeth of Hungary.

'She was a princess,' Sister Veronica told Chiara approvingly. 'And married at fourteen. But when her husband died she founded one of the first women's houses for followers of Saint Francis. And gave all her money to the poor.'

Married at fourteen, thought Chiara, younger than I am now!

175

Simone had now finished the left wall and was working on the last picture on the right.

'Here is Saint Martin renouncing arms,' he explained when they came close to look at his work. 'He is rejecting the earthly knighthood he accepted in the previous scene.'

Silvano admired the painter's skill in showing the different characters in the scene, but now he also felt that the Saint had chosen the harder way when he decided to stop being a soldier and follow the religious life instead. He looked at Saint Martin's bare feet, no longer wearing the boots and spurs of his knighthood.

No hawk and horse for him now, he thought.

Chiara was looking up at the ceiling. Simone had painted it to look like the heavens themselves, deep blue and scattered with gold stars.

'Is that ultramarine?' she asked.

'No,' said Simone. 'That is azurite, but coarse ground to give the intense colour.'

Chiara remembered Sister Veronica's advice when she ground the vivid blue pigment herself at the convent.

As Silvano's gaze followed Chiara's and then travelled down the left wall, he saw again the face that he had noticed on the first visit, the one whose down-turned mouth made him think of Simone himself.

'Is that you, Ser Simone?' he asked.

'Yes, I am sometimes so short of models to draw from that I must use myself,' laughed the painter. 'But only as a last resort. Still, I needed a sceptic for that painting so my suspicious looks are appropriate.'

'What's the story of that one?' asked Silvano.

'Saint Martin is reviving a dead child, whose desperate

176

mother begs him for the life of her son,' said Simone. 'Some in the crowd can't believe their eyes.'

'And there is one of our Order.' Sister Veronica pointed out to Chiara a nun in a grey robe.

'But didn't you say that Saint Martin lived hundreds of years ago?' objected Silvano. 'Long before Saint Francis or Saint Clare?'

'He was born nearly a thousand years ago,' said Simone. 'That is why the chapel must be ready for his millennium celebrations. I admit I have taken a liberty in including a Poor Clare. There's a Franciscan friar too, like you and Brother Anselmo. See, there at the back, gazing up at that tree. That tree is the miraculous one that Saint Francis caused to grow in Siena by planting his walking staff in the ground.'

'But didn't Saint Martin resurrect the child in the middle of a field, according to the story?' asked Anselmo, his eyes twinkling. 'Here he seems to be doing it in the city – your city, by the look of it.'

Simone spread his hands in a gesture of resignation. 'I am homesick,' he said simply. 'You have been to Siena, Brother, so you know what a jewel it is. I have been away a year and now that Pietro has joined me I miss my home more than ever. I want to get this chapel and the figures in the transept finished within the next few months so that I can see my native city again.'

Silvano was silent, thinking of his own home in Perugia, and he saw that Brother Anselmo was thoughtful too. What did he think of as home? Would he say Giardinetto now or did he still sometimes long for Gubbio, the place where he had been young and in love? Silvano realised how little he really knew about the Colour Master.

177

'Why did you make yourself the man suspicious of the miracle, Ser Simone?' asked Chiara. 'Don't you believe in miracles?'

'Of course I do,' said Simone, light-hearted again. 'It's just that the painter is an observer, the man outside the scene, so if I put myself inside one, I still look sceptical.'

'We could do with an impartial observer in Giardinetto,' said Anselmo quietly, so that Sister Veronica would not hear.

'There is no news then?' asked Simone in the same low voice.

'No,' said Anselmo. 'We are no closer to finding the culprit. And some of the brothers are whispering against Silvano and myself. I don't know if we shall survive the visit of our Minister General.'

'But that is terrible,' said Simone. 'Apart from anything else, I can't lose my best pigment-grinders if I'm to get the frescoes finished. But I'm jesting, of course. We must see what we can do to find the real killer.'

'We've tried,' said Silvano. 'We went through all the brothers and couldn't come up with any reason for the same man to murder both the merchant and Brother Landolfo.'

'Then there are only two possible conclusions,' said Simone. 'Either there were two different killers and Giardinetto has been the victim of a dreadful coincidence ...'

'That's what Abbot Bonsignore thinks,' said Silvano.

'... or, we are quite wrong to look for reasons and connections, and the killer is insane. The murders have been committed randomly by someone without motive or reason.'

'But that means anyone could be next to die,' said Chiara, fearful for the first time.

'Then we must just make sure there is no next victim,' said

178

Simone. 'This is more important even than my paintings. Tell me everything you know about every brother in the friary.'

In an inn two roads away from where the painter discussed murder with the followers of Saint Francis sat Umberto, drinking deeply of the red wine poured for him. He was musing on what he had been told in the friary at Giardinetto.

'Brother Anselmo,' he said to himself, slurring the name. 'Or should I say Domenico? You think you've got away with it, don't you? You kill my brother, persuade his stupid widow to appoint your puppet Bonsignore as her representative. And then what? You suddenly discover that you have lost your faith? Leave the Order and after a decent interval – ha! What would be decent for a murderer and his drab? – you offer yourself to my brother's widow. And who is her guardian and protector? That old fool of an abbot! And then you have everything that was Ubaldo's – his house, his land, his business, his wife.

'But you haven't reckoned on one thing. Umberto will not leave his brother unavenged. You shall have none of it – not one scudo!'

CHAPTER FOURTEEN

Minister General

aron Montacuto was eating his midday meal with no relish at all. His wife, Margarethe, had always been pale, like their son, but now her face across the table from him was almost bloodless and no smile ever reached it. Their little daughters, Margherita and Vittoria, normally such a joy to him, sat silent as their parents, toying with their food.

The Baron cursed the day Silvano had ever set eyes on the comely wife of the sheep farmer. With the farmer's death, the Baron's family had been shattered at a stroke. The sentence still hung over Silvano's head; it would be death for him to set foot in Perugia again until the real killer had been found. And until Silvano could return, the Montacuto family was a shadow of its former self.

A servant came in and announced the arrival of the Abbot of Giardinetto. A light flashed in the Baron's eyes but he quickly suppressed his elation.

'Show him to my study and bring him refreshment,' he ordered. 'Excuse me, my dear,' he said to Margarethe. 'I have eaten my fill and Bonsignore is one of my oldest friends.'

'Of course,' said his wife listlessly. 'It will give you pleasure to see him.'

But the joy that Bartolomeo felt in clasping his son's

protector in his arms soon turned to alarm.

'He is well and he is safe – so far,' said Bonsignore cautiously.'

'What do you mean "so far"? Is his secret out?'

Bonsignore sighed. 'That is the least of our worries, but yes, somehow Silvano's history is now known in the friary.'

'Tell me everything,' said the Baron.

In the de' Oddini household a more satisfactory conversation was taking place. Vincenzo had a most unusual commission to convey to his son.

Gervasio had always been a mystery to him. The family had too many children for their father to know them all well but he had a better sense of all his other sons and daughters than he had of this youngest boy. 'You have become friendly with the widow Angelica these last weeks?' he began.

'Yes, father,' said Gervasio meekly, trying to keep the excitement out of his face. He knew what was coming. 'We are on good terms.'

'Well it seems as if Monna Angelica would like to be on even better terms,' said Vincenzo drily. 'She has asked me to enquire whether a marriage would be acceptable to you.'

'A marriage to her?'

'Of course to her! What do you think she is – a professional matchmaker?' said Vincenzo.

'What do you think of the idea, father?'

Vincenzo tried not to shudder. He thought it would be a terrible come-down for a son of a noble family, however impoverished, to marry a common peasant, however wealthy.

181

But he could not advise Gervasio against it. There would not be enough patrimony to support him after Vincenzo's own death and this was a great opportunity to get his hands on considerable wealth. And the widow was pretty, there was no arguing about that, if a bit coarse. As long as Gervasio liked her, his father could raise no objection. He had made enough money himself out of advising her and could not afford to offend her.

'I think, if you like the lady, I should be happy to give my blessing to your union,' he said, through gritted teeth.

'Thank you, father,' said Gervasio. 'Then I am happy to become her second husband. Let us announce the engagement immediately. We would like to have the ceremony as soon as decently possible, considering her status as widow.'

'As you wish. Now, would you like me to visit her or shall you take your answer yourself?'

'I shall go myself, father, if that is agreeable to you,' said Gervasio.

'Perfectly agreeable,' said Vincenzo. 'I shall tell your mother.'

And as his son left the room, he felt as if he had, in some indefinable way, been the victim of a conspiracy.

'Two more murders!' thundered Bartolomeo da Montacuto. 'Under the same roof as my son?'

'Well, two murders,' said the Abbot. 'I doubt they are connected to the one in Perugia.'

'What have I done?' the Baron moaned, his head in his hands. 'All I wanted was to protect my boy and it seems I have sent him into the lions' den.'

'We are doing everything possible to protect every member of the community,' said Bonsignore and his old friend noticed for the first time how haggard he looked. 'The Minister General is coming on a visitation and will interrogate every brother.'

'But meanwhile, Silvano is under suspicion again?' asked Bartolomeo. 'If his history is known and the first victim was stabbed, surely the other friars would think of him as the most likely assassin?'

'I can't deny it,' said Bonsignore. 'But his mentor, Brother Anselmo, is also under suspicion since he wooed the first victim's wife in their youth.'

'And this man is looking after my son?'

'He is our Colour Master. Silvano works under him in the colour room, grinding pigments for the painters in Assisi. He seems to like the work.'

'But do you think this Brother Anselmo is the murderer?'

'No,' said Bonsignore. 'I would stake my life he is not. But it must be someone in my care and I can't bear the thought that any of the friars would do such a thing.'

The Baron sat back in his chair, mollified. 'Do you think Silvano is still safe with you?' he asked. 'Should I try to find him sanctuary elsewhere?'

'I think it would be very dangerous to move him now. But I cannot promise that I can keep him as safe as I should like. After all, I could not save Brother Landolfo.'

The two men were silent.

'I almost forgot,' said Bonsignore. 'I have brought letters from Silvano, for you and for the Baronessa.' He took rolled parchment from the scrip at his belt.

The Baron took them eagerly. 'I shall wait to give Margarethe hers,' he said. 'She must not know it came with you. It is vital that she shouldn't know where Silvano is hiding. I'd better read it myself first, in case he gives anything away.'

'Shall I go out with Celeste to hunt meat for the Minister General?' Silvano asked Bertuccio the cook.

'Not a bit of it,' said Bertuccio. 'I have strict orders from the Abbot. Michele da Cesena is a stickler for poor living. He has just written a paper about how all Franciscans must go back to the original rule of the Saint – no luxury, no property, no self-indulgence. It's going to get him into trouble, mark my words.'

Bertuccio was a lay brother, so Silvano didn't know how much he really knew about Franciscans. Ever since he had arrived in Giardinetto, Silvano had found the rules relaxed for him but he could still tell that some brothers were more abstemious than others. Brother Landolfo, in spite of his jolly appearance and role as provider of hospitality, had eaten and drunk very little, while some other brothers clearly enjoyed the pleasures of the table.

The brothers' attitudes to property were hard to tell. All friars had the same coarse grey robes and maybe a psalter or breviary. No one wore any ornament, except for the Abbot's plain pectoral cross. The brothers wore sandals only if they had to undertake a long journey; usually they went barefoot.

But Silvano had not been into any of the senior friars' private cells, except the Abbot's and Brother Anselmo's. Could

184

some of them have chests full of sumptuous cloths and jewels? It seemed very unlikely. Silvano knew the story of how the wealthy young Francis had renounced all his possessions, even down to the clothes he wore, and turned away from his noble family to found an order based on poverty, to try and get back to the life of Christ.

He remembered how his old friend Gervasio had feared and dreaded the prospect of becoming a friar but Silvano had not found it hard to fit in. It helped, of course, that he knew he had another life to return to. It would have been different if his entire future lay in the Order.

Silvano found himself dreading the visit of this grim-sounding Minister General. He was anxious too for Abbot Bonsignore to return from Perugia. Not only would he have seen Silvano's father and delivered his letters, he might have news of the sheep farmer's murderer, something that could clear his name in Giardinetto.

Anselmo and Silvano now worked in silence in the colour room. The atmosphere was heavy with suspicion. Simone had advised them to look for signs of lunacy in other friars, so they had started to treat the other brothers with the same caution they were experiencing. It made Silvano feel closer to the Colour Master but the more they scrutinised their fellow friars, the harder it was to say who was sane and who not.

Brother Fazio was definitely a little eccentric about his illumination colours but that didn't make him mad. Gregorio the Lector was strict – Silvano thought he was the kind of friar the Minister General would approve of – but he was a fair man and not mentally unstable. Brother Rufino, the Infirmarian, and Valentino, the Herbalist, were a bit territorial with one another. But really neither Anselmo nor

185

Silvano could single out one of the brothers as any madder than any man outside the Order. They had their quirks and peculiarities, but no more than other groups of men and it was still fantastic to think of one of them as an insane assassin.

'It is settled!' said Gervasio, lifting Angelica in his arms and twirling her round. She laughed with relief and when he put her down, he was a little out of breath. Surely she hadn't always been so heavy?

'We are to be married at your convenience, my love,' he said.

Angelica regarded him complacently. Now this was more what a husband should be like! He was young, slim and good-looking – and he came from a good family. He wouldn't scrape her face with an unshaven cheek or belch over his food. Gervasio would be as elegant an ornament to her house as any tablecloth or vase she might order.

She did not deceive herself that he was more in love with her than with her money. She knew that she could please him, though, and that was enough. She wasn't in love with him either but he brought to the match what she had brought to her first marriage – youth and looks and pleasant ways – and she was ready to make the bargain.

For his part, Gervasio was light-headed with relief. He would not have to fear the life of a shoeless religious; his future was assured. And Angelica was a lovely creature. A bit plump and perhaps more so since being widowed, but it suited her. She was fair and rosy and a most attractive armful.

He would not find his marital duties at all irksome.

But best of all, she was rich! He would no longer have to worry about his mounting debts, his bills at the tavern, his gaming losses. Angelica could write them off with a stroke of the pen.

They kissed passionately, each so filled with relief that it served just as well as real ardour.

'My darling,' murmured Gervasio, caressing her shoulder, surprised by the warmth of his own feelings.

'Dearest,' she replied, her eyes closed in ecstasy. How delicate and exciting his touch was! Oh, she could be a real wife to this one! She had a fleeting recollection of another young man with big grey eyes and a poem. But she put him out of her mind.

Gervasio was thinking of Silvano too. He still had that poem in his jerkin. He didn't know where his friend was now but he hoped he was safe. He hadn't really meant him to suffer when he stabbed Angelica's husband. But it had been very handy his coming along the street at that moment.

❧

'He's here, he's here!' said Brother Matteo excitedly. He was at the door of the colour room when the Minister General and his chaplain rode into the yard at Giardinetto.

'He's stabling his horses,' Matteo continued his commentary. 'And now old Gianni is pointing the way to the Abbot's cell. Oh no, that's too bad. One of us should go and escort him. No, it's all right. Father Bonsignore must have seen him from his window – he's come down to greet him.'

'He's back then?' asked Silvano, surprised.

'Oh yes, he got back last night,' said Matteo. 'He must be very tired.'

The Abbot was indeed far too weary to handle the Minister General's visit as well as he should. Michele da Cesena was a terrifying person to entertain. His ascetic, almost fleshless face was dominated by fanatical, black eyes and he had no time for social niceties.

After the briefest of greetings and declining all offers of refreshment, which his chaplain looked a little wistful about, the Minister General asked to see the sites of the two murders. His chaplain sprinkled the guest room and the refectory with holy water, while the Minister General prayed long and fervently on his knees on the flagstones.

'We held a service of purification,' said Bonsignore, when Michele da Cesena eventually rose.

'Good,' nodded the Minister General. 'Now, I shall need to use your cell and interview every friar from yourself to the youngest novice – lay brothers and servants too. I shall hear all their confessions.'

And one of them will freely confess to murder, I suppose, thought the Abbot, but all he said was, 'I have of course heard confessions from them all since the deaths.'

The Minister General ignored him. 'My chaplain will make some notes,' he said. 'In a matter as serious as this, the secrecy of the confessional may be waived.'

As the Abbot followed him to his own cell, he felt displaced from his own house and his position of authority. He sighed and squared his shoulders; he had had no choice but to send for his superior and the knowledge that he was in for a very uncomfortable fifteen minutes was in a strange way comforting. This harsh, uncompromising friar would take the burden from him and, if anyone could solve the terrible crimes at Giardinetto, it would be Michele da Cesena.

The tension in the friary was palpable. Everyone knew why the Minister General was there and everyone expected to be questioned. Work continued but no one was concentrating. As each friar returned to his task after his interrogation, he faced a second one from the brothers around him. 'What was it like? Were you scared?' asked the younger friars and novices, forgetting the normal deference they would show to their seniors.

Brother Anselmo was with the Minister General for a long time, causing much speculation in the colour room. The friars shifted uneasily and looked often at Silvano and he didn't know whether it was because of his closeness to the Colour Master or because of their own suspicions about him.

When Anselmo returned, he looked grey and strained and they were all relieved when the bell rang for Sext. The midday meal came straight afterwards and the Lector read from the Book of Revelation, imposing silence on the brothers with a quelling look.

Michele da Cesena did not appear in the refectory and nor did the Abbot.

'The man must eat surely?' whispered Brother Taddeo at the lower end of the table.

'Perhaps Bertuccio has taken something to the Abbot's room?' said Silvano.

'The Abbot is not in his room,' said Monaldo the Librarian, who had already been questioned. 'I think he is praying in the chapel. The Minister General has taken over his quarters.'

The questioning lasted all that day and into the next.

Michele and his chaplain appeared briefly at supper, eating and drinking a little of the deliberately plain fare provided by Bertuccio, and then went back to work. The Minister General was offered the guest room but chose to sleep a few hours in the Abbot's cell. His chaplain joined the junior friars in the dormitory but would not be drawn on his master's work.

And still Silvano had not been called.

Word got around quickly in Perugia that the beautiful widow Angelica was going to remarry. It wasn't long before it reached the ears of Baron Montacuto. He experienced a rapid series of emotions: surprise, that his old friend de' Oddini could sanction the marriage of even a youngest son to the widow of a sheep farmer; relief that this took the light of enquiry off his own son, since Angelica had clearly not been in love with Silvano and, finally, suspicion.

The most convincing reason for Gervasio's marriage must be lack of money. And if he was short of money, perhaps he had been in debt? Bartolomeo da Montacuto decided that he must put his investigators on to young Gervasio de' Oddini; a terrible misgiving was building in his mind.

He had read Silvano's letters and was moved by how much the boy was missing his family. He had been careful too to keep his news neutral; no one would guess he was writing from a religious house. When Margarethe came into the Baron's room, he hadn't the heart to keep her letter from her any longer.

'I have news my dear,' he said stricken by her wasted look.

190

'A letter from Silvano.'

Instantly the mother's face brightened and she practically snatched the roll from her husband's hand. She read breathlessly.

'He is well; he is safe!' she said, clutching the parchment to her breast as if the skin were her son's own, for her to stroke and kiss.

'I told you, dear heart,' said the Baron, embracing her. 'I promised you I would keep him safe.'

He was not going to tell her that Silvano was shut up with at least one and possibly two murderers; let her enjoy the happiness of the moment.

'But when will we see him again?' asked Margarethe, resting her fair head on her husband's broad chest. 'When will Silvano come home?'

'Soon now, my dear, very soon,' said the Baron, patting her shoulder. 'I think I might have found out something that means he will be back with us before too long.'

CHAPTER FIFTEEN

The Colour of Blood

he Minister General called Silvano to the Abbot's cell shortly before Nones in the afternoon of the second day of his visitation. The walk from the colour room to the main house had never seemed so long to him.

He found Michele da Cesena sitting sternly in the Abbot's chair, the tired chaplain occupying a high reading desk.

'You are not a genuine novice,' was the Minister General's opening remark; it was not a question.

'I am not,' said Silvano.

'Your circumstances have been explained to me by your Abbot. Sanctuary is an honourable tradition and I do not dispute his right to offer it to you. However, in the light of what has happened since your arrival – in this previously peaceable and unremarkable community – I do question his judgment.'

'I am not guilty of any murder, Father, neither the one I was accused of in Perugia nor either of the ones here. I am as anxious as anyone to discover the culprit.'

'Describe your movements on the night the merchant Ubaldo was stabbed.'

'I went to look for Brother Anselmo in his cell. He had not been well at dinner and I was concerned about him.'

'You have developed an attachment to Brother Anselmo?'

Would you have gone in search of any other brother who had been taken sick?'

Silvano hesitated. 'Probably not. I am . . . close to Brother Anselmo. He is my master in the colour room and he has been kind to me.'

'If you were a real friar, I should admonish you about that. We are not to prize any brother over another, any human being over another. Our Lord himself exhorted his disciples to leave their families and follow him. Any human attachment is a distraction from the Lord's work.'

'But I am not a real friar,' said Silvano quietly.

Michele da Cesena frowned at him, his shaggy brows knotted over his piercing eyes. Then the grim face seemed to relax a little.

'No. And I should tell you in all honesty that, since you are not, I have no jurisdiction over you. You do not even have to answer my questions, though I advise that you do.'

Harsh but fair, thought Silvano. 'I am willing to answer your questions,' he said.

'Good. Was Brother Anselmo in his cell when you went to look for him?'

'No. He came up while I was standing outside his door.'

'And where had he been?'

'For a walk in the grounds. He said he needed some fresh air.'

'That was what he told the Abbot. And that he needed to wrestle with a desire to go and confront the merchant.'

'Then if that is what he said, I for one would believe him,' said Silvano.

'Ah, but we have established that you have a special closeness to Brother Anselmo,' said the Minister General. 'It

193

diminishes the value of your opinion on this matter. What about the other murder? Where were you when Brother Landolfo was poisoned?'

'Exactly where when the poison entered his body, I can't say,' admitted Silvano, trying to be scrupulously precise with this exacting inquisitor. 'But I was there when he was taken ill. Virtually all of us were. It happened in the refectory.'

'And Brother Anselmo was there too?'

'Yes. He tried to help Brother Rufino, who was looking after Brother Landolfo.'

'But unsuccessfully.'

'Yes. It was too late. Brother Landolfo started to have fits and died very quickly.'

'You have denied any involvement in the deaths of these brothers,' said the Minister General. 'Do you know who was involved?'

'I have thought of little else since they happened,' said Silvano. 'I still have no idea.'

'Who could have administered poison to Brother Landolfo?'

'Well, the cook, I suppose, Bertuccio. He is a lay brother.'

'I have questioned Brother Bertuccio and he denies it.'

'He had no reason to kill Landolfo, it's true. He liked him – everyone did.'

'Someone apparently did not,' said the Minister General drily.

'Well, I suppose anyone in the refectory could have put poison in his food,' admitted Silvano.

'Who has access to arsenikon?' asked the Minister General.

'Brother Anselmo,' admitted Silvano, caught off guard.

'But also Brother Fazio. He uses it for his manuscripts and we don't make much of it in the colour room, though I have seen some there. Any brother could have got it from there or from Fazio's cell.'

Michele da Cesena suddenly whipped out a dagger and held it less than an inch from Silvano's face.

'You know what this is?'

Silvano had flinched only slightly. With a great effort of will he kept his head steady. 'It is a dagger, Father. Since no friar carries one, I assume it is the one belonging to the merchant. But it is too close to my eyes for me to distinguish.'

The Minister General lowered the weapon and offered it to Silvano, handle first.

'Take a better look, then. Give me your opinion.'

Silvano took it uneasily and weighed it in his hand. 'It is a good weapon, well balanced.'

'Do you miss your own?'

'No,' said Silvano honestly. 'Since it was used to kill a man, I have not wanted to carry a dagger of my own.'

'And yet that is what it is for, is it not? Why did you ever carry one?'

'To defend myself. The city can be a dangerous place.'

'So it would seem,' said Michele da Cesena.

'I thought it would have gone back to Gubbio with all his other possessions,' said Silvano, handing the knife back. The blade had been cleaned but he sensed the blood on it still.

'The Abbot thought it would be insensitive to include the weapon that killed him among his belongings. I doubt any of his sons will want to carry it.'

The Minister General eyed Silvano as if weighing his soul. With a swift blow, he struck the dagger into the table in front of him, where it quivered, the hilt making the shape of a cross.

'Pray with me!' he suddenly ordered, pointing to the ground.

The two men knelt on the flagstones and the chaplain put down his pen, flexing his fingers.

Michele da Cesena prayed tirelessly aloud and Silvano's knees were screaming for mercy long before he had finished. But he joined in when he was required, giving the right responses.

'And now I shall hear your confession,' said the Minister General at last, getting to his feet but indicating that Silvano should remain kneeling.

Silvano glanced towards the chaplain; he had never heard of public confession.

'Take no notice of him,' said the Minister General. 'Just tell me your sins.'

Chiara was making a rich red in the colour room. Although she had had no further experience of dragonsblood since her first day, she knew quite a lot about hematite. 'Blood stone' Sister Veronica called it and it was a hard natural rock of a purple colour. It was so strong it had to be pounded in a bronze mortar before it could be ground more finely on a slab.

Chiara pounded at her allocation of blood stone with a will. If only she could get the lumps out of her thoughts as easily! She had not been sleeping well since the artist Simone had suggested that the murderer might be a lunatic. At night her thoughts went round and round in her head, and when

196

she did sleep, the nightmares came. Hooded figures with dripping daggers jumped out at her from the shadows. Ghostly assassins lurked behind every door.

'Don't break the mortar, Sister,' said Sister Veronica and Chiara realised that she was letting her feelings show.

To stay or to go was still her main dilemma. And that was confused by her growing feelings for Silvano. Even if she pushed those feelings aside, she couldn't leave the convent without knowing that the terrible crimes committed so nearby had been solved. True, she would be safe in Gubbio, and not just from shadowy killers, but she could not forget that every sister and brother in Giardinetto would still be in danger. And one brother in particular, whose fair body she could not bear to think of being stabbed or poisoned.

Perhaps this visit from the Minister General would flush out the murderer? Everyone said he had a formidable intellect. Chiara was a bit apprehensive about his visit to the convent; he was due to celebrate Mass there as soon as he had finished questioning the friars next door.

'He's here,' announced Sister Eufemia, coming to the door of the colour room. 'You are all requested to come to the chapel.'

The sisters' chapel was more like a long bare room; it had no bell tower and little by way of decoration. The sisters sat on benches and there was a rough stone slab for an altar with a wooden cross and two wooden candlesticks at the east end. On the wall behind it was an old panel painting of the Crucifixion. Chiara looked at it more critically now than when she had first come to Giardinetto. She could tell what pigments had gone into its painting and could compare it with images she had seen at Assisi.

But it was still a strong piece of work, strong enough to draw her gaze again in spite of the dark figure standing in front of it. The Minister General's chaplain acted as server and the Mass was conducted with severe dignity. As one of the youngest sisters and the most recent novice, Chiara took the Host last. As she raised her face for Michele da Cesena to place the consecrated bread in her mouth, she caught a glimpse of the dark brow and glittering eyes and it was all she could do not to pull away.

Had he discovered anything? It was impossible to tell. He certainly wouldn't tell her, the least significant member of the convent. Perhaps he would have news for the Abbess?

Monna Isabella was expecting a visitor. When he was shown in to see her, he found her in the merchant's old office; she saved her sitting room for social visits now.

'Ah, Ser Bernardo,' she greeted him.

Bernardo came into the room nervously, unsure why this wealthy woman had sent for him.

'I wanted to talk to you about your sister,' said Isabella.

'Chiara?' asked Bernardo. It was the last thing he had been expecting.

'Only she is not called Chiara any more, is she?' asked Isabella. 'Her given name has been taken away from her and she is now Sister Orsola.'

'You have met her, Madama?'

'Yes. You may have heard that my husband died at Giardinetto. Your sister helped to take care of me when I went to bring home his body. I was very taken with her – and her situation.'

'Her situation, Madama? It is not different from that of many young women without dowries.'

'I don't doubt it. But she has no calling and I have offered her a place in my home. And a dowry too, should she ever need one. She will live here and be my companion and friend. I have only one daughter and she is too young to be a confidante.'

Bernardo was uncomfortable. Isabella's generosity made him feel as if he had wronged his sister and he had convinced himself that he had done his best for her.

'Since you handed your sister over to the nuns,' said Isabella, 'I don't feel I have to ask your permission to invite her into my household. But I take it you don't have any objections?'

'No,' said Bernardo, bemused. If she wasn't asking his permission to give Chiara a home, why had she summoned him? 'It is very kind of you.'

'Another widow, from Perugia, is setting herself up as a wool merchant in Gubbio,' said Isabella. 'And I have decided to keep on my husband's business myself.'

This sudden change of subject perplexed Bernardo even more. He hadn't heard of women running trading businesses and now here apparently there were two! Did this formidable lady want to train Chiara up to follow in her footsteps?

'I shall need a manager,' Isabella was saying. 'And I wondered if you'd be interested in working for me?'

Bernardo was stunned. This was the answer to his prayers. Since Isabella's husband must have had business premises, he could sell his own small trading post and pay off

199

his debts. Monna Isabella must surely be his guardian angel! And if she wanted to be Chiara's too, so be it.

The Minister General was on the road out of Giardinetto. He was profoundly disappointed in his mission. In spite of rigorous questioning, intimidation and threats of eternal damnation, he still had no idea who the murderer was. He wrestled with his feelings, knowing that it was more the idea of his diminished authority that distressed him, than the absolute failure to identify a murderous brother.

He was silent on the journey back to Assisi and his chaplain was grateful; he had heard enough words in the last two days to last him for a long time.

They encountered a lone horseman, who raised his hat, passed them, stopped and turned and retraced the horse's paces.

'Forgive me, Father, but are you Michele da Cesena?' the stranger asked.

A curt nod encouraged him to continue. 'I believe you have been investigating the merchant Ubaldo's murder at Giardinetto? I am Umberto, his younger brother. May I ask if you have had any success?'

'I have not,' said the Minister General, with a brow of thunder.

'Perhaps I could offer you a piece of information?' suggested Umberto.

And there on the dusty road he told the Minister General what he had heard about Brother Anselmo at Giardinetto.

Michele da Cesena had heard the same story from

Anselmo's lips: his youthful passion, the loss of his beloved and his nearly twenty years of devotion to the religious life since; his shock at seeing Ubaldo at the friary and hearing his wife spoken of; his decision not to confront the merchant but to let sleeping dogs lie.

But now, away from the influence of Anselmo's own sincere voice and truthful eyes, it sounded different. A sordid story of jealousy, sexual rivalry and revenge.

Striving not to show that he had been taken in by one of his own friars, the Minister General listened carefully to what Umberto had to say.

'Thank you for your help,' he said stiffly at the end of the bereaved brother's tale. 'I shall go back to Assisi and ponder what to do. Meanwhile, perhaps you would like to have this.'

He took from a sack at his saddle the dagger belonging to the murdered man. Umberto looked at it in fascinated horror. He took it from the Minister General, bowed and turned his horse's head back towards Gubbio.

Brother Anselmo went to celebrate Mass at the convent, unaware that the Minister General had already done so. If he had stopped to think, he might have realised it was likely, but he was still too distracted by his own recent interview with Michele da Cesena.

The Abbess explained the situation tactfully and offered him nettle tea in her room.

'How is everyone at the friary?' she asked.

'Still reeling from our visitation,' said Brother Anselmo ruefully. 'It was a punishing experience. But I do not think it

201

has shed any light on our problems.'

Mother Elena was a sympathetic listener. 'Perhaps the murderer has repented under questioning?' she suggested.

'Even if that is so, he will always be a danger as long as he is at large,' he said. 'Murder is not the kind of sin that can be absolved through confession without also being punished.'

'A life for a life,' said the Abbess.

'Yes, I'm afraid so. Whoever it is cannot hope to be allowed to continue in our Order. Imagine what Saint Francis would have thought of that!'

'How is young Silvano?' asked Elena.

'Why him particularly? He is no worse than the rest of us. Bruised by his encounter with our Minister General, I imagine. He is not a gentle questioner.'

'Do you know that our youngest novice, Orsola, has been offered a home by Monna Isabella?'

The apparent change of subject showed Brother Anselmo that the Abbess saw more than most people realised. She had noticed, as he had, the growing attraction between the two young people. He had to steady his voice and control his expression in speaking of Isabella.

'So Sister Orsola will leave the convent?'

'She is considering it,' said Elena. 'You see, she has no vocation. And I have no desire to keep her here against her will.'

And Silvano will leave one day too, thought Anselmo. There will be nothing to stop them finding love together. A wave of pain and regret swept through him, followed instantly by remorse that he should begrudge any young couple their happiness, particularly two people he was fond of. But suppose they found that happiness under Isabella's

202

roof? Wouldn't that remind her of her own lost youth and love? Anselmo couldn't help feeling that it would be a source of painful pleasure to her.

He took his leave of the Abbess in pensive mood and arrived back at the friary to find a message for him from the Abbot. The subject of his thoughts had sent to say she would like to visit the friary on the following day to discuss her business affairs with Abbot Bonsignore. And she had requested a private meeting with Anselmo.

Umberto had been tempted to stop at Giardinetto again on the way home and confront this scheming Brother Anselmo on the spot. But he didn't even know which friar he was. And he could hardly ask the Abbot to introduce him to the man he wanted to kill.

He had convinced himself that Anselmo was his brother's murderer and that the Minister General, in giving him Ubaldo's dagger, had been entrusting him privately with a mission to see justice done. Umberto knew nothing of the religious life and had no idea that Michele da Cesena would have been horrified by any such interpretation.

His brother's dagger, tucked into his jerkin, burned Umberto with an almost sacred flame. He had all the evidence he thought he needed of Anselmo's guilt, the blessing as he saw it of the Church on his enterprise and the appropriate weapon with which to carry it out.

When he next returned to Giardinetto, it would be as an avenger. And he relished like a sweetmeat in his mouth, the prospect of telling Monna Isabella how her lover had died.

CHAPTER SIXTEEN

Digging up the Past

very nervous man was being shown into Baron Montacuto's private room. He was pale and sweating and refused to give his name. He would say only that he had been sent by the person investigating Tommaso the sheep farmer's murder for the Baron. Such an introduction ensured his admission.

The Baron was eager to hear whatever the man had to say; as an experienced huntsman, he could sense that the prey was almost his.

'Whoever you are, tell me what you know about the sheep farmer and his moneylending,' he commanded.

'I am a younger son myself,' the man began nervously. 'And I was unwise with the allowance I had from my father. Gaming, drinking, women – your lordship knows how it is.'

The Baron nodded encouragingly and poured the man some wine, even though he despised anyone who did not live within his means, whatever they were. He had the good fortune of never having been short of money for his needs and he had husbanded his land and resources well. There would be more to leave to Silvano than Bartolomeo da Montacuto had received from his father.

'Well,' said the informer. 'I heard through the grapevine that there was a man in the city who would lend money at interest, even though it was against the law. When one is desperate, one will do anything. I was ashamed of my debts and did not want my father to find out about them, so I went to this man.'

'And he was?'

'Tommaso the sheep farmer. He had a lucrative second business in lending money illegally. Because the loans were without security, he could and did charge extortionate rates of interest – thirty per cent and more. I was soon in even more difficulty.'

'How did you extricate yourself?' asked the Baron, noticing that the man was reasonably well clad and did not look ill-fed.

'I had a stroke of luck,' said the informer, bitterly. 'My father died.'

He stopped to drink and Montacuto could see he was hiding the tears that had sprung to his eyes. He wiped his mouth on his sleeve, pulled himself together and continued.

'There was just enough money for me to pay Tommaso off. I thought I was a free man at last, even though a poor one. I had used all my patrimony and was without work. My family . . . no one had needed to earn his living before but I had wasted all my inheritance on old debts contracted when I was young and foolish and the interest charged by the sheep farmer had made matters worse. Still, at least I could hold my head up with my family and I began privately to seek honest work.'

'What happened?'

'Tommaso came to me and said that if I did not find him more debtors, he would tell my mother and older brother what my past had been.'

The Baron held his breath; he could smell his quarry now.

'When you have lived the life I did, you know who is gaming too deep and spending money he does not have. It did not take long for me to find another youngest son who was in debt.'

'And that was?'

'Are you sure that my name can be kept out of this?'

'I do not know your name,' said the Baron. 'You will be paid well for this information and you may have to repeat it to the Council. But if the man you name today proves to be Tommaso's murderer, he will not be a future danger to you. You can remain under my protection until his execution.'

Montacuto knew that he risked scaring away his prey but it was a calculated risk; he sensed that this disgraced man longed to redeem himself and he was giving him a chance.

'I do not wish him ill,' said the informer. 'I only wish he had killed Tommaso before I fell into his clutches. Or that I had had the courage to do what he did. The moneylender was evil, fattening himself on the misery of others. But it isn't right that your lordship's son should suffer when he is innocent.'

'The man's name?' pressed Montacuto.

'Gervasio de' Oddini.'

The Baron let out a great breath of relief. He poured himself some wine and offered the informer more. At this moment he felt like clutching him to his breast and kissing him on both cheeks.

'De' Oddini?' he said, as casually as he could manage.

'Gervasio, the youngest son,' said the man. Now that he had named him, it seemed that his tongue had been loosened and he couldn't tell Baron Montacuto enough. 'I knew he was in debt and I happened to tell him one day in the inn that I knew a way he could borrow money. He knew about the interest – I didn't deceive him – but he was desperate, as desperate as I had been.'

'You know that he is about to marry the moneylender's widow?'

'Yes. That was another reason I was willing to come and see you. It's not right. I can understand his killing the old bloodsucker, but it doesn't seem right he should take the man's wife and money as well.'

'And you know that he is the murderer?'

'I'm almost certain. You see, Tommaso had a list of debtors, how much money he had lent and what the repayments had been. All of us who were in his clutches knew about that list. He never let it off his body except when he had it out to make marks on it.'

'It was not found on him when he was killed.'

'No. The murderer knew exactly where to find it and took it after his dagger pierced Tommaso's heart.'

'Except that it was not his dagger,' said the Baron grimly. 'It was my son's.'

'De' Oddini had time to retrieve only one thing.'

'The list would have implicated him, and the dagger my son,' said the Baron. 'That would not have been a real choice to a man like Gervasio.'

'He must have made it in an instant but he was in too deep. He had killed Tommaso to cancel his debt and he needed that list.'

'How do you know this?'

'The night of the murder, Gervasio was in the inn. He was excited and was drinking heavily. He claimed to be upset

207

about your son's exile. 'It looks bad for my friend,' he kept saying. But as the night wore on – and he was buying all the drinks, this young man with debts – he mentioned one or two other names on the list as possible suspects.'

'Did all of the debtors know each other's names?'

'No. Tommaso was very secretive about it. I didn't know any others apart from Gervasio, of course, because I had introduced him myself. But I was suspicious when he mentioned other debtors by name because he wouldn't have known any either – unless he had the list.'

'And who were they?'

The informer mentioned two names, one of which was one of the debtors the Baron had tracked down himself. He sat back, satisfied. This was enough to convict Gervasio and bring back Silvano.

'Thank you,' he said. 'You have given me back my greatest treasure.'

It was hard to say which of them was the more nervous. Abbot Bonsignore had offered to be present at their meeting but both Isabella and Anselmo had preferred to face each other alone. It was a meeting that both of them had known would happen ever since they had seen each other in the friary yard at Giardinetto.

All through the earlier conference with the Abbot, Isabella had been distracted, thinking of what was to come. Brother Anselmo had been in the colour room, making terra verde again; it was the most soothing job he knew. But after Nones, he got the message from the Abbot that Isabella was ready to see him.

They met in the Abbot's cell. When Anselmo entered, they were both flustered, not knowing how to greet each other. Isabella offered him her hand and he took it as if he would like to kiss it but thought better of it. She said 'Domenico,' by mistake, even though she had been practising 'Brother Anselmo' in her head for hours.

'This is extremely awkward,' said Anselmo, after they were both seated. 'I never expected to see you again.'

'And yet Giardinetto is not far from Gubbio,' said Isabella. 'You must have thought about that when you accepted a place here.'

Anselmo acknowledged it. 'I felt safe from any encounter as long as I could avoid visiting my old town. I never dreamed that you would come here.'

'And was it so very terrible to see me? Have I changed so much?' asked Isabella in a small voice.

'It is precisely because you have not changed at all, except to become even more beautiful, that it was – is – so very terrible,' said Anselmo seriously.

'So, you still have some feelings for me?'

'More than any friar should have for a woman.'

Isabella sensed her fate sounding in her ears like a tolling bell.

'You don't ask about my feelings for you,' she said.

'I have no right,' said Anselmo. 'I cannot ask for what might be a balm to my ears as a layman, since I am a religious and have made binding vows.'

'It is not unheard of for a man to leave the religious life, even after he is professed,' said Isabella.

'And is that what you would have me do?'

She was silent, unable to speak.

'You have no idea,' said Anselmo, bitterly, 'what I have been through to rid myself of my love for you. Do you think it is easy for a man to make those vows I have made to Saint Francis and to God? Poverty was not a great trial, though it has sometimes irked me not to have my own books. I have continued my scholarship through the library here and at my previous houses. Obedience has been harder – you know I was not a very compliant man even from my youth. But I have wrestled with it and submitted myself to the Order and to my Abbot. Bonsignore has made that easy here.'

He got up and walked restlessly round the small room, so that his back was to her and his voice muffled when he spoke again.

'But chastity! I had to give up my dearest hopes of our love and come into the brotherhood while I was young and lusty, knowing that you spent every night in bed with that man. Night after night I wrestled in agony with my thoughts of the two of you together!'

Isabella could not bear it.

'Stop,' she implored him. 'Do not torment yourself and me. Every night that I spent with Ubaldo, and believe me they became less and less frequent as the years went by, was as much a torment to me as it was to you. You can't believe that I ever came to love him, or to enjoy his embraces!'

'It does not matter,' said Anselmo. 'Men are different from women. It was not desire I was struggling with, at least not alone. It was jealousy. Had you loved Ubaldo and rejected me for him, I might have found it easier to bear and perhaps to forget you but, as it was, I could only suffer.'

'My poor Domenico,' said Isabella.

'But I did suffer and I offered my suffering to God,' he continued. 'I battled through the stormy seas of longing and jealousy for years and at last came into calm water. I am now reconciled to my loss and to my life as a religious. I no longer suffer in body or mind.'

'So you do not wish to come back to me?'

'I cannot.'

'Then I shall not mention it again,' said Isabella. She struggled to contain the grief that threatened to overwhelm her.

Brother Anselmo was no more composed. Several times it seemed as if he would say more but in the end he sat with his eyes cast down and it was the widow who brought their interview to an end. She rose and went to the door.

'Goodbye, Brother Anselmo,' she said. 'I see that Domenico is gone for ever.'

She did not look back or she would have seen Anselmo stretched prostrate on the cold floor, like a man who had barely survived an ordeal by torture.

Michele da Cesena pondered what to do for a long time. At last, he sent a message to Abbot Bonsignore at Giardinetto.

The friary needs cleansing of the devils within it. I am sending to Giardinetto a most precious relic. There have come to me at Assisi the remains of the Blessed Egidio, one of the first companions of Saint Francis, and I wish to see them buried with due honour and ceremony. The brotherhood will pay for an appropriate casket and I shall myself accompany the blessed bones to Giardinetto before they are interred here in Assisi.

This will go some way to purifying the friary of the evil within. I should also like to interview Brother Anselmo again. This visit and the arrival of the casket will take place within the next few days. No time must be lost in exorcising the devils from Giardinetto.'

The Abbot was overwhelmed when he read this letter. The Minister General was doing them a very great honour in letting the bones of the Blessed Egidio rest at Giardinetto even for a few hours and he did not doubt their effectiveness in ridding the friary of the evil that had taken up residence there. But he was worried by the reference to Anselmo. It seemed as if the Colour Master's problems were piling up.

Monna Isabella was getting better at hiding her feelings; she did not give way to them until she was alone in her private sitting room. She had been to see Chiara after her interview with Brother Anselmo and even then had managed to appear calm and in control.

'Have you thought any more about my offer, Chiara?' she asked. Isabella never called her Orsola; that was one of the things the girl liked about her.

Chiara had indeed thought a lot about going to live with Isabella. Silvano had not asked her to stay, not to leave Giardinetto. How could he? For, if she were to stay it would have to be as a sister, eventually a professed one, and such a person could not be subject to the whim of a sixteen-year-old boy, no matter how big his grey eyes or how long his black lashes.

No, she must decide her own fate without reference to

212

whatever might happen to Silvano.

'I think I should like to come and live with you very much, Madama,' she said.

'But that is wonderful!' said Isabella. 'The best thing that has happened today.'

'Only . . .'

'Only?'

'Not just yet, if you will forgive me,' said Chiara impulsively. 'I don't want to seem ungrateful but I should like to stay here until I know that everyone is safe. I mean Mother Elena and the sisters.'

'And the brothers, of course,' said Isabella with a wan smile.

'Yes, the brothers too,' said Chiara, suddenly very interested in her feet.

'I understand, child,' said Isabella quietly. 'I too fear for the safety of those I love at Giardinetto. Come to me in Gubbio when the murderer has been found and dealt with and we shall be women of business together. You shall find your brother in my house from time to time. He has agreed to be my business manager.'

'Bernardo?' said Chiara, amazed. But already she could see herself, dressed in fine gowns giving orders to the brother who had abandoned her to the grey sisters of Giardinetto. It was a mean thought and she repressed it; it just showed how unsuited she really was to life as a nun. But Isabella's news certainly gave an added piquancy to her offer.

It was not until Isabella was alone that the effort of the day's scenes fell with all their weight on her and she wept as she had when she and Domenico had first been separated. She still loved him just as much; the white hairs among the

213

brown and his thin drawn face excited only compassion and tenderness in her. If he was not exactly as he had been, then neither was she. And they both knew who was to blame for that.

She did not really believe that Domenico, Brother Anselmo as she must learn to think of him, had ceased to love her either. That was what made their separation even harder to bear. She felt, as she often had in dreams, that something exquisite had been dashed away from her lips at the moment of its enjoyment.

Her body ached as if a carriage had run over her bones and her head hurt. She sent for vinegar and got her maid to bathe her temples but it gave her little ease. In vain did she try to rest that night; sleep would not come.

In some ways it would have been easier if Ubaldo still lived. If they had found out that her old love now lived nearby, it would have made no difference; Isabella would still have been bound to the merchant. But – now that her long years of servitude were over and she would be free to marry again after a decent interval – to find him now! It was too cruel.

She fell at last into an exhausted doze, worn out by grief and dry of all tears.

'What are you making?' asked Simone.

He had a rare half hour away from his frescoes and was wandering alone in the complex of buildings that made up the Basilica and its attached friar house. In a workshop he had come across Teodoro, a goldsmith whom he knew slightly from Siena.

214

The goldsmith was measuring sheets of crystal.

'Good evening, Simone,' he said. 'It's a commission at short notice. Michele da Cesena has ordered it himself for a coffin.'

'The Minister General is dying?' asked Simone.

'No, no, certainly not. At least not as far as I know, Heaven preserve him,' said Teodoro. 'This is for the remains of the Blessed Egidio. I must have it ready within days so that the holy bones can be transported to Giardinetto.'

'To Giardinetto? Why? Surely they will not bury such a sacred relic there?'

'I have no idea. A humble craftsman doesn't ask questions when the great Michele da Cesena gives him an order.'

'I know what you mean,' said Simone. 'But perhaps it is in order to cleanse and purify the friary. You know there have been murders there?'

'Yes, I heard,' said Teodoro. 'You think Assisi will lend the bones of the Blessed Egidio to the grey friars? And that the murders will stop?'

'I hope so,' said Simone. 'Perhaps when the brothers are in the presence of so much sanctity, the murderer will be moved to repentance and will confess. I should like to see the devils driven out of Giardinetto.'

CHAPTER SEVENTEEN
Death's Head

ngelica's father had made one rather feeble attempt to reassert his authority over her since her husband's death.

'You should by law come back to my house and bring your dowry with you,' he said.

Angelica snorted. 'And how much would that buy?' she taunted him. 'As I recall, you could scrape together very little to make your bargain with my husband. I was my own dowry and I shall revert to myself.'

'But you have neither child nor husband,' objected her father.

'And soon I shall have both,' she said. 'I am engaged to be married to Gervasio de' Oddini. By next year I shall bear the name of a noble house – and a child too.'

Her father looked both gratified and shocked. A child of his married to a noble, even a penniless one, was an elevation in rank that the family had not dreamed of. They had thought a sheep farmer a significant step up. But he didn't like to think that his own daughter could be of such easy virtue as to be bearing another man's child so soon.

Angelica cared just enough for her father's good opinion to tell him the truth.

'It's not Gervasio's,' she sighed, patting her rounded

stomach. 'But he doesn't need to know that. I can confuse him about the date the baby was made once we are married. Which had better be soon.'

But everyone will think Angelica was dallying with him while the husband was still alive, thought her father. What other reason could there be for such a hasty marriage? Out loud he said, 'Well, we are agreed on one thing at least. Let de' Oddini make an honest woman of you as soon as may be. You won't lack for a dowry this time.'

'I know,' said Angelica. 'And I'll have a good business in Gubbio too.'

A servant came in, very agitated, and whispered in her mistress's ear. Angelica clutched at her heart and looked as if she might swoon.

'The Council have arrested Gervasio,' she told her father. 'They say that he is Tommaso's murderer!'

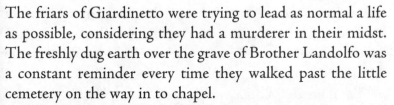

The friars of Giardinetto were trying to lead as normal a life as possible, considering they had a murderer in their midst. The freshly dug earth over the grave of Brother Landolfo was a constant reminder every time they walked past the little cemetery on the way in to chapel.

Brother Anselmo had been preoccupied and uncommunicative ever since his meeting with Isabella, but he ran the colour room as steadily as before. Silvano felt cut off from the Colour Master's thoughts though and this made him feel lonely, lonelier than he had since arriving at the friary.

He took to missing services and riding out more often on Moonbeam. In a novice it was disobedience; in a sanctuary-

217

seeker, it was sheer folly. But no one tried to stop him. Abbot Bonsignore was too caught up with his own problems to take much notice.

On one of his unofficial outings, he ran into Brother Valentino, the Herbalist. The friar had been almost invisible in his grey robe against the rocky hillside and it was the horse who saw him first, pulling up short to avoid running him down.

'Hello there, young Silvano,' said Valentino good-naturedly. 'You gave me a scare.'

'I'm so sorry, Brother,' said Silvano, dismounting. 'I didn't see you. What are you doing?'

'I am gathering wild thyme,' said Brother Valentino. 'My stocks have been rather depleted. I want to dry as many herbs as possible because the Abbot has asked me to take over from Landolfo as Guest Master.'

'He wants you to do that as well as grow and keep the herbs?'

'Yes, but it is not ordinarily a demanding job. We don't have many visitors in Giardinetto. But now we are to receive quite a party from Assisi. They are bringing the relics of the Blessed Egidio and will leave them in the chapel overnight, before taking them back to Assisi for burial in the tomb our Minister General is having built.'

'I'm not sure I understand about these relics. I know it's a great honour but what exactly will they do?'

'They are the bones of one of Saint Francis's early companions. Someone who passed his daily life with the Saint. They are so holy that they will surely drive out the evil that has lodged in our house. And I think the Minister General believes it will cause the Devil to come out of whichever brother killed Landolfo and he will confess his crime.'

'I hope he's right,' said Silvano. 'Will you ride back with me? You can ride Moonbeam and I will walk beside you.'

Valentino looked at the grey horse and the hooded hawk with some apprehension.

'No, thank you. I have not found all I need yet. But it is a kind offer.'

He waved to Silvano and the boy got back on his horse and rode away thinking that he had never had a conversation with the Herbalist before. And then he thought, suppose Valentino was not harmlessly collecting wild herbs? Maybe there was some kind of naturally growing plant that contained arsenikon?

He dismissed the idea as soon as it came. Brother Valentino was a kind and gentle man, who used his herbs for healing. He couldn't imagine him deliberately poisoning anyone, let alone stabbing anybody.

Silvano stabled Moonbeam himself and put Celeste back on her post. He had missed Nones, and suddenly realised that Brother Valentino must have missed it too. Silvano hurried to the colour room, where an acrid smell met his nose.

'Ah, Silvano,' said Anselmo. 'We are making caput mortuum.'

'Death's head?' asked Silvano. 'What is that?'

'It is an ochre rich in red mineral deposits, but when ground and mixed with water, it makes a wonderfully dark purple, suitable for robes.'

Anselmo seemed almost his old self, happy to be explaining and demonstrating the colours that he loved. Silvano smiled at him. They worked till Vespers, then walked to the chapel together, stopping to cross themselves by Landolfo's grave.

219

'Did you know that Brother Valentino is Guest Master now?' Silvano asked Anselmo.

'Yes, I heard that,' said Anselmo.

They both looked round the chapel for the Herbalist but there was no sign of him.

'Perhaps he is still out collecting herbs?' whispered Silvano.

But the Abbot came in and they began to say the Office.

Valentino was not present at supper either and Silvano felt uneasy. It was most unusual for a brother to miss a meal. He saw Anselmo speaking to Bonsignore and the Abbot beckoned him over.

'Brother Anselmo tells me you had some converse with Brother Valentino this afternoon?' he asked.

'Yes, Father. I was out in the hills exercising my horse and I found him gathering herbs.'

'Did he come back with you?'

'No. I offered him my horse but he said he hadn't finished his task.'

'When was this?'

'About mid-afternoon, at the time of Nones,' said Silvano. 'I noticed he wasn't at Vespers. Has he not been back at all?'

The Abbot shook his head. 'He came to me after the mid-day meal and asked to be excused Nones. He said he wanted to pick herbs. Perhaps we should go to his storeroom and see if he became so absorbed in putting his plants away that he missed the Vespers bell?'

The Abbot, Anselmo and Silvano excused themselves from the refectory, leaving a buzz of speculation behind them. A heavy feeling lay in all their hearts. But there was no lifeless Brother Valentino in the storeroom. Still, he had been back. There were two baskets full of fragrant, freshly picked herbs. He had left them on a bench, as if in some hurry.

They went to Valentino's cell, which was likewise empty.

'Perhaps he is in the refectory now?' suggested Silvano.

They went back and were met by the silent faces of the friars all turned towards them. The Abbot strode to the head of the table and rapped on it with his wooden cup. It was not really necessary; every eye was on him.

'Brothers,' he said, 'we are concerned for the safety of Brother Valentino. Has anyone seen him since he returned from his herb-gathering?'

Silvano suddenly felt grateful that they had found the baskets. If anything had happened to Valentino on the hillside, it would look bad that he had been out of the friary at the same time.

'It was his turn to ring the bell for Vespers,' said Brother Taddeo. 'I saw him hurrying across the yard.'

'And did the bell ring?' asked Bonsignore. Like all of them, he was so used to the sections of the day being portioned out by the ringing of the friary bell that he couldn't say whether he had gone to Vespers because of its sound or because his body just knew it was the right time.

But there was general agreement that the bell had rung.

'And no one has seen him since then?' asked Bonsignore. There was silence. 'Well, he was not at Vespers, so perhaps we should go to the bell tower. He might have collapsed.'

Silvano really hoped that was the explanation, even though he didn't like the idea of Brother Valentino having some kind of seizure because he had hurried back and then rushed across the yard. He wished the Herbalist had accepted a ride on Moonbeam.

The evening meal was abandoned and all the friars followed their Abbot to the bell tower with a sense of foreboding.

It was a simple brick tower with only one bell in the open cupola at the top. Several flights of stairs wound up inside it to where the bronze bell hung, but it was rung by a heavy rope that hung down inside the tower. Silvano had been inside the tower only a few times since he was not allowed to ring the bell by himself and was not on the rota of friars that did it before services.

The little procession stopped outside the wooden door at the bottom of the tower.

'Come with me, Brother Rufino,' commanded the Abbot. 'If Valentino has fallen ill, we may need you.'

But when they pushed open the door, it was clear, even in the gloom of the shadowy tower, that Valentino was beyond Rufino's help, or anyone else's.

He swung from a beam, his grey robe long and shapeless, obscuring his feet. The hem dangled only a few inches from the floor. His face was congested and purple, his tongue lolling out of his mouth. There was a bloody bruise on his forehead.

A collective gasp went up from the brothers as Bonsignore and Rufino rushed inside. Anselmo and Silvano were right behind them. The Abbot himself took the weight of the body while Rufino and Anselmo undid the cord. They lay Valentino on the flagstones. The Abbot closed his staring eyes and cast his own cloak over the corpse. He intoned a Latin blessing over the dead friar and all the brothers said, 'Amen'.

The news was quick to reach Assisi. It ran round the Basilica and reached Simone and Pietro the next morning as they breakfasted with their assistants outside their workshop in the grounds.

'Another murder?' said Simone, while Pietro tried to remember which brother was the Herbalist.

'The Minister General is taking the relics of the Blessed Egidio today,' said Teodoro the goldsmith, who had come to bring them the story, knowing their interest in Giardinetto.

'You finished the casket then?' asked Simone.

'It took me all day and all night for three days,' said the goldsmith, yawning. 'And that was with my assistants helping me. But I am pleased with it.'

'May we see?' asked Pietro.

Teodoro took them into the Upper Church, where the casket lay on two trestles before the High Altar. It was a magnificent piece of work. Sheets of crystal were let into the side and lid of the casket, which surrounded a lead coffin holding the sacred bones. It was made of polished pink-veined marble, and every hinge and corner was decorated with gold.

Simone and his friend Pietro knelt in veneration before the holy relics. But first and foremost they were artists and it was the workmanship and artistry of the casket which had impressed them as much as what it contained. They walked out into the cold morning sunshine praising Teodoro's work.

'It was worth losing sleep over,' said Pietro, clapping the goldsmith on the back.

'Thank you,' said Teodoro. 'The Minister General seems pleased.'

223

'So I should think,' said Simone indignantly. 'It is absurd for such a commission to be given at such short notice. You have done in days what any other artist would have insisted on taking weeks if not months to design and make.'

As they walked across the green, they saw a small procession approaching. A carriage drawn by two horses was accompanied by several horsemen, Michele da Cesena among them.

'I showed you my casket just in time,' said Teodoro. 'I think they have come to take it now. Giardinetto's need is more urgent than ever.'

'How should you like a ride out into the country?' Simone asked Pietro.

'Very much,' said Pietro, 'but I have work to do and so do you.'

'Donato and the others can continue while we are away. And you have your own assistants. Besides, we could collect some more pigments from the friars.'

'Do you think Michele da Cesena would appreciate our presence?'

'We are not froward friars for him to glare at. And we can't help it if we happen to be at Giardinetto to collect our colours while he is there.'

Silvano had slept badly, with terrible nightmares. He thought he would never expunge the image of Valentino's ghastly purple face from his memory. He had been hanged by his own rope belt and that somehow made it seem much more cold-blooded of the murderer. No one suggested that

224

the Herbalist had taken his own life.

It seemed as if the other young friars and novices had passed an equally restless night. Faces were pale and voices quiet. But they had not had their supper the night before and they were hungry. So they were all present in the refectory to break their fast.

Compline and Matins had not been said and only a few friars had gone to the chapel for Lauds in the early morning. When the bell rang for Prime at daybreak, everyone looked fearful. Who would have been brave enough to enter that bell tower after what it had witnessed the night before?

As they approached the chapel, they saw that the bell tower door was wide open and it was Brother Anselmo pulling vigorously on the rope. The Abbot was there too, blessing the tower with holy water and carrying a wooden cross before him.

Silvano felt a surge of affection for both men. They were strong and determined to carry on with the religious life of the friary, no matter what new horror was thrown at them. When the brothers had filed into the chapel, the Abbot came and addressed them before they said the Office.

'Brothers in Christ, this death of another brother is a terrible blow to us all. Even to the murderer among us.' He stopped and raked the small congregation with his gaze. 'If that killer is here in this chapel, sanctified to our beloved Saint Francis, I pray him to come forth and confess. Let the devils within him be called out and exorcised so that he may be free to repent and go to the Lord.'

There was an uneasy silence in which no man dared look at his neighbours.

'Let us pray together for the salvation of the soul of

225

Brother Valentino, whose body lies in the infirmary. May he today find himself in bliss, even though he went to his rest unshriven. And we also pray for Brother Landolfo and Ubaldo the merchant. Rest eternal grant unto them, O Lord.'

'And may light perpetual shine upon them,' responded all the brothers.

'May they rest in peace.'

'And rise in glory.'

After the Office of Prime had been said, Bonsignore spoke again.

'Later today our Minister General will come from Assisi with the bones of the Blessed Egidio. The casket will lie here all day and all night and any brother is free to come and pray by it at any time. There will be a service of blessing immediately after Vespers. The relics will be taken back to Assisi after Terce tomorrow morning. I shall be in my cell until the arrival of the party from Assisi, if any brother wishes to speak to me. Meanwhile, you are all to carry on with your work as normal.'

He left the chapel with a firm step, like a man fully in control of his house, though that was far from how he felt.

The friars dispersed to their tasks and did their best to behave normally but they were deeply frightened.

'It is a good thing that Michele da Cesena is coming back,' said Brother Anselmo to Silvano. This is too great a burden for Father Bonsignore to bear alone.'

'What do you think will happen?' asked Silvano. 'Will he call for the friary to be dispersed?'

'It is very possible. We could all be looking for new houses by this time tomorrow.'

'Shall we make colours as usual?'

'We must. It is what the Abbot wants and what will keep us sane.'

'But not the murderer.'

'No. I fear Simone is right. One of our brothers must have lost his mind. Brother Valentino was enemy to no man, as sweet a soul as Landolfo. There could be no other reason but insanity.'

'Perhaps we should not make death's head purple?'

Anselmo looked at him sympathetically.

'No. We shall make a more cheerful colour today.'

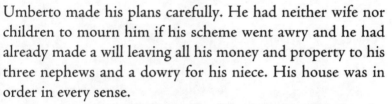

Umberto made his plans carefully. He had neither wife nor children to mourn him if his scheme went awry and he had already made a will leaving all his money and property to his three nephews and a dowry for his niece. His house was in order in every sense.

Now he was drinking deeply. Like his older brother, he was able to drink heavily without impairing his ability to ride. But it made him even more dangerous. He was going to go to Giardinetto, armed with Ubaldo's dagger, and take vengeance on his brother's murderer.

The only pity was that his sister-in-law would not know about it until after the event. And if he should be so unlucky as to miss his mark and be himself killed by the friar, however unlikely that might be, he would miss the satisfaction of seeing her grief over the loss of her paramour.

Umberto brooded about this and eventually sent his man with a message to Isabella:

'Am gone to Giardinetto to avenge my brother. U.'

227

He sat back, satisfied that he had tied up every loose end, and drank another two goblets of wine. He had never killed a man before. And his intended victim was a man of God – supposedly. But that did not deter him. Umberto did not expect to be sent to Hell for murder or sacrilege. He saw himself as the wielder of justice, justice that had so far been denied to his brother.

'It is up to me,' he said to himself, his voice beginning to slur. 'There is no one left in our family to avenge Ubaldo but me. His sons are too young. And I won't let that so-called friar get away with murder.'

He called for his horse.

CHAPTER EIGHTEEN

Mordant

he soldiers arrived from the Council before Angelica could reach the palazzo of the de' Oddini family. But she was there in time to see them lead Gervasio away in manacles. He cast imploring looks at her and his father but did not, she noticed, protest his innocence.

'On what evidence do you arrest him?' begged Vincenzo.

'Ask Baron Montacuto,' said the Captain.

'Montacuto? But then this is a trumped up case to get his own boy cleared,' protested Vincenzo. 'Don't worry, Gervasio. I'll have you out of prison within the hour.'

'Look after Angelica,' was all Gervasio said, looking his intended wife defiantly in the face.

Left alone, Vincenzo and Angelica were in a state of shock. The father instinctively believed in the son's innocence and was all for going to the Palazzo Montacuto immediately. The beloved, though, had her reservations about the lover. She saw straightaway from the look on his face that he probably was her husband's killer.

Angelica was under no illusions about Gervasio. She remembered that he had been friendly with the young man who had written the poem. And though the red flower had been gained by the one, it had been the other who had vigorously courted her. That was not the action of a true friend. If he could do that, he could just as easily have killed a man and put the blame on someone else. She didn't doubt it.

Nevertheless she still wanted to marry him. He was her safe-conduct to a more elegant life and a way of putting her peasant origins behind her. There must be a way to rescue him from execution. But not at the cost of the Montacuto boy's life. There was something sweet and natural about him in her memory that brought out a new maternal feeling in her.

'Let us try the Baron,' she agreed. 'I shall go with you.'

The solemn procession had arrived at Giardinetto. The Abbot went to meet it with heavy heart. Although it would have been a sinful deception, he wished he could have kept the fact of Brother Valentino's death from the Minister General. After his strictures last time, Bonsignore was still smarting.

He saw now that, as well as Michele da Cesena and his chaplain, there were four other friars from Assisi – and it looked as if the two painters had joined the group as well.

The Abbot and the Minister General performed a perfunctory embrace and then the four friars took the elaborate casket from the carriage and carried it on their shoulders to the chapel, as if the Blessed Egidio had died only the day before, like poor Brother Valentino, whose plain coffin already lay before the altar.

There were two trestles laid ready for the casket and the

friars of Giardinetto filed in behind it, chanting the opening prayer of the Requiem Mass, as if willing the bones to do their work and flush out the murderer from their midst.

But nothing had happened by the end of the service, except for some heartfelt sobbing by some of the younger brothers.

When it was over, Valentino was laid next to Landolfo in the little cemetery. As the Minister General performed the committal, he looked around the graveyard and Bonsignore could tell he was thinking it too cramped for the needs of a house that was going to have a murder every week or so.

When Valentino was safely under the earth, the Assisi party visited the Abbot's cell for refreshment. Simone and Pietro, the unofficial visitors, went to the colour room. Brother Anselmo suggested that all the other friars should take some fresh air while he spoke to the Sienese artists but Silvano stayed to talk to them.

'This is a bad business,' said Simone. 'You must have some idea who's doing this?'

'I have had my suspicions,' said Anselmo, much to Silvano's surprise. The Colour Master certainly hadn't shared them with him. 'But I have no proof.'

'You must be careful,' said Pietro. 'If the murderer suspects you know something, you will be in even greater danger.'

'And you shouldn't try to confront him by yourself,' urged Simone, 'or you will be his next victim. Go and tell Father Bonsignore once the visitation is over and let him help you.'

Anselmo was touched by their concern. 'If I'm still here, I shall,' he said.

'Still here?' said Silvano. 'What do you mean?'

'Father Bonsignore has told me that the Minister General wants another interview with me. I think he has me marked down as the murderer.'

'But that's ridiculous!' said Silvano. 'I thought he was supposed to be a good judge of men.'

'Your loyalty is touching – all of you,' said Anselmo. 'But I think things are coming to a head here. If the Minister General orders me to Assisi, you must look out for the other brothers, Silvano. And our sisters nearby.'

'Do the sisters know about Brother Valentino?' asked Pietro.

'The Abbot sent the stableman to tell them,' said Anselmo. 'He didn't want any of us to leave the friary before the party came from Assisi. Mother Elena has locked and barred the doors. But I am not really afraid for them. The murderer hasn't harmed any of them yet and it would be immediately noticed if someone other than myself as their chaplain left here to visit them.'

'This is unbearable,' said Silvano. 'Do you really think the murderer will confess, because we have the Blessed Egidio's bones?'

'I know that Father Bonsignore hopes so. It is such a personal disgrace to him, what has happened here. And I know he fears that Michele da Cesena will remove him from office. Or disband the house, if the relics do not expurgate the sin.'

Brother Fazio's head came round the door.

'Excuse me, Brother Anselmo, gentlemen. Might I have some gold?'

'You are still working on your Gospel?' asked Anselmo, taking a key from his belt and going to a cupboard in the corner.

'Of course,' said Fazio, looking vaguely at the others. 'God's work must go on.'

'You are gilding the letters?' asked Simone. He was always interested in gold. 'You use mordant gilding?'

Fazio nodded and focused on the painter.

'Water, glair, a little chalk and a little honey,' he said. 'And then the finest slivers of gold.'

'Why do they call it mordant?' asked Silvano, interested in this new aspect of artistry, in spite of the horrors he had seen.

'Because it bites,' said Pietro unexpectedly clashing his strong teeth together, so that Silvano jumped. 'The sticky mixture painted on to the page clings on to the gold like a dog to a bone.'

'I could not have put it better myself,' said Fazio. 'But I believe you use gold in another way?' he asked Simone.

'Yes, we have reached that stage in the chapel,' said Simone. 'For the haloes of the saints, I use a set of punches in the soft gesso and then we paint it over with gold tin. It's less fiddly than mordant gilding but it takes time.'

'I'd like to see that,' said Silvano. He suddenly longed to be in Assisi, thinking of nothing more distressing than colour and form and technique.

Simone patted him on the shoulder. 'I'm sure you will.'

'Ah, we each have our own mysteries,' said Brother Fazio, taking the tiny packet of gold from Anselmo. 'And I must get back to mine. I have a new chapter to prepare.'

Vincenzo de' Oddini listened in despair to the damning evidence against his son. He could not maintain Gervasio's

233

innocence in the face of it. He was particularly shocked to learn of the boy's debts. But he could not let him go to his certain death.

'Please help him,' he begged the Baron. 'Consider if he were your own son.'

'You dare to speak of my son,' said Montacuto, 'who languishes in exile while his mother and sisters waste away with grief because he can't show his face in Perugia? It is *your* son who is responsible for that, stabbing the sheep farmer with Silvano's dagger.'

'I know. It was terrible. But think of the old friendship between our families. Our boys have always been close.'

'It is not wise to remind me of that. What did their friendship mean to Gervasio when he stole my son's dagger to do his dirty work with? Silvano looked up to your son as soon as he could walk. Do you imagine he would ever have done such a thing to him?'

'But perhaps he did not mean to leave the weapon in the body and put the blame on Silvano?'

The Baron grunted. 'If that is true, it makes it little better. But Gervasio intends to marry this – lady,' he said, indicating Angelica, who sat overawed in the great salon of the Baron's palazzo. 'What are we to think of him for that?'

'I do not think that was his intent when he killed my husband,' she said in a small voice. 'It must have been the money. But we have a future together now. I beg you to be generous. I . . . I am expecting a child.'

Both the Baron and Vincenzo were so surprised by this announcement they didn't ask if the baby was Gervasio's; they just assumed it. Angelica was relieved that she didn't have to lie.

'I beg of you,' said Vincenzo, falling to his knees. 'Don't visit your vengeance on my unborn grandchild. Let him have a father and this woman a protector. Let them leave Umbria and start a new life in another city.'

'It is no longer up to me,' said Montacuto. 'The Council have the evidence and they have him. The law must take its course.'

'You can do it,' said a quiet voice. The Baronessa had entered the room silently and had been listening for some time. 'You can ask for the sentence to be commuted to exile and a fine. You and Silvano.'

'Margarethe,' said Montacuto. 'Don't distress yourself about this. We shall get Silvano back. And soon.'

'But does another parent have to lose his child?' asked the Baronessa. 'And a pregnant mother her husband?'

She took Angelica by the hand. The widow felt large and clumsy and brassy in her new finery next to the slim and delicate Baronessa. She had the same large grey eyes as the young man who had written the beautiful poem.

'My dear,' said the Baron. 'It is different. Gervasio de' Oddini is guilty of a crime. Our son had to flee for his life when he had done nothing wrong. Would you let a guilty man go unpunished?'

'Will it not be a punishment to leave his family, his friends and his city for ever?'

The Baron was silent. Suddenly his wife and the pretty blonde widow of the sheep farmer were both kneeling before him beside his old friend Vincenzo.

'Get up, get up,' he said testily, helping the women to their feet with more tenderness than his voice showed. 'I shall refer the matter to my son. If Silvano agrees to clemency, I shall try

235

to help Gervasio escape the full penalty of the law.'

Chiara was shivering with cold and fear. Since the Abbess had told them about the latest murder, she had repented her decision to stay in Giardinetto. The friary seemed cursed and she was frightened for Silvano as well as herself. Now she had absented herself from the colour room and was looking out of the grille towards the brothers' chapel. No one had come to reprove her; discipline in the convent seemed to be breaking down.

She had seen the arrival of the relics from Assisi and noticed the painters riding behind. From here too she could watch while another coffin went into the ground and the friars dispersed. It was agonising not knowing what was going on. At any minute she expected to hear the bell toll to announce another death. Or to see another corpse carried into the chapel.

But what she did see was even more terrifying. The dead merchant Ubaldo riding back into Giardinetto on his horse! Her heart was beating fast and she wanted to cry out to warn the brothers that the world had turned upside down and the dead walked again. But gradually she got hold of her senses and remembered that Ubaldo had a younger brother. Peering as hard as she could, she thought she could discern differences between them after all.

This one was taller, though he had the same slumped posture on his horse as Ubaldo when the sisters had met him on the road from Assisi the night he was murdered. Chiara guessed that he had drunk too much. But what was he doing

236

in Giardinetto? The sight of him filled her with dread, even once she had realised he was a living man. She wondered whether to go and tell the Abbess, but what could Mother Elena do?

Night was beginning fall in the friary of Giardinetto. Candles were burning at the head and foot of the casket of the Blessed Egidio. The evening meal had been consumed in silence, to the clear annoyance of Umberto, the unexpected visitor. Michele da Cesena was much stricter than Abbot Bonsignore and expected the Lector to read at every meal while the friars ate in silence, even when visitors were present.

When Umberto had arrived, loudly demanding to see Brother Anselmo, he had been told that the Colour Master was closeted with the Minister General. This confused Umberto, who thought that the Minister had handed over the task of retribution to him. But he could do nothing but fume.

Anselmo had not come to supper after his meeting with Michele da Cesena. The Abbot had told Umberto frankly that there was no room for him to lodge at the friary that night. He had not been best pleased to see Ubaldo the merchant's brother unannounced and the worse for drink on such a difficult day. Now Umberto had to decide whether to ride on to an inn in Assisi or turn back to Gubbio. And he still didn't know how to get Anselmo alone.

The friars went to bed early, a practice that Silvano still found irksome. He went for a few minutes into the chapel and knelt before the casket. There were another one or two friars there, silently praying. He didn't stay long. He couldn't raise the enthusiasm for the holiness of these relics that seemed to come naturally to the real friars.

He wondered whether to go in search of Brother Anselmo but it felt too uncannily like the night Ubaldo had died; he didn't want to tempt Fate by repeating his actions of that day. So Silvano went back to his thin straw mattress and turned restlessly for a few hours before falling asleep.

No one rang the bell any more for the services that took place in the hours of darkness; the friars moved automatically to the chapel to say Matins and Lauds.

But somewhere between Lauds and Prime, Silvano was woken by the unmistakeable whinnying of Moonbeam. He got up immediately, casting his cloak round him against the early morning air and ran to the stables. Moonbeam was restless and frightened, his eyes rolling. And he was not the only one. The other horses in the stable seemed infected with the same fear.

'What is it, boy?' asked Silvano, stroking his horse between the ears. But even that familiar caress did not soothe the animal. Celeste too was fluttering on her perch, though whether alarmed by the horses' behaviour or her by own fears was impossible to tell.

Silvano went out into the yard. The sky was light and there were flocks of birds wheeling erratically, as if they didn't know what direction to take. There was an eerie quality to the light and he suddenly felt afraid. The ground under his feet began to tremble and he fell to his knees. Immediately he knew what had been frightening the animals.

'Earthquake!' he cried, as loudly as he could, running towards the house to waken the brothers. Soon they were all out in the yard, clutching on to each other and to any bit of wall or tree they could find as the ground seemed to slide beneath them. A fissure opened between the chapel and the friars' house – about six inches wide. A hot blast came from the vent.

And then all was still and silent again.

Michele da Cesena took charge and ordered the brothers into the chapel. Many of them had to step across the gap that had opened in the earth.

'It is a sign from the Lord,' he said severely as soon as they were all inside. 'Nothing has been damaged but a great rift has opened between your dwelling and the House of God. It symbolises how the evil of the murders has separated every man here from the love of Our Creator. On your knees, Brothers! And pray as you have never prayed before that the culprit comes forth.'

But again no one stood up to admit the crimes. No one had been moved by the bones of the Blessed Egidio to confess anything and even God's wrath rending the earth brought no admission now.

Silvano cast his eyes warily round the chapel. It had become a routine to check the friars against his mental list and they were all there, even Brother Anselmo. Silvano breathed a sigh of relief; it seemed ridiculous to be glad that no one had died in the night. No one injured by the earthquake and no new murder.

Michele da Cesena and his party were going back to Assisi after breakfast. And the painters had already gone the day before, taking more packages from the colour room in their saddlebags. Silvano liked to think that life would go back to normal in the friary but he knew that couldn't be.

'How is it with you?' he asked Brother Anselmo as they left the chapel together.

'I have been better,' said Anselmo, with a wintry smile. 'The Minister General made it very clear that I am the chief suspect for the murders here – even though I had no reason for violence against Brother Landolfo or Valentino. My history with Ubaldo is enough to darken my name.'

'Did you see his brother last night?'

'Umberto was here?'

'Yes. He was looking for you. And he was drunk.'

'I'm glad I didn't meet him,' said Anselmo. 'Has he gone?'

'I think so,' said Silvano. 'Father Bonsignore said there was nowhere for him to stay.'

The two went into the refectory and broke their fast with a good appetite. Anselmo had missed the evening meal the night before and Silvano was always hungry. While they ate their porage and coarse black bread with honey, they saw the stableman come in and speak to the Abbot. Bonsignore's brow creased with concern.

'Has anyone seen Umberto from Gubbio?' he asked, breaking the silence in the refectory. 'His horse is still in the stable.'

Silvano and Anselmo looked at one another with apprehension. The Abbot too had his fears. He immediately asked the Minister General if he would let the four friars who had come with him from Assisi search the friary for any sign of Umberto. All the Giardinetto friars were to remain in the refectory.

It was an awkward hour. No one wanted to eat or drink much, in case it looked heartless in view of Umberto's possible fate, but the shock of the earthquake had made all the brothers hungrier than usual. Brother Gregorio resumed the lectern and read to them from the Acts of the Apostles. Conversation was impossible.

Eventually, the Assisi friars returned. They had been into every cell and storeroom, even the infirmary, stable and bell tower, but there was no trace of Umberto.

'We shall return to Assisi,' said the Minister General, 'and take the bones of the Blessed Egidio back for burial. The sin is so thick on Giardinetto that not even those holy relics have been able to clear it. And as a safeguard, I shall take Brother Anselmo back with me. He can travel in the carriage with the casket – it might do his soul good.'

And with that he whirled out of the refectory, clearly disappointed with Giardinetto and everyone in it.

Silvano rushed to say goodbye to Anselmo.

'Don't worry,' said his mentor. 'The truth must come out. I can't be judged for what I didn't do. And nor can you. One day we shall both be vindicated.'

Silvano felt more wretched than he had since the night he arrived in Giardinetto. He wished more than anything that he could visit Chiara at the convent, but that was out of the question. It seemed a very long time since he had cared about a pretty blonde in Perugia. And then, as if by thinking of his home town he had conjured him up, he saw a messenger ride into the yard, wearing the Montacuto livery.

It was only minutes before Silvano was called to the Abbot's cell.

'You are free, my son,' said Bonsignore, delighted to have some good news to convey. 'Another man has been convicted of the sheep farmer's murder and you are completely cleared.'

241

'Who?' said Silvano, too dazed to express any gratitude.

The Abbot consulted his message. 'A young man called Gervasio de' Oddini. Do you know him?'

CHAPTER NINETEEN
A Burial

or Silvano, still reeling from the earthquake and the removal of Anselmo, this new turn of events was like being hit by a shovel.

'Gervasio?' he repeated, as if he hadn't heard the Abbot correctly.

'Yes,' said the Abbot. 'Apparently he planned to kill the farmer and marry the widow.'

'Gervasio is going to marry Angelica?' asked Silvano, still dazed.

'Well, he was. Their betrothal had just been announced when he was arrested. But look, here's a letter to you from your father explaining it all.'

Silvano took the package. 'So I am free to go back to Perugia?'

'You may leave whenever you wish,' said Bonsignore kindly. 'I am very happy for you.'

Silvano could not take in such double-edged news. He was free of suspicion at last but his freedom was bought at the cost of the loss of his best friend and of his idealised view of Angelica. And at the same time every sinew of his body and thought in his head was tensed towards the drama at the friary; he could not just wrench them back to his old life at a moment's notice.

243

'I don't want to leave Giardinetto,' he said. 'At least, not for Perugia. But with your permission, Father, I should like to go to Assisi, to see if I can help Brother Anselmo.'

'You have my blessing,' said the Abbot. 'And you had better have this too.' He went to a deep chest in the corner of the room and drew out a bundle.

Silvano took it back to the empty dormitory and unpacked the clothes that belonged to his former life. As he drew the fine muslin shirt over his head, the soft touch of the material felt sensuous and unaccustomed. He saw a red stain on it and started with horror; was that the sheep farmer's blood, shed by Gervasio? No, it was all that was left of Angelica's flower, and almost as repugnant to him. There was a sword in the bundle too and it felt strange in his hand.

His father's messenger was waiting to take a response back to Perugia but Silvano asked him to wait at the friary. The messenger had ridden hard from the city to Giardinetto and was quite happy to cool his heels for the rest of the day. He stretched out in the sunshine by the cemetery gate, quite untroubled by being near the fresh graves or the rift in the earth that gaped like another.

Silvano almost ran down the stairs and out to the stables. Stopping only to ask the stableman to feed and exercise Celeste, he saddled up Moonbeam and turned the horse's head towards Assisi.

From her station at the grille in the convent door, Chiara watched them go. Apart from sleeping and eating, nothing had removed her from her post. Seeing Silvano leave in his nobleman's clothes cast her into despair. He must be going back to Perugia and she would never see him again. And he hadn't even come to say goodbye! But then two thoughts consoled her.

First, if he was no longer dressed as a friar, he no longer needed sanctuary. He must have been cleared of the murder he had been accused of. And then she realised that he didn't have his hawk with him. Surely he would not leave without his hawk? It was agonising not knowing.

'Sister Orsola,' said a quiet voice. It was the Abbess. 'Come away from the door. I think it is time you left us. It has been clear to me for a while now that your heart is not with us in the convent. The outside world is calling you and I think it is time for you to go to Monna Isabella.'

Mother Elena led Chiara to her cell. There she gave her back the clothes she had arrived in and took off her white veil.

'Your hair grows fast,' she remarked, smiling. It had not been cut again since Chiara's arrival in Giardinetto and was a profusion of dark brown curls.

Chiara hung her head. 'I'm sorry, Mother.'

'What for? For having healthy hair?'

'For being no good as a nun. It wasn't my wish to be professed.'

'I know,' said the Abbess. 'And now, thanks to the kindness of Monna Isabella, you have the opportunity to leave the convent with honour and live a life you are more suited to.'

'What must I do?' asked Chiara. 'How will I get to Gubbio?'

'The widow will come for you; I have sent word to her. But put your secular garments on and do what you will till she gets here.'

245

There is nothing to stay for, thought Chiara, bleakly. Suddenly she couldn't wait to get away from Giardinetto, although she had been happier there than she had ever dared to hope.

'Do not grieve,' said Mother Elena. 'You have not disgraced yourself here. Sister Veronica thinks highly of your work in the colour room and I have seen myself that you are a good-hearted and willing girl. In my own opinion, I think your brother was wrong to send you here. But we have enjoyed having your youth and energy in our house.'

'I have enjoyed my time here too, Mother,' said Chiara, and meant it. 'And I shall never forget your kindness. Or Sister Veronica and the other nuns.'

Chiara could scarcely see her way out of the room for tears. She went back to her dormitory and changed back into her old clothes. They felt strange and restricting after the loose grey habit. She unpicked the hem of her petticoat and removed the ruby cross and gold earrings she had sewn in when she left her family home.

As she put them on, she felt that Orsola the grey sister was gone for ever and that Chiara had returned. But then she felt overdressed and gaudy and almost took them off again. She was vigorously brushing her hair when she heard the sound of carriage wheels clattering in the yard.

It was only a minute or two before Isabella burst into the dormitory, flushed and agitated. She was pulled up short by the sight of her young protégée in her secular clothes.

'Chiara,' she said, taking the girl's hands in hers. 'You look lovely.'

'What is the matter?' said Chiara. 'You seem upset.'

'My brother-in-law Umberto sent me a disturbing

message yesterday,' said Isabella. 'He said he was coming to Giardinetto to avenge Ubaldo. When I spoke to his servants, they said that he had been drinking heavily when he set out and had told his steward where to find his will. I came as soon as I could but there isn't a moment to lose. We must visit the friary before I take you home.'

Even as she felt the contagion of fear from her patroness, Chiara felt her heart leap at the word 'home'. Together they went to the Abbess and told her where they were going. For the first time Chiara stepped out of the convent without feeling self-conscious.

But that soon disappeared when they arrived at the friary. All the brothers looked at her the same way: one brief glance of spontaneous admiration, swiftly followed by a downcast look at their feet. Both women were appalled when they saw the vent made in the ground by the earthquake. It seemed as if the wrath of God had fallen on the friary of Giardinetto.

The Abbot was surprised to see them and even more so when he knew why they had come.

'I'm sorry to tell you that Brother Anselmo has been taken away for further questioning in Assisi,' he said.

'But he is unharmed?' asked Isabella. 'My brother-in-law hasn't hurt him?'

The Abbot sighed. 'More bad news, I'm afraid. No, not about Anselmo – he is physically safe. But your brother-in-law has disappeared. He turned up unexpectedly last night, the worse for drink and asking for Brother Anselmo. This morning he had gone but his horse was still here. We searched the friary but there was no sign of him. Everyone fears the worst.'

'But Anselmo is in Assisi?' pressed Isabella, unconcerned

247

about Umberto as long as he had not carried out his implied threat. 'Then we shall go there, Chiara.'

Silvano stabled his horse near the Basilica and hurried into the Lower Church. He found Simone at work as usual in the Chapel of Saint Martin.

'Good heavens!' said the painter admiringly, looking down at him from the scaffolding. 'I wish I'd had you as a model when I was painting Saint Martin as a knight. What a pity I've nearly finished the cycle.' He was gilding the elaborately punched halo of the Saint in the picture of Martin renouncing arms for the religious life, on the right-hand wall.

Silvano looked round the chapel. It was true. The round platform had been lowered to not much higher than ground level and Simone was working on the last picture in the sequence, even though it told one of the early stories. The artist had to work backwards so that visitors to the chapel could read the pictures from the bottom upwards, eventually raising their eyes to the starry heavens on the ceiling.

'Brother Anselmo has been brought back here for further questioning,' Silvano said dully, unable to concentrate on art today. 'The Minister General thinks he killed Umberto.'

'Umberto? There was another killing after we left?'

'No. I mean they don't know. But Umberto has disappeared and Michele da Cesena has really taken against Brother Anselmo.'

Simone jumped down lightly from the platform and wiped his gilding brush carefully before joining Silvano. The painter put his arm round the young man's shoulders.

'Try not to worry. They can't do anything to Brother Anselmo if he is innocent. And I'm guessing you've had good news about your own case, since you are no longer disguised as a friar?'

'Yes,' said Silvano, trying to sound enthusiastic. 'They have found the real killer.'

'But that's wonderful news!' said Simone. 'Congratulations.'

Silvano decided not to tell him why it wasn't such good news; Anselmo was more important. The two men went out into the sunshine, where they bumped into Teodoro, the goldsmith.

'Good day,' said Simone.

'Good day. I hear that the Blessed Egidio made nothing better at Giardinetto.'

'No, I'm afraid not. There were no confessions.'

'They are burying him today,' said Teodoro.

'Who?' said Silvano, suddenly scared.

'The Blessed Egidio, Monsignore,' said Teodoro, looking curiously at the young nobleman and wondering who he was. 'They're putting him down in the crypt. But I reckon they'll have trouble getting the casket down the stairs. It was heavy enough when I made it but the friars who took it to Giardinetto reckon it's heavier now. They say it's because of the load of sin piled on it there.'

Simone and Silvano looked at one another with the same thought.

'Where is the casket now?' asked Simone.

'Back in front of the altar,' said Teodoro, and scratched his head as his two interlocutors took off rapidly up the steps to the Upper Church.

249

Silvano and Simone arrived out of breath and had to compose themselves; they were going to have to ask someone to open the casket.

Angelica was not allowed to see Gervasio but the guards let his father go down to visit him. He was shocked to see how his son had deteriorated in just a few hours. His cheeks were stubbled, his hair unkempt and wild. His eyes were dull and he already looked like a prisoner. Vincenzo could not bear it.

'I have been to Montacuto,' he said.

'How will that help me?' asked Gervasio listlessly.

'I think I can persuade him to help you get away,' said Vincenzo under his breath. 'I think it was Angelica who did the trick. She told him about the baby.'

The effect on Gervasio was impressive. He shook off his lethargy in a moment. 'Baby?' he said stupefied.

'Yes, and that got the Baronessa on your side. I think she will be able to sway him.' Vincenzo had decided to say nothing about Gervasio's life depending on Silvano's mercy.

He could not understand the wan smile that his son gave him.

'Then thank God for the baby,' said Gervasio.

Vincenzo left the prison with heavy heart. He had to get Gervasio out of there before he lost all will to fight for his life. He had gone beyond worrying about his son's guilt, which now seemed certain. All he cared about was getting him out of prison and away to some distant place where he could be safe.

250

It was the Minister General who had to be fetched in the end. He came into the Upper Church with a brow like thunder followed by a friar with iron tools. He barely glanced at Silvano, obviously not recognising him dressed as a noble; he was focused entirely on what they were about to do. Michele da Cesena ordered the great doors to be closed; he did not want any pilgrims to witness the approaching violation.

'Only the seriousness of this case and your reputation with my Order can justify this act,' he said to Simone. 'To open the casket of the Blessed Egidio is an act of desecration I agree to with the utmost reluctance.'

Simone inclined his head. 'I would not ask for it, Father, in any other circumstances.'

The friar with the tools hesitantly approached the casket and crossed himself awkwardly before levering up the lid. Simone and Silvano both helped him lower the heavy marble and crystal lid to the floor and then he tackled the lid of the lead coffin inside. It was soft and easier to open.

As soon as the young friar had pulled the lead lid back, they were all assailed by the smell of death. But it wasn't the ancient and fleshless bones of the Saint's companion that gave it off. The stiff body of Umberto had been squashed into the coffin on top of them and he lay there with a bruised and livid face and staring eyes.

Instinctively, the friar put his sleeve over his face and turned aside, choking.

'So,' said the Minister General, impassive. 'There was another murder at Giardinetto. Brother Giovanni,' he ordered the friar. 'Fetch Brother Anselmo here.'

251

The young friar was happy to leave. But, as he opened the heavy door, Isabella and Chiara slipped in. He tried to stop them entering but Isabella was determined to see the Minister General and pushed past him.

Michele da Cesena was not pleased to see her; he indicated to Simone and Silvano to stop the women coming any nearer to the casket. It was with a shock that Silvano recognised Chiara behind the widow. For an instant they gazed as if seeing each other for the first time. And in a way they were, since they had both cast aside their grey disguises. Seeing the admiration on Silvano's face, Chiara allowed herself to hope.

But the situation was hardly romantic.

'It is him, Madama,' said Simone gently. 'Your brother-in-law's body has been found in the casket. There is no need for you to see him.'

Isabella sat down on one of the benches. She felt only relief that Umberto was gone and had not succeeded in hurting Anselmo.

As if summoned by her thoughts, Brother Anselmo himself entered the Basilica. He walked slowly up towards the party by the altar.

'Well,' said the Minister General. 'It will not surprise you to know that we have found Umberto's body.'

Anselmo crossed himself. 'I am sorry to hear it.'

'Sorry that he is dead or that the body has been found? I imagine you thought this corpse would go undiscovered to the Blessed Egidio's burial?'

'I have not seen Umberto of Gubbio for nearly twenty years,' said Anselmo. 'I did not kill him.' He looked towards Isabella. 'Could the lady not be taken from this dreadful scene?'

The Minister General nodded to Silvano as if noticing him for the first time.

'You, sir, Montacuto is it? Will you see the women safe to the guest house here? And ask Brother Giovanni to send more friars with a proper coffin for this poor man. I shall come to talk to you soon, Madama, and find out about his family.'

Simone went with the others; he was glad to get out of the Upper Church, with its deadly secret.

Isabella seemed loath to leave Anselmo to Michele da Cesena's mercies but Chiara persuaded her. Once outside, the fresh air revived them.

'You are a free man, I see,' said Isabella to Silvano. 'I am happy for you. I just wish the true murderer could be found at Giardinetto too so that Brother Anselmo could also be cleared.'

'Brother Anselmo told us he had some idea of who the murderer is,' said Silvano.

'Who?' asked Isabella, then quickly said, 'No, don't tell me. I am just glad Anselmo is here, even if he is in the clutches of the Minister General. At least he won't be facing someone even more dangerous.'

The women were not at all inclined to wait for Michele da Cesena to interview them, so Simone offered to show them his paintings. They were only too glad to get away from the horrors in the Upper Church and walk down the outside steps to the glowing and gilded jewel box of the chapel below.

'Look, Silvano,' said Chiara. 'Simone has given his falconer a glove.'

It was true. Simone had repainted the fist on the falconer on the extreme left of the picture in which Saint Martin was

253

made a knight. It was a light bluish-grey and almost invisible but it was now there.

Silvano felt absurdly pleased. With all the death and devastation going on around him it shouldn't have mattered. But to have influenced even a tiny detail in the work of a great master like Simone – why, that might endure for centuries, long after he and Chiara and Gervasio and Angelica had all turned to dust.

'You were right, of course, about the glove,' said Simone from behind them. 'I have never kept a hawk myself so I got that wrong.'

'You have rings on the glove where you tie the bird's jesses,' Silvano explained to the women. 'When she comes back to your wrist, you draw the line through them and make a knot. Look, you can see that Simone has painted the line in.'

'That must be hard to do with the bird sitting on your wrist,' said Chiara.

'You have to learn to do it one-handed,' said Silvano.

And then it was as if the world slowed down around him. He could see Isabella's mouth moving as if she spoke, but he heard nothing. The colours and shapes of Simone's pictures swirled slowly round him. Silvano suddenly knew who the murderer was.

'So you still deny having anything to do with the murders at Giardinetto?' The Minister General pressed Brother Anselmo.

'I could do no other, even under torture,' said Anselmo. 'I have never raised my hand in violence to any man. I had no

254

reason to want Umberto of Gubbio dead. But still less those dear brothers who were murdered at the friary.'

'I should like to believe you,' said the Minister General. 'Your record as a religious is impeccable. But in your secular life before you joined the Order, you did have reason to hate the merchant Ubaldo. You are the only friar with any motive for any of the murders. Umberto certainly believed that you had killed his brother.'

'But he must have thought I had done it in order to make Monna Isabella free to marry me,' said Anselmo. 'And to do that I would have to give up my professed vows as a friar. I have no intention of doing that.'

'That is true,' said Isabella.

The two friars turned; they had not heard her come back up into the Upper Church.

'I asked you to take the ladies to the guest house,' said the Minister General to Silvano, with some asperity.

'We have found out something important,' said Silvano.

But Isabella interrupted him.

'I came to Brother Anselmo and asked him to leave the Order and come back to me,' said Isabella, her eyes fixed on Anselmo's face. 'He would not. He said that his life was dedicated to the Church and he would not break his vows. Would he have done that if he had killed my husband to be with me?'

Michele da Cesena did not answer straightaway. But then he simply asked, 'Who else could it be?'

Silvano stepped forward eagerly. 'Forgive me, Father,' he said. 'But I think I know. It's . . .'

Anselmo stopped him. 'Don't say it,' he said. 'Too many people have suffered from unjust suspicions. We need absolute proof.' He turned to the Minister General. 'Let me go back to Giardinetto with this young man and confront the suspect. If it is as I believe, we can bring him to justice here.'

'But that is much too dangerous,' exclaimed Isabella. 'Whoever it is has killed four people already. Surely he will try to kill you too if you accuse him?'

'I shall be with him,' said Silvano. 'And I am armed.'

'Don't let them go,' implored Chiara. 'At least not alone. Send some others of your friars to protect them.'

Michele da Cesena hesitated. At last he knelt and prayed before the altar, in front of the bones of the Saint's companion and the newly dead body of Umberto. When he got to his feet, a group of friars was entering the church with a wooden coffin.

'Go,' he said to Anselmo. 'I believe you are innocent of any crime. Go and take this young man with you. And bring me back the murderer.'

CHAPTER TWENTY

Dead White

he messenger from Perugia stretched and yawned. He had spent a pleasant day doing nothing. A nice old friar had brought him bread and cheese at midday and he had lain in the sun for several hours. When it got too hot, he had transferred himself to the shade of some yew trees and slept on, oblivious of his surroundings.

As the friars trooped out of the chapel after saying Nones, he woke up. If the young master didn't give him a message soon, he would be hard pressed to make it make to Perugia before nightfall. But, even as he had the thought, Silvano came back. The big grey horse clattered into the yard, followed by a lady's carriage.

So there is another woman in the case, thought the messenger, who had heard rumours about Angelica. And indeed Silvano handed down a very pretty young girl from the carriage. Perhaps those were her parents, that handsome woman and the rather ugly man with the down-turned mouth? Silvano was lucky the girl took after her mother in that case. But there was also a friar; maybe the young master had rushed off to Assisi to get married? The messenger settled down again with his back against a tree. If that were the case, young Silvano would have a long letter to write to his father.

There had been little conversation in the carriage on its way back from Assisi. Simone had talked to Isabella about art and Chiara had sometimes joined in. Brother Anselmo had listened in silence. They all knew that what they really wanted to talk about was unspeakable. Silvano rode alongside the carriage and cast many a longing look through the window. It would be good to settle the matter of the murders once and for all, thought Anselmo, and let these young people get on with their lives. Yet, if he was right, he was taking all of them into danger.

Isabella had insisted that they should accompany Anselmo back to Giardinetto but now that they were here, she did not know what to do. She didn't want to let Anselmo out of her sight. He settled the matter by taking her and Chiara to the Abbot.

'You are back!' said Father Bonsignore, delighted. 'Does that mean the Minister General has acquitted you?'

'He no longer believes me responsible for the murders, Father,' said Anselmo.

'But that is splendid news! You and young Silvano cleared on the same day.'

'There is bad news too,' said Anselmo. 'We found Umberto. His body was in the casket with the holy relics.'

Bonsignore's good humour quickly evaporated. 'Another murder,' he said quietly. 'And the bones of the Blessed Egidio desecrated! But if the Minister General has let you go, perhaps he knows now who is responsible for all these deaths?'

'No, he doesn't know,' said Anselmo. 'But we do,' indicating Silvano. 'At least we think so. We should like to speak to him now but you must keep Monna Isabella and Sister Orsola, I mean Chiara, safe here with you.'

Before the Abbot had time to ask anything else, the three men left the cell.

'We shall go first to the colour room,' said Anselmo. 'That would be natural and will not put the murderer on his guard.'

The friars and novices were still working on their porphyry slabs; Anselmo had been absent for only a day and had left them tasks to get on with. Matteo looked up at their entrance and smiled to see Silvano no longer in his novice's robes.

'I'm going back to Perugia, Matteo,' said Silvano. 'They have found out who really killed the man there and I am free to go home without a stain on my character.'

There was a little smatter of applause in the colour room. Silvano had been a popular worker there.

Anselmo was showing Simone some cinnabar so Silvano sat down at the long table; they were obviously not going to confront the murderer straightaway. He felt the package from his father, which he had thrust into his jerkin and forgotten about. He pulled it out now and read the letter.

Gervasio, Angelica and Tommaso the sheep farmer now seemed to him like characters in a story – a tale told on a winter evening perhaps. It all seemed so far away compared with the beautiful girl who had smiled at him from the carriage window and the moment of revelation he had experienced in Saint Martin's chapel.

He still didn't know if Gervasio had planned to incriminate him in Tommaso's murder or just stolen his dagger because it was better than his own, as he had apparently told the Baron. It was of course inexcusable to kill a man but he could imagine something of the desperation that drove Gervasio to do it. Ever since they had been boys, the

259

older friend had been aware of his family's lesser fortune and the fact that he was a youngest son and not his father's heir.

And now he was going to marry Angelica and become a father himself – at least if Silvano said the word. Silvano did not know if his friend deserved to escape execution but he did know that he had seen enough deaths at Giardinetto not to want to be responsible for another. And he wasn't jealous about Angelica any more. His ideal woman was no longer plump and blonde and rosy. His idea of the perfect woman was a real person, now drinking herbal tea with the Abbot.

Silvano put the letter away with a secret smile. Perhaps he would be a father himself not long after Gervasio? He could hardly imagine it; it seemed a world away. He suddenly remembered the messenger. He should go and find him and send him back to Perugia.

He slipped out of the colour room and soon found his father's servant in the cemetery. The man jumped up brushing grass off his livery.

'Yes, master?' he said.

'Please tell my father that I give my assent to the question he asked me.'

'Is that all?' said the man. 'No letter for me to take back?'

'Not today,' said Silvano. 'I shall probably be home myself soon enough. Just tell my father what I said and take my love to him and my mother and sisters.'

He watched as the man headed towards the stables. And then he saw Brother Fazio going towards the colour room.

260

'Ah, the painter,' said Brother Fazio. 'How is the gilding going?'

'Very well,' said Simone. 'And how goes the Word of God?'

'It progresses slowly,' said Fazio. 'Brother Anselmo, can you let me have some verde azzurro?'

'Certainly,' said Anselmo, going over to his jars. 'Have you been using your lead-white today, Brother?'

'No,' said Fazio. 'I prepared the page yesterday. I am ready to illuminate it now. Though I shall not get much done before Vespers.'

'I am glad you have not,' said Anselmo, escorting Fazio towards the door with the jar in his hand. 'I think the bianco di piombo is not good for you.'

It happened in a flash. As Silvano stepped back through the door, he saw Brother Fazio drop the jar and then the flash of a blade.

'Quick,' Silvano shouted as he sped towards Brother Anselmo. 'Fazio is the murderer. He has a dagger!'

But it was too late. Fazio had raised the blade and caught Anselmo in the forearm he had flung up to save himself. The two men fell to the floor, struggling with the knife and in a moment everyone else in the colour room was trying to pull them apart. Fazio fought like the madman he was and there was a cry ending in a gurgle. Blood was spreading on the floor of the colour room.

'I can't bear this,' said Isabella. 'We must go and see what is going on.'

261

'Has Brother Anselmo shared his knowledge with you?' asked the Abbot. 'Do you know whom he suspects?'

'He shares nothing with me,' said Isabella bitterly. 'I am nothing to him now. But I still can't sit here while he might be getting himself killed!'

There was an agitated knock on the door and Matteo the novice burst in.

'Please come to the colour room straightaway, Father,' he panted.

'What is that on your habit?' said Isabella horrified. 'Is it some red pigment?'

Matteo looked at his stained garment and shook his head. He was clearly in a state of shock. They did not wait to ask him any more but hurried from the cell.

They reached the colour room and saw Anselmo sitting propped up on one of the grinders' benches. The sleeve of his habit was rolled up and Silvano was staunching the blood from a deep wound with strips torn from his own shirt. Brother Fazio lay on the floor, very still.

'Father,' said Anselmo. 'Michele da Cesena was right. I am a killer.' His eyes rolled up into his head and he slid down the bench.

Isabella gave a cry and ran to him. Chiara looked at the still body of the Illuminator on the ground.

'Is he dead?' she asked Silvano.

He nodded. 'He tried to kill Anselmo. We all did everything we could to separate them but in the commotion, Fazio got hurt.'

'More than hurt,' said Bonsignore, who had turned the body over and now closed Brother Fazio's eyes.

'Brother Anselmo was fighting for his life,' Silvano pleaded with the Abbot. 'Fazio had a dagger and was trying to kill him. It was a fierce struggle and Anselmo wrested the dagger from him but Fazio wouldn't give up. I think he fell on the blade as much as Anselmo wielded it.'

'The wound is just under his ear where one of the great blood vessels lies,' said the Abbot, examining the body. 'It was bound to be fatal.'

Isabella was clasping Anselmo in her arms. Silvano came and put his round Chiara.

'Are you all right?' he asked.

She nodded, but she was trembling. She hadn't seen any of the other bodies since Ubaldo the merchant's. They had shielded her from the sight of his brother's in the Basilica. It didn't seem real now, with Brother Fazio stretched out on the floor in a pool of blood and Anselmo unconscious and bleeding.

Brother Rufino came bustling in; Matteo had fetched him from the infirmary.

'Let me see, let me see,' he said, so scandalised by what Isabella was doing that he almost pushed her out of the way. 'Brothers,' he beckoned to some of the friars once he had looked at Anselmo, 'help me get him to the infirmary. He will be all right. No vital organs or blood vessels involved.'

❧

It was hours before the friary had any sense of coming back to order. Abbot Bonsignore had sent the stableman with an urgent message to Michele da Cesena in Assisi. He had himself gone to the Abbess to tell her that the weeks of terror were at an end. And he had insisted that Brother Fazio's

263

body should be laid in front of the altar in the chapel.

'He was a brother, one of us, and whatever his crimes, he will soon stand before a higher judge than the Minister General,' he said.

And then he set a team of younger friars to scrubbing and mopping the flagstones of the colour room.

While Bonsignore busied himself with putting his house to rights, the others all stayed in the infirmary, in defiance of Brother Rufino's wishes. Anselmo was conscious but very pale. Rufino had absolutely refused to let Isabella help him, so she sat in a chair by the window, with Chiara by her side.

Silvano would not leave Anselmo's bedside. He kept seeing the scene in the colour room replaying itself in his head, this time with a different outcome. Fazio's knife rose and fell and landed, not on Anselmo's arm but in his heart.

Silvano shook his head to get the image out. It was replaced by a swarm of questions. And he was not alone. As soon as the Abbot joined them in the infirmary and had assured himself that Anselmo was going to live, he asked for an explanation.

'How did you know it was Brother Fazio? And why did he do it?'

'I had suspected for some time that he was poisoning himself with some of the strong substances he had been working with,' replied Anselmo. 'Particularly the bianco di piombo. But there was also the arsenikon in the orpiment and realgar he loved to use.'

'You mean that all the materials of an illuminator are dangerous enough to drive him mad?' asked the Abbot.

It was Simone who answered. 'Many are to be handled

only with care. Dragonsblood and even vermilion contain poisons.'

'And he was devoted to what he called "the two kings" – he told us himself,' said Silvano.

'Two kings?' asked Bonsignore.

'Zarnikh and sandarach, as the Persians call them,' said Simone. 'Orpiment and realgar, as we know them. They are a brilliant yellow and red but no good for us mural painters because they turn black on walls. And they do contain arsenikon.'

'That's what killed Brother Landolfo,' said Rufino. 'Brother Fazio must have put some in his food. He sat next to him, remember.'

'It is not outright dangerous unless consumed in a large quantity,' said Simone. 'Orpiment is even used as a physick for sparrowhawks, Silvano, when they are afflicted with an ailment. But Landolfo must have ingested a great deal in a short time for him to die so quickly.'

'He did die quickly,' said Silvano.

'Then why didn't Brother Fazio die from all these poisons?' asked Chiara.

'Because he ingested them over time, in quantities so small they did not kill him,' explained Simone. 'But it is as Brother Anselmo said, prolonged exposure to lead-white will bring about all sorts of ailments, even without the two kings of colour – fits and eventually paralysis.'

'Brother Fazio did have fits,' confirmed Rufino. 'I have treated him myself – with mugwort.'

'And he made all his lead-white himself,' added Silvano. 'He showed me the shed where he did it.'

'He was well known for it,' said the Abbot. 'And he liked

to show new brothers how it was made.'

'Really?' said Simone. 'But it smells so bad.'

'Fazio had no sense of smell,' said Anselmo. 'I think that was why he didn't realise that he was being exposed to so much danger.'

'I don't understand why he went mad instead of just becoming ill,' said Isabella.

'Madness is an illness too,' said Brother Rufino. 'And with such a mixture of poisons, it is not surprising that it affected his brain.'

'But I still don't understand why he killed my husband,' said Isabella. 'Or any of the others.'

'I think he was intensely jealous of me,' said Anselmo, 'because he considered himself to be an expert of all manner of colours, and then when I came to Giardinetto the Abbot decided to set up a colour room and appointed me Colour Master. I thought that Brother Fazio had come to terms with it, but his initial resentment must have been fuelled by the poisons he was ingesting.'

'So he wanted suspicion to fall on you?' asked Bonsignore. 'But that means he knew of your past, er, association with Monna Isabella.'

'It was only Fazio's sense of smell that was impaired,' said Anselmo grimly. 'He had a very acute sense of hearing and I think it was his habit to listen at doors. That way he knew what I had told you when I first came here, about my secular life and the reason for my profession as a friar. And I think, as a bonus, he must have overheard you tell Brother Ranieri why Silvano was under our protection.'

'Then why was Brother Landolfo his second victim?' asked Silvano.

'I think,' said Anselmo, 'that Fazio told Landolfo what he had heard. That was how the rumours about Silvano first circulated in the friary.'

'I certainly heard it from Landolfo,' said Rufino. 'Though he didn't tell me where he had picked it up.'

'Then, when all the friars were suspicious of Silvano, Fazio killed Landolfo so that he wouldn't reveal the rumours had started with him,' said Anselmo. 'I think he was quite mad by then. He didn't care if it was Silvano or myself under suspicion.'

'But how did he administer the poison?' asked Rufino.

'It would have been easy enough to conceal the poison in his sleeve,' said Anselmo. 'And he always sat next to Landolfo.'

'This is terrible,' said Silvano. 'If I hadn't come here, Brother Landolfo would still be alive!'

'Don't forget I said it was jealousy of me that prompted the first murder,' said Anselmo. 'And you know there was some suspicion of you, Silvano, after the first murder, because of the way it was done.

'He was happy to make known the information about your past but he also spread around my history too. Very effectively, as it happened, because the Minister General and Umberto both believed I had killed Ubaldo – and possibly some of the brothers here too.'

There was silence and Silvano saw that Brother Rufino looked a little embarrassed. Bonsignore thought he would have to hear many confessions in the coming weeks.

'Then why did he kill Brother Valentino?' the Abbot asked.

'As to why, I don't know,' admitted Anselmo. 'Fazio had been working with dragonsblood that day and I think he was becoming more and more deranged. Some quite small comment of Valentino's might have incensed him and made him his next victim. But it was young Silvano here who realised how he did it.'

'I was talking to Ser Simone about falconry,' explained Silvano. 'And about how you have to tie the bird to the glove one-handed. I remembered that Fazio was equally skilled with both hands. He could have rung the Vespers bell with one hand while stringing Valentino up by his belt with the other.'

'Not if Valentino were conscious, surely?' said Rufino.

'I don't think he was,' said the Abbot. 'You remember the bruise on his forehead? I think Brother Fazio was waiting for Valentino in the bell tower and knocked him out straight-away.'

'So it was Fazio who rang the bell and then slipped into the chapel,' said Rufino. 'And Brother Valentino was already dead.'

'He must have been enormously strong,' said Simone doubtfully. 'To string a man up single-handed and that man a dead weight.'

'He was very strong,' said the Abbot.

'And he had to ring the bell at the same time,' said Silvano. 'Because the friars knew it was Valentino's turn and might have seen him going towards the chapel. Any delay and they might have looked into the bell tower.'

'He must have tied his own belt to the beam already and then, when Valentino was dead, taken his belt off him to put round his own waist,' said Anselmo, with a shudder.

'A madman can be very logical and ruthless,' said the Abbot.

268

'But what about Umberto?' asked Isabella. 'Do you know the how and the why of that murder?'

'It was another attempt to incriminate me, I'm afraid,' said Anselmo. 'I didn't see Umberto that night. I was unwilling to go into supper after the questioning the Minister General had given me. But I gather Umberto was drunk and openly seeking me. I expect Fazio thought if he hid the body in the casket, it would be found here and look bad for me. He didn't know I was to be ordered to Assisi and that the casket would also go there unopened.'

'But how did he kill him?' insisted Isabella. She had got up and drawn near to the bed as the exposure of Fazio's crimes had gone on.

'He was hit on the head and then sealed in the coffin,' said Simone. 'Since Umberto was drunk, it must have been quick.'

'And Fazio took Umberto's dagger,' said Silvano.

Rufino brought the weapon over from the table where it had been laid aside when taken from Fazio's neck. It was clean now.

'I never thought to have to handle this weapon again,' he said. 'Either it is Ubaldo's or the brother's dagger was identical. See the "U" and the family crest.'

Even Isabella couldn't say which it was.

'What will happen now?' asked Chiara.

'As soon as I have word from the Minister General, we shall bury Brother Fazio,' said the Abbot.

'What, in the cemetery next to the friars he killed?' asked Simone.

'Certainly,' said Father Bonsignore. 'He was a friar too. And, though it was not a case of possession by devils, Fazio was just as much changed from his true self by the poisons

269

that inhabited his body.'

'I agree,' said Anselmo. 'He was a good man, undermined by jealousy, whose mind was warped by the materials he worked with. The real Brother Fazio would never have committed murder.'

'You friars amaze me,' said Simone, shaking his head. 'Your capacity for forgiveness is endless.'

'What shall you do, Ser Simone?' asked Silvano.

'I shall go back to Assisi and finish my paintings,' said Simone. 'I have to be back in Siena for St Luke's Day. Every member of the Artists' Guild must carry his candle to the Cathedral on that day. Pietro and I must both be there but he will have to come back. His work in Assisi is barely begun.'

'It will soon be October,' said Rufino. 'The nights are drawing in.'

They looked instinctively towards the window, where the sky was beginning to darken.

'I cannot get back to Assisi tonight though,' said Simone, frowning. 'I came in Monna Isabella's carriage in the heat of the moment, with no thought of how I would return.'

'Please lodge with us tonight,' said the Abbot. 'I'm sure that the Minister General will come in his carriage tomorrow and you can travel back with him.'

'At least we can all sleep peacefully in our beds tonight,' said Brother Rufino. 'It will be the first such night for a long time.'

'It is too late for me to set out for Perugia tonight too,' said Silvano. 'May I spend one last night on my straw mattress in the dormitory, Father?'

'Of course,' said Bonsignore.

'We, on the other hand,' said Isabella, 'shall go back to

270

Gubbio. You know that Chiara is coming to live with me?' she asked the company in general. 'Please feel free to visit us, if your work ever brings you to Gubbio, Ser Simone.' But her eyes went to Anselmo and Silvano. 'I expect to see you as soon as life has returned to normal here, Father Bonsignore. I am sure that there will be papers for you to witness.'

Silvano walked the two women to the stables.

'May I come and see you in Gubbio?' he asked Chiara. 'I have so much to tell you.'

She looked towards Isabella, her new protector and chaperone. The older woman smiled at her.

'I should like that,' said Chiara. She suddenly felt shy of this young nobleman with whom she had spent so many easy hours when they were both dressed as novices.

'The true murderer has been found in Perugia, as well as in Giardinetto,' said Silvano. 'And it was my best friend Gervasio,' he added bitterly.

In the infirmary Brother Anselmo was protesting that he was well enough to come to supper in the refectory.

'And what will you do, friend?' asked Simone. 'Will you return to the colour room when your arm is healed?'

'You are worried about your supplies?' said Anselmo. 'I don't know what is going to happen. I shall have to wait and see what the Minister General says to me. All I know now is that I should like to retire to bed and sleep for a hundred hours.'

271

CHAPTER TWENTY-ONE
A Merlin for a Lady

he Baronessa Margarethe da Montacuto was in her little parlour when the sound of running feet and excited barking reached her ears. Perhaps it is another message from Silvano, she thought, jumping up and dropping her grospoint. But it was better than a message. Her son himself burst in, dishevelled and dirty but sound and full of life, followed by his deliriously happy hound.

'Madre,' he said, lifting the Baronessa off her feet and swinging her round.

'Silvano!' she said, breathless. 'Oh my darling boy! Are you all right? Your hair needs cutting. And whatever has happened to your shirt?'

'I used it to bind a man's wounds, mother,' he said truthfully, putting her down and looking at her soberly.

The Baronessa clutched at her throat. 'Mon Dieu!' she said. 'Where have you been that such dangerous things happen?'

'I left Perugia because of such a danger, remember? But don't worry, mother. I have been safe,' said Silvano. 'Though others have died.'

'You are different,' said Margarethe, with a mother's perceptions. 'I think you have come back a man from wherever you have been.'

272

Just then Silvano's two sisters came running in. They threw themselves on his back, screamed at the state of his clothes and protested that he was growing a rough beard.

'I must change my clothes and brush my hair before presenting myself to my father,' said Silvano, laughing.

'And put on some cologne,' said Margherita. 'You smell of horse.'

'And shave your face,' added Vittoria.

'Too late,' said the Baron, easing his bulk into the little parlour. 'I'll take him as he is.'

And he clasped Silvano in his arms.

It was difficult to persuade the Council of Perugia to show clemency towards Gervasio. Only the Baron's and Silvano's pleas, joined with those of the victim's widow could have done it. The evidence that Tommaso had been acting illegally as a moneylender was also seen as mitigation. After many anxious hours for the de' Oddini family and Angelica, the sentence was commuted to exile and a huge fine. The fine was to be paid jointly to Tommaso's widow and the state but the money for both fines had of course to come from Angelica herself, since Gervasio had none of his own.

'So you are not to have any punishment at all?' Silvano said to Gervasio when he had been released. He had come to the gaol to confront his old friend and was waiting for him outside. 'Even the money you pay is given by your wife-to-be and half of it comes back to you.'

'I don't blame you for being angry,' said Gervasio, biting his lip.

'Angry?' said Silvano. 'I am not angry. I am just relieved to be back home.' And he surprised himself by realising that this was true.

'I didn't mean them to think it was you, you know,' said Gervasio.

'Then why did you steal my dagger?' asked Silvano.

'It all happened so quickly,' said Gervasio. 'I took it the night before when we walked back from the tavern. I'd always envied you that dagger of yours. I don't think I really meant to kill him, you know. But I was desperate about the money and the dagger made me feel I had some control. I meant only to threaten Tommaso but when I saw him in the street the next day, I had a moment of madness. The dagger was in my belt and I just knew I could rid myself of my problems with one blow.'

'But you left my dagger in the body,' said Silvano. 'You must have known I would be suspected of the murder.'

'I didn't mean to,' said Gervasio. 'But you came along the street! I couldn't believe it. I had only seconds before you saw me and, to my shame, I took Tommaso's list, which would have implicated me, and left the dagger . . .'

'Which implicated me,' Silvano finished for him.

'You must hate me,' said Gervasio.

'I should do,' admitted Silvano. 'But I have seen enough of hatred and killing.'

They were silent for a while, each wrapped in his own thoughts.

'It isn't true that I go unpunished, though,' said Gervasio. 'You know that Angelica is pregnant? Well, the child is not mine, even though my father thinks it is. I have never lain with her. I shall have to bring up the sheep farmer's sprog as my son and heir.'

'Perhaps it will be a daughter and she will favour the mother?' suggested Silvano.

'You are not even angry that I am going to marry your . . . the woman you admire?'

Silvano laughed. 'Not at all,' he said. 'All respect to your betrothed, but I do not admire her any more. My heart is given to another.'

Gervasio looked at him curiously. He owed his life to Silvano and the younger man had changed. He could no longer patronise him.

'I shall miss the city,' Gervasio said, as they walked together towards the Platea Magna where their adventure had begun months before. Again they walked past the Franciscan church. 'But at least I don't have to fear being sent to join the grey brothers any more.'

'It wouldn't have been that bad you know,' said Silvano seriously. 'There are worse things than living in a friary.'

Chiara had settled into Isabella's home as if she had been born there. She was soon a great favourite with the children. The boys were unthreatened by their mother's affection for her and Francesca was thrilled to have an older girl in the house – and such a pretty one.

The two women threw themselves into Isabella's new business as a merchant. There was one awkward moment when Bernardo came to get some orders from the house and met his sister again for the first time since he had left her in Giardinetto.

He scarcely recognised her in her fine light green velvet gown but she saw his glance fly to the ruby and pearl cross and she knew he was thinking: so she did take it with her!

But he was nothing but polite and Isabella said he was proving to be a good manager. The greatest challenge was the competition from Angelica's new business, which was thriving. But then one day the widow of Perugia was again announced and shown this time into Isabella's office.

Chiara was there too as the women had been working over the accounts. They were both wearing long aprons and had ink-stains on their fingers.

They look happy, thought Angelica wistfully. She had come on an errand that made her heartsore in spite of the prospect of her married life with Gervasio. She had enjoyed being a businesswoman for the short time it had lasted.

'Monna Angelica,' said Isabella. 'Welcome. Come and sit down.'

Her sharp eyes had taken in that her rival was a lot plumper than on her last visit.

Chiara saw only a voluptuous fair-haired woman, dressed elegantly in black mourning.

'Chiara, dear,' said Isabella. 'Will you ring for some tisane for our visitor? Something suitable for her delicate condition.'

'Oh,' said Chiara. 'Of course. Excuse me, Madama. Please have my seat.'

How terribly sad, she thought. She expects a child but from her black dress her husband must be dead.

'You have heard of our visitor, I'm sure,' said Isabella when the servant had come and gone. 'Monna Angelica also has a trading station in Gubbio, since her husband sadly passed away in the summer.'

276

'Angelica,' stammered Chiara, 'of Perugia?'

It was Isabella's turn to be surprised. 'You know each other?' she said.

'Your companion has the advantage of me,' said Angelica, puzzled. 'I'm afraid I know nothing of her.'

Chiara was now blushing deeply. 'It is just that Silvano mentioned you,' she said. She could not take her eyes off the pretty widow; so this was the woman Silvano had been in love with!

'Silvano da Montacuto?' said Angelica. 'You know him? He was suspected of my husband's murder at first, you know. So he was hiding in Gubbio all the time! But that's incredible – I might have bumped into him at any time on my business trips here.'

Neither Chiara nor Isabella felt that Angelica needed to be disabused of that idea. Chiara longed to ask if Angelica had seen Silvano recently but she felt too jealous to ask.

'Even Gervasio didn't know where he was, you know,' Angelica confided to the two women. 'He'll be so amazed when I tell him. We are going to be married, you know, Gervasio and I. Young de' Oddini – he came with me the last time I was here.'

'I remember,' said Isabella. 'Congratulations.'

Silvano's friend, Gervasio, thought Chiara. The one who really killed her husband. What an extraordinary woman!

'The thing is,' said Angelica. 'We are going to leave Umbria and set up house elsewhere. Maybe somewhere further south. Perhaps Rome – that would be elegant, wouldn't it?'

'You are leaving?' said Isabella. 'But why, when you have just set up such a successful business here?'

'Oh, you know, family matters,' said Angelica. She couldn't hope to keep Gervasio's disgrace a secret from these women for ever, not if they knew Silvano, but at least she didn't have to tell them about it herself. 'The point is, I wondered if you'd like to buy me out?'

Michele da Cesena did allow Brother Fazio to be buried at Giardinetto. Umberto, of course, was carried to Gubbio where in time he was buried in the family vault built for his brother in the Cathedral. The Minister General carried out another purification service himself in the friary and a second one in the convent of Saint Clare, just to be sure. There was no question of the nuns and friars attending a service together this time, not with Michele da Cesena as celebrant.

Father Bonsignore was to keep his office of Abbot. The Minister General acknowledged that there was nothing he could have done in the face of Fazio's madness and cunning. And when all this was settled, he sent for Brother Anselmo.

'It seems that I was wrong about you,' were Michele da Cesena's first words to the Colour Master. Anselmo bowed his head in acknowledgment; he imagined that the Minister General did not often apologise.

'The evidence looked bad against you, but if you hadn't come to me with your suspicions in Assisi, there might have been more deaths in Giardinetto.'

'There were deaths enough,' said Anselmo. 'And the last one should have been avoided.'

'Ah, yes,' said the Minister General. 'We must speak of that. How is your wound?'

'It is healing well, thank you,' said Anselmo, who still bore his arm in a sling. 'I have done little colour-grinding in the past week. But Brother Rufino thinks I will recover full use of my arm.'

'That is good to know. But what shall you use that arm for in future, Brother?'

This was what Anselmo had been dreading. 'I await your decision, Father,' he said, humbly.

'You have shed blood in the friary,' said Michele da Cesena. 'Not on the sanctified ground of the chapel like Fazio, it's true. But within the walls of a religious house dedicated to peace and to the teachings of our blessed founder, Saint Francis, you killed a man.'

'I killed a man,' agreed Anselmo.

'You do not try to justify yourself?' asked Michele da Cesena. 'You do not remind me that you acted in self-defence or to disarm a murderer?'

'Both you and I know that it makes no difference,' said Anselmo wearily. 'What matters is that I did it, not why.'

'Do you want to remain in the Order?'

'You know that I cannot, Father.'

'Then I release you from your vows as a professed friar,' said the Minister General. 'Take the amount of time you need to make your arrangements, but you must leave Giardinetto.'

'What did you make of her?' asked Isabella when Angelica had left.

'I thought she was very pretty,' said Chiara in a small voice.

279

'She is not as pretty as you,' said Isabella.

'Really?'

'Really. And I'm sure Silvano thinks so too.'

'Then why hasn't he come?' asked Chiara. 'He said he would come and he hasn't.'

'I don't imagine that his family would have been keen to let him go again so soon. And perhaps it took time to sort out everything in connection with Tommaso's murder?'

'But that is settled now,' protested Chiara. 'You heard her. She is getting married to Silvano's friend, even though he did kill her husband, and they will run away together to start a new life.'

'And we shall have a second wool business in Gubbio.'

'You are right,' said Chiara, shaking her curls as if to shake all thought of Silvano out of her head. 'We should go back to our books. Everything is going to get much more complicated.'

'For my part, I hope Silvano doesn't come too soon,' said Isabella gently. 'I don't want to lose you when I have only just welcomed you into my home.'

Chiara squeezed her hand affectionately.

'What would I do without you?' said Isabella. 'It will be some years before my children are old enough to be rational companions.'

'Perhaps you will marry again?' said Chiara. 'Not that I am planning to leave you, of course.'

'Of course,' said Isabella. 'But no, I shan't marry again. There was only one man to tempt me and he is beyond my reach. I shall devote myself to my business and my family. And maybe one day, when I am old, I shall enter a convent myself. What do you say to that? Do you think Abbess Elena would have me?'

Her eyes were bright and there was a catch in her voice.

'I'll go with you,' said Chiara impulsively, 'if I'm still living here and unmarried. I'm not afraid of the convent any more. I hated the very idea when I was forced to enter it but now I think that, if you did it by choice, you could live a happy and useful life there.'

'Excuse me, Madama,' said a servant, knocking on the open door. 'There is a gentleman to see you. He wouldn't give his name.'

'I am popular today,' said Isabella, straightening her dress and taking off her apron. 'Show him to the parlour. Will you tidy up for me here, Chiara?'

Her fingers were still covered with ink, her hair escaping from her cap of black lace, but Monna Isabella had no idea who her visitor was. And even when she entered the parlour it took a while for her to recognise the man sitting there. He was no longer wearing his friar's robes.

'Anselmo?' she said doubtfully.

'Domenico, once more,' he said, coming forward but stopping short of taking her hand. 'I have left my Order.'

'You are no longer a friar?'

'No longer even a priest,' said Anselmo smiling wryly. 'In fact, I am nothing. I must think about getting some new work. Perhaps I should go as apprentice to Ser Simone in Siena and grind his colours for him?'

'I don't understand,' said Isabella, sinking into her chair. 'Why did you leave the Order?' She hardly dared to hope that it was for her sake.

'I knew it really the minute that blade entered Brother Fazio's neck,' said Anselmo. 'That was the moment I ceased

281

to be a friar, not when Michele da Cesena released me from my vows.'

'Is it a rule of the Franciscans then?' asked Isabella. She felt nothing but bleakness in her heart. Domenico was leaving the Order but not because he loved her. He was taking away the last bar to their being together but he would then leave for ever. This was the last time she would see him.

'No, not a hard and fast one,' said Anselmo. 'But it was as clear for me as if I had lost my faith. I can no longer minister to my fellow man.'

'But you are not a murderer,' protested Isabella. 'You killed a murderer. It was an accident but by doing it you rid the world of a very great evil. Why should you be punished for that?'

'It sounds as if you would like me to remain a friar,' said Anselmo. 'I thought that was the opposite of what you wanted.'

'What I wanted?' said Isabella. 'When has it ever mattered what I wanted? I was torn from my true love and made to marry a man I didn't care for. I was forced to be a good wife to him, to bear his children, entertain his friends, turn a blind eye to his mistresses. And then a mad friar did an evil deed and took that husband's life away. At the same time I found my old love again but did he want me? No, he was married to another now – the Church!'

'Hush,' said Anselmo. He took her hands. 'I have nothing to offer you, no wealth, no job, no position in society. I am an ex-religious and ex-scholar who has killed a man. I have no right to lay my heart at your feet.'

'Your heart?' said Isabella.

'People would say it was for your money, because you are

282

a rich widow. And I could not bear to be thought such a parasite.'

'What are you saying? That if it were not for what gossips would say, you would offer yourself to me? That you love me?'

'I have always loved you,' said Anselmo simply. 'A love like mine doesn't alter because of circumstances. But as a friar I could not allow myself to think about you. I had to lock that love up as if in an iron chest and bind it with chains. But I am a friar no longer.'

'Why did you come here?'

'To see you once more. With the eyes of one who is now free to love you.'

'And free to marry me?' said Isabella softly.

'I would not ask that of you,' said Anselmo. 'It is too much to expect that you would take me back after what was said at our last meeting.'

Isabella smiled for the first time since she had entered the parlour.

'Then it seems as if I must do the asking myself,' she said. 'Domenico of Gubbio, will you do me the honour of being my husband?'

Chiara couldn't think who could be taking up so much of Isabella's time. She had been to supervise the children's bedtime, heard their prayers and ordered supper for herself and the lady of the house. Since she couldn't get on with the accounts on her own, Chiara now had nothing to do.

It was a balmy night, even though late in September, and

283

Chiara went to the window and looked out into the street. At first she thought she was seeing things. A grey stallion was coming along the street under her window, ridden by a very elegant young man in a grey velvet jerkin and a feathered hat. On his pommel sat a hawk.

But it couldn't be Silvano! Young men, even as high born as the heir of Baron da Montacuto, did not take their hawks when they went visiting. She rubbed her eyes and looked again. The horse and man had disappeared. She must be having visions.

But then there was a knocking at the front door and her heart started to beat faster. She went to the head of the stairs but was so surprised to hear laughter and a man's voice coming from the little parlour that she stopped on the top step.

A servant went to the parlour door and Monna Isabella came out, followed by – of all people – Brother Anselmo. Only he was no longer dressed as a grey brother and he had an arm round Isabella's waist. Chiara rubbed her eyes again.

And then Silvano came up the stairs. His plumed hat was under his arm and he carried a small hawk on his left wrist.

'Welcome,' said Isabella.

'Well met,' said Anselmo. 'You know my betrothed, I think?'

'Betrothed!' Chiara and Silvano exclaimed at the same time.

And so he saw her. And ran up the remaining steps to stop on the one beneath her.

'Chiara,' he said, making a formal bow. 'I have brought you a gift.' He held out the bird to her. It was tiny, Chiara saw now, like a miniature version of Silvano's peregrine falcon.

'For me,' she said, puzzled. 'It's very kind of you and a very

284

pretty bird. But . . .'

'It is a merlin,' said Silvano, grinning widely. 'A lady's hawk.'

'But I don't go hunting and I'm not a lady,' said Chiara.

'But you might be one day,' said Silvano. 'In fact I very much hope you will be.'

'Why did you send no message?' whispered Chiara.

'I tried to write but the words seemed artificial on the page,' said Silvano. 'Besides, I wanted to bring the merlin in person. It is a kind of a message.' He was still smiling and Chiara, feeling her heart lift, began to smile too.

'I know I am not worthy,' said Silvano. 'I know after what I have told you before that I must convince you that I am worthy of your trust and love. But I want to try. Please tell me that you believe me.'

'Yes, please tell him,' said Monna Isabella.

'Put the poor boy out of his misery,' said Anselmo.

But Silvano didn't look at all miserable. This time he felt his beloved really did return his feelings.

Chiara went down the stairs towards her suitor.

'What chance have I, if you are all conspiring together?' she said.

She reached out to Silvano. And he carefully transferred the glove with the merlin on it to her left hand. He took the right one in his own and looked as if he would never let it go.

Italy and the Region of Umbria

Venice

Siena

Rome

Naples

Gubbio

Giardinetto

Perugia

Assisi

Umbria in detail

List of Characters

PERUGIA

Silvano da Montacuto, the only son of a noble family
Barone Bartolomeo da Montacuto, his father
Baronessa Margarethe da Montacuto, his Belgian mother
Margherita and Vittoria, his younger sisters
Gervasio de' Oddini, his best friend
Angelica, the object of his affections
Tommaso, her husband, a sheep farmer

GUBBIO

Chiara, daughter of a once wealthy family
Bernardo, her brother and guardian
Vanna, Bernardo's wife
Monna Isabella, a married woman
Ser Ubaldo, her husband, a wealthy wool merchant
Ser Umberto, his younger brother

THE HOUSE OF SAINT FRANCIS IN GIARDINETTO

Father Bonsignore, the Abbot, an old friend of Baron Montacuto
Brother Anselmo, the Colour Master
Brother Bertuccio, the cook, a lay brother
Brother Fazio, the Illuminator
Brother Gianni, the stableman, a lay brother
Brother Gregorio, the Lector
Brother Landolfo, the Guest Master
Brother Matteo, a novice
Brother Monaldo, the Librarian

Brother Nardo, the Cellarer
Brother Ranieri, the Novice Master
Brother Rufino, the Infirmarian
Brother Taddeo, the Assistant Librarian
Brother Valentino, the Herbalist

THE HOUSE OF POOR CLARES IN GIARDINETTO
Mother Elena, the Abbess
Sister Cecilia, a novice
Sister Elisabetta, a novice
Sister Eufemia, the Novice Mistress
Sister Felicita
Sister Lucia
Sister Orsola, see Chiara of Gubbio
Sister Paola, a novice
Sister Veronica, the Colour Mistress

THE BASILICA IN ASSISI
Simone Martini, painter from Siena
Pietro Lorenzetti, another Sienese artist, old friend
and rival of Simone
Lippo (Filippo) Memmi, Simone's friend and later his
brother-in-law
Tederigo, Lippo's brother
Donato, Simone's brother
Marco, a journeyman
Teodoro, a goldsmith from Siena

Michele da Cesena, Minister General of the Franciscans
The Minister General's Chaplain

291

The Divine Office

Friars, monks and nuns say the Hours of the Divine Office, that is the eight sets of prayers recited at specific times of day. When they can't get to a church to do so, they say them privately. At the time of *The Falconer's Knot* the services and times would have been roughly as follows:

Matins	Midnight
Lauds	3 a.m.
Prime	6 a.m. (dawn)
BREAKFAST	
Terce	9 a.m.
Sext	Noon
LUNCH	
Nones	3 p.m.
Vespers	6 p.m.
SUPPER	
Compline	9 p.m.
BEDTIME	

HISTORICAL NOTE

Background

Giardinetto, unlike Perugia, Assisi and Gubbio, is an invented place, as are the Franciscan friary and the convent of Poor Clares there. All the characters in this novel are fictional except for the painters Simone Martini and Pietro Lorenzetti, and their assistants, and the Minister General of the Franciscans, Michele da Cesena.

In the Middle Ages in Italy, the word 'convent' was used for the religious house of either friars or nuns, but I have followed the modern usage in giving the Poor Clares a convent and the Franciscans a friary.

The Falconer's Knot takes place in the summer and early autumn months of 1316 – the early fourteenth century, or Trecento as the Italians call it. I have taken the consensus view of art historians that Simone Martini had finished his frescoes in the chapel of Saint Martin in Assisi by 1317, some months after the action in the book, and that Pietro Lorenzetti's work was started after Simone's, and was influenced by him.

There is no historical evidence that I could find for where the pigments were ground for the artists working on the Basilica in Assisi. But such work was sometimes undertaken by friars and it has suited my narrative purposes to build a whole edifice on some very slight references in the literature, especially from Cennino Cennini's *Il Libro dell'Arte*. The colour rooms and Colour Mistress and Master are my own invention.

I have been in touch with art historians and mediaevalists, have visited Assisi, Perugia and Gubbio for research, and have read and consulted a huge number of books and journals about falconry, pigments, fresco-painting techniques of the early Trecento, life in the Franciscan and Poor Clare Orders in the Middle Ages, and the status of widows in Umbria and Tuscany.

But I have taken some huge liberties, in particular in letting a young Franciscan novice, albeit a sham one, spend time with a young novice Poor Clare. This could not have happened in fourteenth century Umbria. But earthquakes did and do!

The Falconer's Knot is not an academic treatise, but a novel so, with a novelist's magpie instinct, I have seized upon the bright and shiny fragments which caught my eye and discarded much else that didn't. I hope that the many authors whose theories I have read and the kind academics who let me consult them will forgive this single-minded tendency of the storyteller. It is certain that any historical errors or stretching of the truth are mine and not theirs. It only remains to say that no one but myself ever suggested that the great Simone Martini was ever involved in any murders, even in the role of detective.

Women and Society in the Middle Ages

It is hard for us to put ourselves in the position of a woman in the Middle Ages, whether that of a teenage girl or a middle-aged wife or widow. Meg Bogin, author of *The Women Troubadours*, puts it better than I can: 'Throughout the Middle Ages women were the pawns of men. Depending on their class, they lived in varying degrees of comfort or misery. Only in the most exceptional circumstances did they have any say in their own destiny. Marriage was a creation of the aristocracy, an economic and political contract designed to solidify alliances and guarantee the holdings of the great land-holding families. Following the rise of commerce, it was adopted by the bourgeoisie for these

295

same reasons – as a means of maintaining and advancing their economic and political status . . . Love or affection had little to do with the making of marriages.'

And she goes on to say, 'Women of all ranks, even those who held property, were wards throughout the Middle Ages, always under the official guardianship of a man.'

Not that men had it easy either. Life expectancy was short, much shorter than today, and those who worked on the land, growing crops and looking after animals, had to do so in all weathers and without the benefits of modern farming techniques. Peasants might have looked up to merchants, whose power began to grow in the Middle Ages, but both had to show respect to the aristocracy.

The country we now call Italy was divided into many little principalities and dukedoms. Counts, barons and marquises abounded. Only the nobles – people with titles – were known by names like da Montacuto (from Montacuto) or de' Oddini (one of the Oddini family). Ordinary families did not have established surnames in the fourteenth century. So a man might be known as Tommaso the sheep farmer or Ubaldo the wool merchant, which a hundred years later might be passed down as the surname Farmer or Merchant. Simone Martini's name means 'Simone son of Martino'. Surnames in Italy, as in England, were formed from place names, fathers' names, nicknames (like Rosso for a redheaded man) or the words for occupations.

Simone Martini
Very little is known of the life of this most sophisticated of Trecento painters. He was probably born in 1284, in Siena. And probably (this word comes round a lot when you try to

research Simone Martini's life) he was apprenticed to Duccio di Buoninsegna from the age of twelve to twenty. His reputation was made by the commission to paint the *Maestà* – Mary in Majesty – in the Palazzo Pubblico in Siena, when he would have been only thirty-one.

Shortly afterwards he went to work on the Saint Martin frescoes in the Lower Church of San Francesco in Assisi, paid for by the late Cardinal Gentile da Montefiore. By 1317 Simone was a knight and was getting many commissions for paintings. In 1324 at the age of forty, he married Giovanna, the younger sister of his fellow painter Lippo Memmi.

The great poet Petrarch, who befriended Simone in Avignon, implies that he wasn't very handsome and it was suggested first in 1957 that the sceptical observer with the downturned mouth in the fresco *St Martin Reviving the Dead Child* might be a self-portrait.

Simone was in Avignon, where the Papal Court was, by 1336. Petrarch mentioned him in two sonnets and got him to paint the portrait of the poet's beloved Laura. Sadly it hasn't survived. Simone died in Avignon in 1344 but was buried in Siena. He had no children.

You can see images of all the paintings in the Saint Martin chapel at Assisi described in this book on the Internet at: http://www.wga.hu/tours/siena/index_c2.html

Websites are frequently subject to change and may not be permanently online or updated regularly. If you find this website is no longer working, just type 'Simone Martini' and 'Montefiore' into a search engine and you will find other websites that feature the works of art which appear in *The Falconer's Knot*.